Advance Praise

"The author has a fun, dynamic style... the narrative recalls Carl Hiaasen's work with its balance of humor and suspense and its big cast of oddballs."

— *Kirkus Reviews*

"*Dirty Myrtle* is the kind of book that grabs you by the collar and doesn't let go. Kennedy Weible drops you into the sweaty, neon underbelly of Myrtle Beach and makes it impossible to look away. This is crime fiction with a big heart and a wicked sense of humor... a rowdy, big-hearted thriller that earns its laughs and its bruises."

— *Book Below*

"I've been recognized as an actor, director, and producer, but the first thing I identify as in my mind is a late-'90s Myrtle Beach bartender. I swear I've poured drinks for every character in *Dirty Myrtle*. Kennedy Weible nails the peculiar, hilarious chaos of that world in a way I could never describe to people. It's a thrill ride full of wild, idiotic characters who stumble, trip, and accidentally crash their way toward redemption. That's exactly how I remember the underbelly of the Grand Strand."

— Kevin Kane, actor, director & producer (*Life & Beth, Law and Order: SVU,* Martin Scorsese's *The Irishman*)

"I've been waiting a long time for someone to explore the enigma that is Myrtle Beach. Kennedy has answered my prayers at last."

— Brandon T. Snider, best-selling author of *The Dark Knight Manual* and writer/actor (*Inside Amy Schumer, Late Night with Conan O'Brien, Chappelle's Show*)

Dirty Myrtle

Dirty Myrtle

Kennedy Weible

First Edition

Library of Congress Control Number: 2025948874

Casebound ISBN: 978-1-62720-680-8
Paperback ISBN: 978-1-62720-681-5
Ebook ISBN: 978-1-62720-682-2

Design by Jenna Mattern
Editorial Development by Jenna Mattern
Promotional Development by Eleanor Salvatore

Published by Apprentice House Press

Loyola University Maryland
4501 N. Charles Street, Baltimore, MD 21210
410.617.5265
www.ApprenticeHouse.com
info@ApprenticeHouse.com

For Amanda,
my north star.

Chapter 1

Sailor pushed through the rising alarm of her hangover and plucked a half-smoked joint from where it was poked through the tab of an empty Coors Light can. She stuck it in her mouth then rested her head in her hands, breathing deep and feeling the contours of the hangover, getting the shape of the thing. It felt sticky and high-pitched. A small miner was chiseling away rhythmically at the inside of her skull with his hammer and pick, trying to get through. Sugary drinks, that's what did this to her. The syrupy shots, margaritas and rum and Cokes that gave Myrtle Beach hangovers that little something extra: the sugar crash.

Her phone buzzed. It had been doing that off and on for about ten minutes now.

Sailor stood and steadied herself. She spotted a lighter on the floor and navigated her way down to get it and then back up. She wobbled, lit the joint, inhaled, and exhaled. "Hey presto," she said quietly to herself. The sun pressed against the blinds she never opened. She gave the buzzing phone what it wanted and answered. It was a service call, forwarded to her phone from the main number. She took the details from the client, saying finally, "Alright. I'll be over in an hour." Sailor reached to put the phone back on the milk crate that served as her nightstand. She missed. The phone hit the floor with a clatter.

The softly snoring lump under the covers in Sailor's bed tugged gently at the corner of her attention. With the phone silent and a few rips off the joint circulating, she felt prepared to address it.

Short blond hair sprouted near the pillow. Sailor lifted the sheet a little and saw the pale ass of the woman she had brought home. A tourist, she remembered, a volleyball coach in town for a tournament. *Well alright*, she thought. *Still got it.*

Sailor left the woman sleeping and went to the bathroom to brush her teeth, alternating the toothbrush with the joint until it was dead. She dropped the roach in the toilet, peed on it, flushed, and went into her kitchen to make coffee. While it brewed, she got in the shower and washed away last night's debauchery and a little of the hangover. When she was done, she combed out her brown hair in the smeary uneven oval she had cleared with her palm in the fogged mirror. The bangs she had given herself six months back had grown out and weren't so much bangs anymore as simply visual impairments. She combed them straight down and, looking through the brown cataract they created, clocked where they fell against her cheeks. A problem for another day. She brought her fists up to either side of her head and flexed her biceps. Work had toned her arms and shoulders revealing a capacity for muscle she didn't know existed within her limbs. It was the only thing she liked about her job.

When Sailor came out of the bathroom, the woman was sitting up on the mattress, staring unhappily around the room. Her hair was in an uproar, a short blond mob in a panic, running in multiple directions at once. She had small, deep-set eyes, startlingly blue, like they were backlit. Her cheeks were full and round above a small mouth that was, just then, frowning.

"We lost," the woman said.

"Feels like a win from where I'm standing," Sailor said, pulling on underwear and jeans and stepping into her boots.

"The semis," the woman said. "We lost to Tabor City."

Sailor remembered the volleyball tournament. "Oh, yeah, well, you know, those Tabor City girls are real beasts on the," she wracked her brain, "court?" She hoped volleyball was played on a court. She clipped her bra in the back and pulled a long sleeve, waffled Henley over it, then a short sleeve button-up for Air Down There HVAC with its logo patch on the left breast and her name in red cursive stitching on the right. The woman was eyeing her. "There's coffee. If you want some. On your way out," Sailor said. She grabbed her tool bag off the dresser and found another unfinished joint under it. "Hey presto," she said, grabbing it.

"You're leaving?"

"That's the glamorous life of HVAC repair," Sailor said. "Always on the go."

"You care if I take a shower at least?" the woman asked.

"Knock yourself out," Sailor said. "The towel is," Sailor looked around and spotted it behind her on the floor, "right here." She flipped it into the air with her foot and caught it. She tossed it onto the bed. "That's one hundred percent real cotton too, I'll have you know."

The woman stared at the wet towel, the mattress on the floor, the state of the bedroom. "You don't have a clean one?"

"That one's pretty clean. I only use it after I shower so..."

"You only have one towel?"

"My second one is in the shop. They don't know what's wrong with it. Maybe the hem? That's the best I can do for you at the moment." Sailor headed for the door.

"Aren't you worried I'll rob you when you leave?" the woman called after her.

"Lady, you couldn't find anything in here worth stealing if I gave you a week," Sailor called back. She shut the door and went to her car.

Sailor started the engine of the little Honda. She put the joint she found under her tool bag into the ashtray for later. The previous night she had started at Shuckers, having beer and oysters and fries with Tayto and Julie, then they had migrated to Señor Frog's. That's where the high-octane sugar cocktails entered the picture along with the volleyball coach. Lula, that was her name. Sailor squinted through the glare on her windshield at the door to her end-unit, the crumbliest side of the single story house divided into three uninspired apartments. Lula was in there now doing what? Showering? Standing in the kitchen by the coffee maker realizing there were no clean coffee cups? Or regular cups for that matter. Lula was the first person Sailor had touched non-platonically since she split up with Harper six months ago. *Take that, Harper*, Sailor thought. She had a brief impulse to call Harper and brag, but realized almost immediately that she didn't want to brag, she just wanted to tell her because she had always told her everything. At the deepest level she wanted Harper to tell her what to do next—Sailor knew that whatever she was supposed to be doing, it wasn't running away from her own apartment—and the disgusting part was that if she called and asked, Harper would absolutely offer guidance. There had always been the lingering whiff of novice and instructor between them, though they were practically the same age.

Sailor backed out of her space in a hurry before she thought too much about it. Who gave a shit about Harper and the woman Harper lived with now? Sailor went ahead and sparked the leftover joint and called her sister, Carrie. This was partly to think of something else and partly because she knew Carrie had met their friend Chess, the divorce attorney, that morning, more than eight months after finding out her husband was seeing another woman. Sailor wanted to check up on her.

Sailor downshifted her brain into the gear where she felt angry on behalf of her sister. That was better. Carrie answered after a couple rings.

"What are you doing up?" Carrie asked, instead of saying hello. "I figured you'd be in bed till three after last night. Heard you went after it pretty hard."

"From who?" It wasn't that Sailor expected discretion from Tayto and Julie, but it felt a little early for them to have already worked the phones.

"From you. You texted me like a million times. One said, 'Boys get sun.' Another says, 'Going mud diving.' They're all drunk-text gibberish."

Sailor looked at her text messages muttering, "'Boys get sun'? What does that— Oh. That was definitely supposed to say 'Bout to get sum.'"

"About to get some what?" Carrie asked. "Wait. Oh. Ew, don't translate the rest."

"Sorry."

"Well, congratulations, I guess. Do you need a ride? Did you get some?"

Sailor admired her big sister. She was a nurse who had just worked an overnight shift, taken an early meeting with a divorce attorney because her marriage was over, and still would have come and collected Sailor from a one-night stand.

"No, we went back to mine," Sailor said.

"Oh Sailor, gross! No. You didn't really take her back there, did you?"

"You're overreacting. My place is fine. I'll grant you it has its own flavor but—"

"A smell isn't a flavor. That's what it has. A smell. Are you in the car?"

Sailor was driving down Ocean Boulevard, which ran for miles along Myrtle Beach's shoreline, bordered on either side by luxury hotels, decidedly non-luxury motels, houses and condos, bars and beachwear stores. It terminated on the north end at Dunes Golf and Beach Club, an upscale neighborhood and golf course that hosted PGA tournaments. The south end passed through "The Strip," where lifted trucks cruised up and down for an audience drinking on the sidewalks outside the T-shirt shops, bars, and arcades. Sailor was currently between these two poles, cruising through a residential stretch where older, stately homes held ground with new construction that looked like it was built with fondant. "Got an emergency call from a customer," she answered Carrie.

"Make Dad do it. It's your day off."

Sailor opted to change the subject rather than explain that if she punted the call to their dad she wouldn't have an excuse to run away from her apartment and the woman inside it. "What did Chess say?" Sailor made a mental note to buy some cleaning supplies and a second towel before Carrie came over again. Maybe a scented candle. "I mean, Morgan's cheating on you. It's a spike, right?"

"A spike?"

"Like in volleyball. A slam dunk? Is that better?"

"Apparently, I need proof," Carrie said.

"Can't they pull his phone records?"

"Maybe, yeah. But once I file, he'll delete everything and his lawyer will fight it. Chess says we want the proof first, before we file."

"What kind of proof?"

"Pictures," Carrie said. "Video. I need a private detective but it's—"

"It's what?"

"Expensive."

"How much?" Sailor said.

"Like a couple thousand at least I think."

"You've got that."

"Yeah, still it's just a whole—"

"It's a whole thing, and you don't want some stranger knowing how messy your shit is now that your life has heavy spice," Sailor said. Her sister was a private person. She would hate having a stranger follow her husband just to prove he was a shitheel.

"That's a gross way to phrase it, but yeah," Carrie said. Sailor was always remarkably perceptive, despite being half-stoned most of the time. She read people well.

"So what are you going to do?"

"I don't know. Right now I'm sitting in my car eating a whole pack of gum I found in my purse."

"I'll do it," Sailor said. She was morose about her inability to really help in any way since her sister had confided in her about Morgan and his cheating. Sailor had wanted to go after Morgan right then, chase him out of that McMansion he built for them, maybe throw his shit all over the lawn—her and Carrie stampeding through the house, shouting and wrecking things. That was how she imagined it. Carrie hadn't felt like doing that, of course, so Sailor's sense of vengeance remained pent-up and looking for an outlet.

"You'll do what?" Carrie asked.

"I'll get pictures of Morgan and the floozy. I'll follow him."

"Don't do that," Carrie said. "Chess said it was best to keep family uninvolved. I'll hire a professional. I'm just feeling bummed about the whole thing this morning, is all."

"Dude, I'll handle it. I'll do it for free. It'll be like a second wedding gift, but on the ass end of things," Sailor said. She was excited. She would bust that punk Morgan's bullshit wide open.

"You didn't get me a first wedding gift," Carrie reminded her.

"Then I owe you one," Sailor said. "Wait, I got you something for your wedding. Didn't I put my name on Mom's gift?"

"Mom and Dad paid for the wedding. That was the gift."

"Yeah, that was from all three of us," Sailor said. "Listen, this is perfect. I'll get the pics, you save money and emotional leakage, and Morgan gets divorced so hard in the nuts he can't stand straight for a year. It's perfect."

"Sailor, no."

"Think about it," Sailor said.

"I'm thinking about it now. I can think on demand, it's not something I need to get to at a later time. No."

"I can see we're at loggerheads right now, but we'll come to an agreement."

"Sailor!"

"Hey, guess who I saw last night," Sailor said.

"Sailor, I'm serious—"

"Jug."

That stopped Carrie mid-protest. "Jug? As in Judson Shaw?"

"One and the same."

Jug had grown up next door to their small house in an even smaller house, with his grandmother, Nana Jean. He was the same age as their older brother, JP. He had worked for their father for a time before quitting one day with no notice and leaving town.

"Well that's a blast from the past," Carrie said. "Did he say where he's been all this time?" Jug skipped town more than three years earlier. He was rarely heard from after that. It had been hard on Nana Jean.

"Not to me. He was pretty drunk by the time I saw him."

"Maybe we'll see him at Mom and Dad's tomorrow at breakfast." Their youngest brother, Dex, was coming home from college for Thanksgiving break that night. Their mother wanted all the kids at breakfast the next day. "Do you know if Jug's staying with his grandmother?" Carrie asked.

"I don't know. He didn't last night."

"Why not?"

"Last night he went to jail."

•••

Tusk was still dragging the whole night behind him when he knocked on the captain's open door. The feeling would fade in an hour. His brain would accept being tricked by the morning sun and tell his body things were fine. Then he would cruise along until he could get home and crash. Pending this psychological con job kicking in, he needed to pour coffee that was too hot to drink into an angry stomach that was driving a hostile nervous system. His heart revved, but the wheels spun. He slouched around the station being unhelpful.

Tusk leaned into the open doorway and said, "You asked to see me?"

Captain Lewis looked up from his phone and waved Tusk inside. "Shut the door. Sit," he said. Captain Lewis' short black hair was diluted with gray, but that was the only indication of his advancing years. He wore the short sleeved uniform top that senior ranking officers generally eschewed to show off his muscled biceps and forearms. The day he turned fifty he shaved the mustache he wore as a younger man to give him gravitas. The shave took ten years off his face and since then he stayed clean shaven.

He left the gray in his hair, though. Trying too hard to look young actually made you look older, was his opinion.

"Everything alright?" Tusk took a seat.

"Why? Because you have to shut the door?" Captain Lewis asked.

"It's a contributing factor. When Maroney arrested the mayor's daughter and got put on leave, you called him in here and shut the door. Now he's a waiter," Tusk said.

"Did you arrest the mayor's daughter last night?"

"No."

"Then calm down. And for the record, Maroney arrested the mayor's daughter for changing in her car at the beach."

"Well, that's, probably..." Tusk realized he was going to come up empty-handed and slumped back in his seat, not bothering to finish stammering.

"You don't know if that's illegal or not, do you?" Captain Lewis asked.

"Public indecency?" Tusk guessed.

"Pulling on a shirt and shorts over your bathing suit isn't indecency. Besides, he'd been stalking her for weeks. She had a video. His dash cam backed it up when we pulled it."

"Are you allowed to tell me that?"

"Am I, the captain, allowed to tell you that former MBPD officer Chad Maroney was placed on leave and then fired for stalking the mayor's daughter and arresting her for covering up her bathing suit?"

"Yeah. Are you allowed to tell me all that?"

"No, but what's Maroney going to do about it, arrest me? He's a fucking waiter. Are we done talking about that departmental embarrassment, now?"

"Yes, Captain."

Tusk liked the captain. Captain Lewis maintained only the thinnest veneer of civility and patience with his force, but he was consistent and that was important. And they were both Black. Tusk felt that was a bit of luck in a town like this, with Confederate flag towels in the windows of all the beachwear stores. The flag showed up on hats, bumper stickers, and T-shirts, as well. Tusk imagined there were more Confederate flags in South Carolina now than during the actual Confederacy given the limitations of printing and sewing in the eighteen hundreds. So he cut Captain Lewis a bit of patience, regardless of the man's quirks.

Captain Lewis picked up a folder from his desk and opened it. "You brought in Judson Caleb Shaw last night."

"Yes, sir," Tusk said.

"Pissing in public, huh?"

"While fall-down drunk," Tusk added.

The captain looked up from the folder. "You say that as a euphemism, or—"

"No, he actually fell. A bunch. He was standing when I first caught him, but that was a rare moment. He didn't manage too many more of those."

The captain nodded. Judson Caleb Shaw wasn't the first person Tusk had arrested for pissing in public at Celebrity Square, a prefab oval of bars and clubs with ever-changing names situated at one end of an outdoor shopping and amusement compound called Broadway at the Beach. The "Broadway" in the name came, presumably, from the complex's now-closed Palace Theater. Tusk couldn't recall ever seeing the theater put on any Broadway shows, but he saw ads once saying Jeff Foxworthy was playing there which, he supposed, qualified as the Mamma Mia! of the southern U.S.

The parking lot around Celebrity Square was the place to go when you needed to boost your booking numbers. You could pick up three or four public urination citations in a weekend and barely leave your vehicle. The fine wasn't as handsome as a speeding ticket, but it showed you were doing police work. Judson wasn't the first, but he was undeniably the most cheerful. Tusk waited for him to finish peeing (he had learned early on to let them finish, no point in getting splashed by a surprised drunk just to keep a few more ounces of urine off the asphalt) and said, "Quite a performance. You washed away some of the cigarette butts but none of the gum. I'll score that a seven. Now can you put your hands behind your back for me?"

Judson turned and looked at him, startled but smiling. Tusk felt like he recognized him then, but not enough to get into it. There would be time to figure that out later and see if it mattered.

"Sure man!" Judson called out, laughing a little. He turned and drunkenly waved his arms around behind him.

"How about you put your dick back in your pants and zip up first? Then hands behind your back. Guess I should have been more explicit," Tusk said.

Judson had looked down, laughed at the sight of his manhood drooping out the fly of his pants like uncooked chicken, and said, cackling near hysterical, "Turns out I'm the one who's explicit!"

Then he had fallen over.

"Was he any trouble?" the captain asked.

"He was annoying. Kept singing that Peter Frampton song, *Baby I Love Your Way* the whole drive in. It's stuck in my head now. Can't say I appreciate that, but I wouldn't call him trouble. He's being released in about thirty minutes."

Captain Lewis put down the folder and leaned back in his chair. "Did you instruct him to be quiet?"

"Repeatedly, sir."

"And he failed to comply?" Tusk wasn't sure where this was going. "That's not in the report," Captain Lewis went on. "Failure to comply with an officer's instructions is considered sort of unforgivable, isn't it? An officer gives you an order, you don't follow it, you've broken the law, right?"

"I'm not entirely sure that's how the law works, sir," Tusk said.

"You weren't entirely sure it wasn't illegal to change clothes in your car a few minutes ago either, though, were you?"

Tusk was starting to reconsider how much he liked the captain. "You change in your car and flash your balls to everyone in a Walmart parking lot, that's public indecency. But no judge wants to see a "Failure to comply" charge in front of them because a drunk wouldn't stop singing lame seventies tunes. But I can update the report if you want, sir." This was maybe the wrong attitude to take, but Tusk was exhausted.

However, Captain Lewis just smiled and waved away Tusk's suggestion like they were chatting about nothing more than a movie they had both seen. In fact, he seemed pleased.

"Do you know Mr. Shaw?" the captain asked.

"Kind of, actually," Tusk said. "I don't know him, but I know who he is."

"You make it sound like he's famous."

"We went to the same high school for a little while. Everyone called him Jug back then. He looked familiar when I picked him up. I recognized his name when we were booking him. We weren't friends."

"Bad blood?" the captain asked way too casually for Tusk's taste.

"No, sir. Not at all. I transferred into Myrtle Beach High partway through my senior year. Not the easiest year to make new friends, you know? I maybe spoke to the guy in class or something, I just didn't know him."

The captain considered this. "So, you aren't friends with Mr. Shaw. You know his name and his nickname. You know what he looks like now that you've arrested him. And you didn't go the full nine yards and add a bunch of petty charges to his arrest report just to jam the guy up, even though you could have. It's something a lot of officers do," the captain said. He drummed his fingers on the desk and stared at Tusk.

"Am I in trouble, Captain? Did I do something I'm not following here?"

"Is the closed door still bothering you?"

"The whole conversation, really. Is this guy related to the mayor too?"

"Officer Knight, I'd like to ask you to do something, and I'd like you to do it without a gung-ho, jam-a-guy-up attitude. Using the same calm, reasonable behavior you've already demonstrated when faced with an annoying citizen. I'd like you to keep an eye on Mr. Shaw. Watch him. Take note of where he goes, people he sees repeatedly. Not follow him exactly. And not drag him in here every time he fails to signal when pulling into his driveway. Just watch him. Calmly. Patiently. Do you think you can do that?"

Tusk wasn't sure how to respond. This was the Investigative Division's job, though a lot of patrol officers had pets they followed around and harassed. Just cops who took things personally and found repeat offenders to torment. It was an easy thing for them to justify to themselves, brag about even. Designating your own Joker allowed you to feel like Batman for a reason other than carrying a lot of shit on your belt.

"And before you ask, no, I don't feel like explaining further," the captain said. "I need a favor. Will you do me a favor?"

"Yes, sir," Tusk said, rousing himself from his fog and getting excited. This meeting was turning around. "I can do that. I'd be happy to do that. I want to move to Investigation one day."

"Then let's think of this as some early training," said the captain. "And I want to be clear, this is strictly observation. Casual observation. It shouldn't get in the way of your normal duties."

"I understand, Captain," Tusk said. "And I take it I'll be," Tusk paused to make it obvious he was searching for a polite phrase for something outside of procedure, "updating you privately on my observations?"

"It's a fucking secret, yes. You don't have to use code. Keep it between you and me."

Captain Lewis asking him for this favor was, in itself, a favor. Doing something off the books for a higher-up was a privilege. The kind of thing that got you promoted, assuming you didn't fuck it up. It was dark currency, but it spent. Tusk thought the police force would be the one place you could move ahead without a hustle or the moral lassitude to debase yourself for the crooked entitlement of doing something unethical for the approval of men with lackeys they thought of as their "squad" or "crew." It was just so much extra bullshit to deal with on top of doing your job. He wanted to get ahead on merit and hard work, without dragging an ethically dubious shortcut behind him the rest of his life and career. And here was the captain, a decent man Tusk believed, giving him the opportunity to have it both ways. A favor that was just observation, which wasn't illegal. No roughhousing.

"Understood, sir." Tusk felt brighter, fully awake.

"Well then," the captain looked at his watch. "Guess you better go let Mr. Shaw back out into the world."

•••

The truth was Sailor had already spent time following Morgan back when Carrie first told her about the affair. She had followed his mistress too, a plasticky blond named Nina Capaldi. Nina was slim and fully manicured, far beyond her nails, like a really well-tended lawn. Her hair was always clean and in soft curls, her clothes fitted and stylish. She dressed like she was the center of a reality show. Sailor followed them both for a couple weeks, unsure of her own end-goal. She felt a perverse need to witness the actions of two people trying to go unobserved. Spite, she supposed, plus she was looking for any excuse to be away from the house as much as possible back then. Harper had been doing the same, staying gone all day just to be away from their relationship, neither of them talking about it. They were doing the inverse of Morgan and Nina, sneaking away from one another, secretly being broken up on the side.

Sailor learned, during that period, that Morgan hung out at a sketchy bar off Ocean Boulevard on the south end. Nina went to Grand Strand Bank an awful lot, staying too long to be simply banking but not long enough to be working anything that could be called a shift. Sailor never got further than the sketchy bar and the employment mystery though, because Harper finally summoned the energy to shatter their mutual ennui and began what would turn into a two-month long break up.

Sailor decided to pick up where she left off with Morgan and Nina. Carrie would be grateful in the end, when she didn't have to engage a stranger to do it. Sailor had some time before she needed to be at her client's house, she had told the guy an hour. She drove to the shady bar Morgan favored. She just meant to remind herself where it was but was shocked to see his Range Rover out front in the parking lot. The one with the vanity plate that read: DVLPER. The bar was closed. Morgan's SUV was the only vehicle in the lot. Had he been drunk and taken a car service home? Or ridden with his sidepiece, Nina? Sailor couldn't picture the crispy blond she had followed deigning to enter this shithole bar. It was a squat concrete building with two small windows on either side of a brown front door. Sailor thought it looked like an ashen face with dead eyes. The eyes lit up bloodshot with old neon signs at night.

Sailor picked up her phone and almost called Carrie back before she caught herself. Carrie was already having a lousy morning. A lousy year, really. This wasn't helpful information to dump on her. Plus she kind of specifically told Sailor not to do what she was currently doing. *Document it, Sailor*, she said to herself. *Document it and give it to Carrie to give to Chess.* She took a picture of Morgan's car, making sure to get the sign with the bar's name in the background: Jumper's. The photo looked flat and unimpressive on her phone. She should use a real camera for this. One with a proper lens that could zoom in and still take clear photos. Photos no one would question in court. Photos that would show Carrie she was taking this seriously. Sailor checked the time. She knew where she could get a camera like that.

She went to the Krispy Kreme first, where the Hot Donuts Now sign was lit. She ordered herself a coffee and got two large boxes of originals. Sailor drove to the development where her service call was, the donuts riding shotgun. She passed the house that needed the repair and drove to the back where the new construction was being done. The neighborhood was quiet in the autumn light. The houses sat on less than a quarter acre, defiantly squeezing themselves onto the property like cats sitting in too-small boxes. They were treeless except for saplings, young crepe myrtles that came as options on new construction. You could have one installed out front on the twelve by six rectangle of lawn. There wasn't enough room to put one in the back of a property. Every little bit helped in the summer, the HVACs running nonstop as the neighborhood cooked, shadeless, under the Grand Strand's bare sun. Plus the homes' designs skimped on ductwork to lower overhead costs for the development company, so the places didn't cool efficiently. The units wore out faster running all the time like that for almost seven months of the year. It all kept Sailor and her father busy, but the customers grew increasingly angry over time.

She found the house she was looking for and saw Isaac's truck parked out front. The house was the orange-yellow of construction grade wood inside and out. It smelled of split lumber still damp and dewy from the mill, the scent of the natural world still evident before the drywall and flooring and paint masked it all.

Sailor was friendly with most of Isaac's crew. As she came in, a stout guy they all called Conejo nodded hello before seeing the donut boxes. He rushed to the stairs and called up, "Marinera está aquí. She's got donuts." The hammering and sawing waned, replaced by the stomp of boots on boards as the men poured toward her through the house. Isaac was in the back frowning at a cup he was holding, filled with cigarette butts. He turned when she came in, his wide frame swinging around to face her. He was wearing his usual tattered cotton ball cap with his company logo, his long brown hair curling up around the bottom, some of it meeting and blending into the wild beard he sported. He smiled. "Sailor, our hero," he said, gesturing to the donuts. She opened the box for him to take one, then handed it off to Conejo, who had dogged her heels through the skeletal rooms. The guys plowed through the donuts silently and gave her appreciative little pats on the shoulder as thanks, their mouths full, before dispersing back through the house. The sound of hammers and drills rose again in the morning air.

"I have a call a few streets over," Sailor told Isaac as he swallowed the last of his mouthful. "How's this going? You still ready for me after the holiday?"

Isaac's gaze swept the place. "If the developers had me build this place any cheaper, I'd have to get material from the Dollar Tree," he said. "I think sometimes, well, at least I'm building in an era where they can't legally make me use asbestos, but it's only because it would be over budget. Can you do it the morning after Thanksgiving? Friday?"

This was almost a week earlier than Sailor was expecting. "I can be here. You ahead of schedule?"

Isaac shrugged. "It takes less time to do things half as well. You get done quicker."

"What's with this?" Sailor said, pointing at the cup of cigarettes. "New insulation they want you to use?"

Isaac barked a laugh. "This," he said, "is evidence."

"Evidence?"

"The guys found it this morning. I think someone's sleeping here. After hours. Can't be sure, but I found stuff like this here and also at the other place I'm working down on Ocean Boulevard. You're installing at that one too, actually."

"It's probably just kids," Sailor said. "Be grateful they're putting the butts out at all. Listen, you still got that nice digital camera?" Isaac shot freelance photography when he wasn't miserably building cheap houses. Local surfers like himself mostly. He was always pushing to get Myrtle Beach more recognition for its surf despite the fact that it had almost none.

"I have it," Isaac said warily. "It's still nice."

"Could I borrow it?"

"Will I get it back in the same condition it's currently in?"

"I don't see why not."

Isaac nodded. "I need it back in a few days. A swell is supposed to be coming through."

He was doing her a favor, so Sailor didn't roll her eyes or comment on the swell that would inevitably deliver the Grand Strand barely rideable three foot mush. She just said, "No problem. You won't miss the swell."

•••

Jug had been awake for a while, pretending to sleep. He was only pretending for himself, though, as there was no one else there. He lay on the plastic mattress with his eyes closed, unwilling to commit to wakefulness and face his predicament. It wasn't his first time in the Myrtle Beach jail. Jug was excited to be home, but this wasn't the hit of nostalgia he was looking for. He often made poor decisions. He'd known that for the last three years, but somehow being aware of it didn't stop him from making them. It was like having a disease or condition that flared up on you, he thought. Like hemorrhoids. Knowing you were susceptible didn't stop you from getting them. And just like with hemorrhoids, his bad-decision flare-ups resulted in an unhappy asshole—him.

Jail experienced the same dawn stillness as places less reliant on cinder blocks and bars for their peace and quiet. This was usually the time of day Jug found it easiest to sleep, but he could only hold the horizontal position now, wondering what made him think stopping for a quick beer or ten at one of his old hangouts would be a good idea. He was overwhelmed by the emotional muscle memory of finally being home. It had been a long time since anywhere felt as comfortable as this ridiculous town with its mini golf and dinner theaters and fried seafood joints. It felt like pulling on your oldest pair of jeans after wearing borrowed clothes from someone roughly your same build. Like stepping back into his real life. He suddenly found himself parking outside Stool Pigeons and the next thing he knew he was sitting at the bar.

Parker was the first familiar face Jug saw. He ambled through the door in that same old hat, the brim beginning to fray a bit. Recognition crossed Parker's face like a truck slamming through an intersection, and he grabbed Jug in a bear hug, shouting, "My brother from another mother!" That sealed it, the night was off and running and Jug was back in the warm, neon embrace of his hometown. They raced through six beers each catching up, waiting for Rainy and Haines and Other John who were meeting Parker there when they got off work. There were more bear hugs and shots and beers, then they walked over to Señor Frog's where Julie squealed up to Jug and threw her arms around him. She walked beside him taking baby steps, her high heels limiting her to a trot. There was Sailor, still dressing like two disparate people mashed together, her preferred style—with a floral patterned flouncy feminine top above a pair of baggy men's jeans that looked like they were purchased in the eighties. She grabbed his head and placed an exaggerated kiss up by his temple. Tayto threw her arms around his neck and hung there, lifting her feet off the ground, letting him spin her around once, still in her uniform from her bartending shift, her makeup elaborate and sexy to maximize tips.

Jug vaguely remembered his arrest. He had meant to sleep it all off in the back of his truck. There was a camper shell over the bed and a sleeping pad rolled up back there—he was an experienced rambler now, always prepared. First though, he needed to take a monster piss and he wasn't walking all the way back to the bar when he could go in the parking lot like God intended. Poor decisions.

Jug was in his own cell, a small mercy that suggested just how drunk he must have been. The cops called the individual containment units the VIPs. They were for psychopaths or people too drunk to take care of themselves in the group cells. The dangerously strong or the credibly weak. Everyone deemed somewhere between those two points got tossed in together and had to make do.

Jug heard footsteps, then sounds at the door to his cell. He opened one eye and saw someone looking at him through the wire glass. The window was small, but large enough for Jug to take in the smoothly shaved head, no nicks or cuts, a practiced job. Prominent eyebrows and dark lashes framed light brown eyes the color of honey. The man was not smiling. The door opened and Jug sat up.

Chapter 2

Tusk came straight down from the captain's office to personally release Judson Shaw, aka Jug. Tusk would have to make an effort to get used to that name. He opened the door to the cell and stared at Jug a moment before his eyes moved to the wall above the bare plastic mattress where Jug had spent the night.

"You scratch your name on the wall?" Tusk asked.

The VIPs were small square rooms with cinder block walls. The occupants who stayed in them liked to scratch their names into the paint with their fingernails.

Jug raised an eyebrow. "No."

"I'm going to look at the walls. If I see your name, I'm going to shut this door and walk back out there and write up another arrest report and then I'm going to come back in here tomorrow morning and we'll try this again. If you just tell me now that you scratched your name on the wall, I'm still going to close this door and go write up another report, but I'll come back this afternoon since you didn't make me read through all these other dumb motherfucker's names looking for yours. So. Did you scratch your name on the wall?"

Jug's eyes were bloodshot and his hair was a mess. "Take a look, man. I barely feel alive. I didn't scratch anything into anything."

"Well, I appreciate that," Tusk said. "C'mon. Let's get you out of here."

"You're not going to look?"

"I believe you. C'mon. Got a few things for you to sign and you can be on your way."

Jug stood up and Tusk took in the man he was supposed to follow. Average height, five nine or five ten. A little shorter than Tusk stood at an even six feet. Jug was hungover and had spent the night in jail, so Tusk allowed that he was looking at a particularly low-res version of the man, but it didn't seem too far off from what he figured was his standard appearance. His hair was long, past his ears but not quite to his shoulders, and he wore a few days' worth of five o'clock shadow. He was good looking though, Tusk had to admit, with a friendly face that didn't show its true mileage. His eyes were bright blue, set beneath dark eyebrows, and high cheekbones. Judson was wearing jeans, a long-sleeve T-shirt and was barefoot. The number of white guys who got arrested in flip-flops in this town never failed to impress Tusk.

Tusk led Jug down the hall, past the dozing hoi polloi in the group cells and out to the booking and release area. "Jamie will get your effects," Tusk said, motioning to a sleepy officer with one AirPod in, standing behind the gray counter.

"This is where I get my shoes back," he said.

"Your flip-flops, yeah. You've been here before," Tusk said, meaning the overnight lock-up.

"Passed through a few times."

"What'd you do?"

"Always just having a little too much fun," Jug said. He picked up the pen that Jamie, the sleepy AirPod officer, pushed in front of him and signed the clipboard to take back his thin wallet, folding knife, and cell phone, the only three things he had been carrying when Tusk arrested him. The knife gave Tusk pause. It was a Buck 110, finely sharpened. Jug was carrying so little that each thing seemed purposeful. He didn't even have a set of keys. There was no law in South Carolina that said you couldn't carry a knife, though, regardless of size.

"Hey, shit-for-brains," someone called out. Jug turned. Jamie and Tusk both looked up as the chatter and office sounds of the booking and release area quieted. An arrested man, previously seated on a bench along the wall waiting to be booked, was standing now, hands cuffed behind him.

"It's you," the man said. His black hair was greasy, slicked back, the stubble on his narrow unshaved face was thin, like it was drawn on. "It's you. Yeah, it's you. You know it's you and I know it's you."

"Tweakers," Jug said in an offhand way to Tusk and Jamie, shaking his head. "Always great to have one notice you."

"Don't ignore me, don't ignore me. Do. Not. Ignore me," the man shouted.

"Can someone—" Tusk began.

"I said look at me, motherfucker," the man shouted and charged across the room.

Tusk closed the gap between him and the crazed man in three strides. He hooked his arm around the man's throat, positioned himself behind him and kicked hard at the back of the man's knees. The guy's legs buckled, and Tusk pulled down with his full weight, dropping the man to the ground. It didn't stop his shouting. "Get your fucking hands off me you prick," the man yelled. Then to Jug, "You're fucked, man. Should have stayed hidden away. Stayed hidden. Back to your hidey hole."

Tusk flipped the man onto his face and put a knee on his back, pinning him down. "Get the fuck off me, fucking pig." Tusk looked up toward Jug and the knife that was still sitting on the counter. Jamie didn't seem to have the sense to move it out of Jug's reach, just in case. Jug was just standing there, though, calmly observing the fracas. Two other officers came barreling around the counter and gave Tusk a hand.

"Whose fucking perp is this?" Tusk shouted.

"Mine," said one of the officers, Craig Daniels, who was pressing the man's face into the floor. The man was growling now, still straining, the fight not going out of him.

"Why the fuck aren't you watching him? Or have him cuffed to the bench rail?"

"Fuck off, Knight. I was ten feet away. He came in quiet," Daniels said.

"He ain't quiet now, is he?" Tusk snapped.

"For fuck's sake," Officer Daniels said. He and the other officer hoisted the snarling man between them.

"Out of your hidey hole," the man yelled at Jug. The two officers dragged him through the door back to the cells, most likely to a VIP room. Maybe the same one Jug had just come out of. That prick was definitely going to scratch his name on the wall, Tusk thought.

"Someone you had too much fun with in the past?" Tusk asked Jug, who was putting his phone, wallet, and knife back in his pockets and stepping into his flip flops.

Jug shrugged. "Never seen that guy before in my life. Seemed like a meth head to me. Those dudes just go nuts."

"You don't know that guy?" Tusk asked. The man's anger had seemed awfully personal.

"I'm telling you," Jug said. "Check the waistband of his pants. They cut them open and slip their stash in between the fabric. Most cops don't check. I'll bet you a thousand dollars that guy has a baggie of crank in the waistband of his pants."

"You hang around a lot of meth heads?"

"No, but I get around. You hear things."

"Anyway, police officers know that trick," Tusk said. "We check."

"You think that particular officer checked?" Jug signed the last of his release forms. Normally, Tusk gave fellow police the benefit of the doubt, but having just taken down the perp he had left unrestrained, he was pretty sure Daniels hadn't checked the man's waistband. Jug pushed the clipboard back to Jamie. "That the last one?"

"That's it," Tusk said. He pointed to the door that led to the lobby. "Right through there and out the front."

Jug smiled. "Back in good old Myrtle Beach."

•••

Carrie saw Morgan's car in the driveway and drove past her own house. She wasn't ready for whatever dumb conversation was waiting inside. She needed to think. She drove down the empty street to the cul-de-sac and turned around. Chess had been painfully forthright about the realities of getting a divorce when she met with him that morning. Needing to hire a private detective to document the most painful part of her life certainly didn't do much for her mood. His follow-up question hurt the most, though.

"We need proof he's been unfaithful," Chess said when she balked at bringing in a private eye. "He'll deny it. Then it's your word against his. And what about you? If you're seeing someone yourself..." Chester trailed off, probably reading the look on Carrie's face. She never expected to be asked, never even considered it.

Carrie was mortified. She got up and stomped to the door, turning to hiss at poor Chess, her friend since grade school, "You mousy little shit with your mousy little face."

Chester, being a compassionate friend who Carrie had called far worse after losing games of playground basketball, stopped her by the door and cajoled her back into her chair, saying, "Carrie, for Christ's sake, just listen a minute. You come in here saying your husband's having an affair and you've known for almost a year. And you haven't confronted him? You think I'm shit at my job? That this is the first time I've heard that? It's not. And every time I've heard it, it turns out the person had a revenge-affair before they came in here. And it matters. It matters in how we handle this."

"I'm your friend," Carrie said.

"Who's asking to be my client. You want a friend for your divorce, call Tayto. You want an attorney, then come sit back down."

Carrie retook her seat. Chester went back around his desk to his chair.

"My mousey little face?" Chester felt his jaw line and gently squeezed his nose. "You think my face is mousy?"

It wasn't. Chester was slim, not especially tall, but had normal, non-mousy features. In fact, he had a square, rugged face that tanned well and set off his nearly blond hair.

"No, your face is fine. I'm sorry, Chess. I really am." Carrie pressed the heels of her palms into her eyes to keep from crying. "I didn't mean that. I just didn't want you to know I was," she felt like her mother for a moment, unwilling to verbalize something sexual, "doing that. And then you came right out and called me on it. You must think I'm the biggest asshole."

"I could have been more tactful," Chester said. "Look, I can get you a divorce and I can make it ugly for him, but it'll be painful for you too. I know you're angry, but the best move is to file and settle amicably."

"Why do lawyers never want to actually do lawyer shit?"

"Because the law is hell. It's expensive, it takes forever, and it leaves everyone devastated whether they win or lose. Same as the medical industry. What's better? Making it through a heart transplant or skipping the fries and not needing one in the first place?"

"Chess, I..." Carrie tried to think of how to say she would die if she had to live much longer with a husband who was fucking another woman. When she first found out about Morgan's affair, it was like she was the one with the secret because she didn't know how to confront him. Confronting him was actually more embarrassing than the affair. Storming out of an attorney's office? Giving an earful to some tweaker acting up in the emergency department? She could do these things. Such was the gift of inheriting her father's temper. She was frozen with inaction, though, in the face of Morgan's infidelity. Just because you know how to get angry doesn't mean you know how to dismantle your whole life. She thought having her own affair might get her to a place mentally where she focused less on being betrayed and more on what to do next. That was why she started sleeping with someone else. But sleeping with someone else didn't teach her what to do about Morgan. Now she was in this office trying to put a confident face on all this, a mere inch from crumbling completely if something didn't happen soon.

Carrie had tried to think of how to say all this to Chester.

"Listen," Chester said, not forcing her to finish these thoughts that had no tidy conclusion. "I know it's not as simple in real life as 'file and settle amicably.' It would be great if it was, but it's not. But it's advice I feel obligated to give. Here's what we do. Go to every good divorce lawyer in town. I'll give you a list. Meet with them about representing you. It'll create a conflict of interest if Morgan tries to hire them. That leaves him with a selection of supremely shitty lawyers. Then come back here, we'll make it official and get to work. See what the best plan is. Think more about the private eye. Okay?"

Carried nodded.

"And for what it's worth, I'm really sorry you're going through this. I liked you and Morgan together."

"You did not."

"No, you're right," Chess had said. "I think he's a poser. But I didn't think he was also a shitheel. And I'm really sorry about that for you."

Carrie continued to drive, passing the two finished houses in the neighborhood besides their own, the half-constructed one, and the remaining empty lots. Christ, wasn't Morgan supposed to be selling these things? Whenever she asked about it, he got irritable and told her she didn't understand real estate. She didn't understand how this place was supposedly the success he told her it was when hardly anyone lived there and nothing ever seemed to get built. If this was the real estate business then no, she didn't understand it.

She pulled a U-turn at a stop light and headed back to their house. She knew now that Morgan had started his affair with Nina almost as soon as they moved into their new home. It had been going on for at least six months when Carrie found out. She read it in a text message on his phone when he'd left it on the kitchen counter.

As simple as that.

He had gone to the bathroom before heading out to one of the "business dinners" she was happy not to have to attend. The phone chimed and Carrie glanced at it, a habit of looking at anything that chimed, nothing more. *I'm wet thinking about having ur cock in my mouth. Hurry up.* Morgan's messages popped up on his screen even when the phone was locked. The name was above the message: Nina Capaldi. Carrie heard the toilet flush down the hall and hurried to the refrigerator, opening it, grabbing the first thing she saw. It was a beer. Some high-concept IPA in a can that cost way too much to taste, as it did, like old grass clippings. It was a new thing Morgan liked, or claimed to anyway. He came back into the kitchen.

"Alright, I'm out of here. Might be a little late tonight," he said. He saw her holding the can of beer. "Hey, you're coming around on those? I told you they were good, you just have to get used to the taste."

"Oh. Yeah," she said, opening the beer. The smell of it hit her and she almost gagged. She should have been confronting him. Yelling. Throwing the pretentious beer at his well-coiffed head. She found she just wanted him to leave, so she could think. She took a swig of the beer. It was disgusting. She smiled. "Your phone was going off," she said, like it was an afterthought. Tension flooded his face. He picked up his phone and looked at it. A flush of red began in his neck and went up to his cheeks, fear coming to an instant boil. "You're not late for your reservation, are you?" Carrie asked.

"No, no," he said. He tried to shove his phone in his pocket but missed and it fell to the floor. He rushed to pick it up and hit his head on the island. "Shit!"

"Jesus, are you alright?" Carrie said with reactionary concern, not even faking it. She moved toward him but he got his phone and backed out of the kitchen.

"I'm fine, I'm fine," he said. "Just a little knock. It was just the guys in the group chat. The text you heard. Just people saying they're on their way. I got to go." He went out the door that led to the garage.

Carrie stood listening to the garage door going up and his Range Rover starting and pulling out. Then she laughed. A gut-busting laugh conjured from his blushing, his bumbling, his head smacking the granite countertop. When the laugh had gone, there was nothing left in her, and she sat down at the kitchen island on one of the Italian leather-backed bar chairs Morgan had imported rather than buy the identical ones she had found at TJ Maxx. She sat there for a long time, sipping the terrible beer just because it was in front of her. She was gutted. She hadn't been passionately in love with Morgan, sure, but she had respected him and their marriage.

What was it he said about these gross beers? That you had to get used to the taste? That's what she had done. She had committed herself to him and found she got used to the taste. She liked him, she supported him, and he went out and started fucking someone with the unfairly exciting name of Nina Capaldi and didn't even have the decency to put a password on his phone or turn off his text alerts. She got another gross IPA out of the fridge and opened it. She was particularly enraged by this last point. His fucking phone. The fucking text. Just right out in the open on the kitchen island where they ate breakfast. There were so many options in a smartphone for hiding texts and messages and this dipshit had his mistress's full name in his contacts and text alerts on his home screen. It took a lot of audacity to be that stupid.

Carrie spent the rest of that night angrily staggering around their opulent house. She drank all of Morgan's IPAs. She got used to the taste.

She circled the neighborhood three times, what there was of it, anyway, and arrived back at their house. She pulled her white Suzuki Sidekick in alongside Morgan's Range Rover. Morgan was always trying to sell her beloved Sidekick and "upgrade her to something decent." Before he started fucking Nina Capaldi this had been the thing she liked least about him. It had taken her two summers at a Calabash seafood buffet, first bussing tables and then waiting on them, to save the four thousand dollars to buy the used Sidekick before her junior year of high school. It was her first car and the world had opened up. She loved that car. The top came off if you wanted. Every day she and Sailor would pick up Tayto for the drive to school, singing along to the radio and laughing about everything. They didn't sell them anymore and the local mechanics had stopped servicing hers years ago, but her father managed to keep making any repairs it needed. She never wanted another car.

She found Morgan in the kitchen, standing at the island with his broken fingers under a bag of ice, scrolling through his phone with his good hand. He had been on-site at the one house currently being built and somehow got his hand smashed by some two-by-fours. A few days later he broke his thumb at the same site. If Carrie had felt more generosity of spirit toward him, she might have suggested he stay away from his poorly staffed worksite. Instead, all she had said was, "Maybe you should learn how to handle lumber properly."

"Does it still hurt?" Carrie asked as she came in. She tossed her bag on the counter.

"Only when I'm awake," Morgan said, not looking up.

In banal moments like this, the two of them in the house together chatting about bits of the day, Carrie felt outside her own body. Like she was watching two other people pretending to be husband and wife while deceiving each other. Bizarrely, Carrie sometimes felt like she was the worse of the two of them. She was deceiving Morgan three times to his single lie. She was sleeping with someone else, she was pretending not to know that *he* was sleeping with someone else, and finally, the one that she now knew had been nagging at her throughout their marriage, she had never really loved him at all. The guilt from that—whether it was justified or not—was what had kept her from confronting him. It led her to think having her own affair would even things out. Now, that guilt was only deepening as she realized a piece of her was relieved about his fucking Nina Capaldi because it meant she could leave him. Only she hadn't left him. They had just started living like roommates, pretending things were normal, never addressing the fact that they didn't have sex anymore and rarely bothered to keep up with where the other one was at any given time. From slightly outside her body, Carrie saw two assholes in a nice kitchen and hated herself for being one of them.

"You want to meet at the place tonight or will you be home in time for us to ride together?" Carrie asked, rummaging in the fridge for a LaCroix.

"Meet at the what now?" Morgan's eyes stayed on his phone.

"At Big Lock's for JP's show," Carrie said.

"Oh, I can't make it tonight," Morgan said.

Two assholes in a nice house cheating on one another or not, this was a bridge too far. Carrie slammed the refrigerator door. "I told you about this three weeks ago. I've reminded you over and over. What the hell do you mean you can't make it?" She had promised her brother, who was counting on them to add a little volume to the crowd. Morgan had committed to coming. She was letting him get away with cheating on her for Christ's sake, he could fulfill a single family obligation.

Morgan looked startled by her turn of mood. "I just can't make it. Something came up. What's the big deal?"

"The *big deal* is this is family. You said you'd come. Who's so important you need to be with them rather than supporting your brother-in-law? And your wife."

Morgan flushed. Carrie knew she was leveraging something that wasn't out in the open. It would confuse him, make him wonder if she knew, pushing this whole thing closer to the inevitable confrontation she wasn't ready for. She didn't care.

"What's that supposed to mean?" Morgan said.

"You don't have a meeting at the bank because it's closed. You're not going on-site because no one is working. You're not meeting with suppliers because it's after hours. So, who exactly do you have a thing with that you can't come to the show you promised to be at for the past three weeks?" Carrie said. Morgan took all this in, and Carrie clocked his face as it changed from panicked to self-righteous the moment he decided on a lie.

"I'm meeting a couple who's considering buying a house here," he said, with an expression and tone like he had just confessed to using his extra cash to feed orphans. "I'm taking them to dinner."

"You're taking a couple who wants to buy a house to dinner? Tonight?" she asked.

"We need this sale. I have to go all in with these people. I have to get people into more of these lots."

"You said yesterday that everything was going just great."

"It is going great. This sale is part of it going great. Listen, you don't understand real estate. Sometimes you have to wine and dine them. This is how deals are struck."

"You have to wine and dine people into a three-bedroom, two-and-a-half-bath? And you have to do that tonight? During your brother-in-law's show."

"I support JP, alright? I employ the guy for Christ's sake," Morgan said, getting irritated now. He paid JP cash under the table to do any work he thought he could get away with having a non-professional do.

"He's the only person you employ who shows up. So don't act like it's some kind of favor."

Morgan sighed. He put his phone down. "How much are the tickets to this thing?"

"What difference does that make?"

"Just tell me how much they are."

"It's ten dollars at the door."

"Okay, and what's JP's take of that? Fifty percent?"

Carrie was lost. "I have no idea. Why?"

"It's maybe fifty percent. Fifty percent is a generous guess. So JP would make five dollars if I came to this thing. How about I give JP six dollars? That way he makes more than he would from my attendance, and I don't actually have to go."

"Are you seriously trying to cut some shitty deal?" Carrie yelled.

Morgan's slack face pulled tight into anger. "That is *not* a shitty deal. That is a solid deal."

"You said you would be there tonight."

"Well now I have to work. So does JP want six dollars or not?"

Carrie took a deep breath. This wasn't worth the fight. "Fine. Give me the six bucks."

Morgan deflated. "Now?"

"Obviously. We're talking about it now. You're not coming tonight. So yeah, now." Carrie held out her hand. "C'mon, Mr. Dealmaker, cough it up. Six bucks."

"I uh, I don't actually have six dollars on me," Morgan said.

Carrie let her hand drop. She almost thought better of what she was about to say, but she was sick of thinking better of saying things to people who never gave her a reason to have better thoughts in the first place. She adjusted the settings on her mouth past Stun, past Kill, directly to Eviscerate.

"After that little outburst about your solid deal, you don't have six dollars to close it? The great salesman, everybody. Mr.

Dealmaker. No wonder no one is buying these fucking houses. Try not to get taken for your car and watch at dinner tonight with your buyers, you goddamn clown."

Carrie grabbed her purse, marched to her Sidekick and drove straight to Tusk's house.

•••

Tusk parked in front of his duplex on 79th Avenue North, right off Ocean Boulevard. He leaned back against the seat, closing his eyes and taking a deep breath, gauging how tired he was. He could go to the beach. How many times had he gone to the beach since he moved back here a year ago? Three? Four? You could count them on one hand. He moved to this townhome specifically because it was close to the beach, so he could go all the time. He could go inside, change into his trunks, grab a cooler and a chair and go to the beach. It was close enough he could walk, or ride a bike if he had a bike. He should buy a bike. But who had money to waste on a bike you were never actually going to ride to the beach? If he actually went to the beach twice in the same week he would buy a bike, Tusk told himself. Then he got out of his car and went inside to go to bed. The beach would still be there tomorrow.

Tusk dropped his bag inside the front door. He was pulling his shirt tail out of his pants when he heard something on the second floor of the duplex. Unmistakably footsteps. He drew his weapon and started up the stairs, his breath steady, eyes ahead, following his training. The footsteps were leaving his bedroom, coming toward the small, neutral space that connected his bedroom, bathroom, and guest room. Tusk stopped a few steps down and raised his weapon, anticipating where center-mass would be on whoever was about to come out of his room. That's when he recognized Carrie's perfume. Tusk actually caught the scent halfway up the stairs, but his brain was in defense mode and his nose couldn't get the message of recognition through to the action-cortex right away. He made the connection just as Carrie stepped out of his bedroom wearing only the top of her scrubs, no pants, and found herself staring into the black eye of a gun barrel. Carrie screamed. Tusk lowered the gun, yelling, "What the hell are you doing here?"

At the same time, Carrie was yelling, "What the hell is wrong with you?"

They both stood taking deep breaths. Carrie said, "I brought your keys back and thought I'd surprise you." She gestured to her bare legs. "Surprise," she said.

"I am the most surprised a man can possibly be," Tusk assured her. He took in her legs. Adrenaline was still coursing through him. It would be a shame to waste it. He holstered his weapon and came toward her. "Can we still finish the surprise?"

Carrie nodded. "Nice to know you can control when that thing goes off."

"You got lucky. I was thinking about baseball."

She laughed. Tusk scooped her into a fireman's carry—lousy firemen, he thought, got all the cool shit named after them—and took her back into the bedroom.

Afterwards, they lay in his bed and watched his ceiling fan make its gentle rotations. Tusk reached down beside the bed and took his cigarettes from his pants pocket. "Light me one too?" Carrie asked.

"Since when?" She didn't give him grief over his smoking, which he appreciated, but she didn't smoke and she made faces at the smell.

"Since today I guess," Carrie said. "I quit back in high school."

"You smoked in high school?"

"Once, yeah. Then I quit, cold turkey. Light me one. Today's the day I get back on the wagon."

"Fall off the wagon you mean."

"I said what I said. Getting on the smoking wagon."

Tusk lifted one of his bedroom windows with a *shunt* sound and lit two cigarettes. He handed one to Carrie then sat down on the bed to watch her.

"You're staring," Carrie said.

"I'm curious what's about to happen when you inhale that thing."

"I'm going to work my way up to inhaling by the end. Right now I'm just puffing."

Tusk put an ashtray from his nightstand in the center of the bed. He watched Carrie pull on her cigarette like she was taking a breath before putting her head underwater. Her cheeks inflated like a child holding their breath, then she blew smoke through her pursed lips so hard it made a hissing noise. "Oh my God, stop," Tusk said, laughing.

"What's the problem?"

"You smoke like a punctured tire."

They sat quietly for a few minutes. Then Tusk couldn't stop himself and said, "I know we have this sort of agreement that I don't talk about your husband when you're here and you don't talk about him either. But..." He trailed off.

Carrie sat up and hugged her knees to her chest, the uninhaled cigarette burning between the fingers of her right hand. "Okay," she said. "But what?"

"You know that I like you and I don't enjoy pretending to—"

"Just say it."

"You don't usually show up here unannounced and pantless after an overnight shift. I can feel an edge on you that isn't usually there."

Carrie puffed the cigarette but said nothing.

"Want to talk about it?"

"Can we not?"

Tusk recognized the disappointed look Carrie got whenever he poked too deeply into her mood or feelings. She wished he would just get on board with the spirit of an illicit affair and stop being so goddamn thoughtful.

"Okay." Tusk was embarrassed whenever he did something that summoned *the look.* It made him feel like a kid who stopped the game everyone was playing to remind them it was time to get started on their homework. Something he had, in fact, done as a kid. He wanted to cover what he said with something fun, something cool and nonchalant. "Oh shit, your brother," he said.

"My brother?"

"His live stream."

Tusk grabbed his laptop off the dresser and climbed back into bed. He pulled up JP's website and logged in, turning up the volume.

"You're a member of JP's website?"

"Is that weird?" Tusk asked. "Aren't you a member?"

"Yeah, but out of a selfish interest in keeping him financially independent so he doesn't try to crash with me. I don't actively engage with it."

JP was in Tusk's senior class the single semester Tusk had attended MBHS. Tusk had come to Myrtle Beach with his father back then, choosing to stay with him, deciding there was nothing for him in Florida with his mother anyway besides unsolicited advice from her string of unemployed boyfriends, all proud graduates of his same dingy high school. Why start bogging down in a mud-puddle ecosystem over trite notions about the fun of senior year? He wasn't particularly having fun. Myrtle Beach was north, and that felt enough like moving up. He had enjoyed the anonymity of his semester at Myrtle Beach High. No one had any expectations about his personality, he didn't have to try to be himself. He wasn't paid any attention, kind nor ill. His new classmates were too absorbed in the end of youth's third act.

Tusk arranged the laptop between them. Carrie propped herself up on pillows, saying, "I've never actually watched one of these things he does. Are they good?"

"He has his moments." Though they shared a semester at Myrtle Beach High School, Tusk didn't actually meet JP until later, after his father died. Tusk met JP through a couple other guys on the force. He appreciated the easy way JP had folded him into his social circle, which was most of the reason he followed JP's comedy career, such as it was. Subscribing to his website was an act of gratitude.

Tusk turned up the volume on his laptop and Carrie peered down at her brother's image on the screen. Tusk took the ashtray and the cigarette Carrie was wasting and moved them over to his nightstand. He hadn't really turned his attention to whatever JP was doing yet—he was holding up his phone and seemed to be talking to someone on speaker—when a female voice caught his ear, saying "Jug's back."

"Is that Sailor?" Carrie asked.

Tusk only vaguely remembered Judson "Jug" Shaw from high school, much the same way he vaguely remembered JP. Thinking about it now though, after the surprise of hearing Jug's name, Tusk realized those two had been close friends. The cliques really stood out that semester—everyone conscious of the looming finality. He remembered them together. Not just friends, they were brotherly. Which meant Carrie, sitting in bed next to him, probably also knew Judson "Jug" Shaw.

"Hard to tell through the speaker phone," Tusk said to Carrie. "Sounds like her I guess. Would she know this Jug person?"

JP started having a coughing fit after hearing the name "Jug." He was trying to play it off, but it was obvious the news meant something to him. Tusk wondered what that was about.

"Yeah, of course she knows him. Jug was—"

"Was what?"

"Wait, shh," Carrie said, turning the volume louder.

"I want to ask you something," Sailor was saying now. "Like obviously don't say anything to her about it, but do you think Carrie is having an affair? Lately she's been—" Then JP hung up or the connection dropped.

Carrie stood up from the bed, hand over her mouth. "Oh my God," she said.

"How the hell's she know something like that?" Tusk asked.

Carrie started pulling on her pants and top. "She just knows shit sometimes. She's got this ability to like—"

"She just knows shit?" Tusk said, incredulous. "Like she lives in a mirror and you have to summon her with a rhyming couplet? Uh-uh, this isn't something someone just knows. Did you say something to her?"

"Did I— No! I didn't say anything to her. Did you listen? She didn't know for sure. She doesn't know it's you. She doesn't—" Carrie closed her eyes and said, "Shit."

"What shit? Shit what?" Tusk asked.

"I asked her about you once. Before. Before we started this. If she remembered, she'll have put it together. But she doesn't know, I don't think, so it—"

"You don't think?" Tusk shouted. Carrie stared at him and Tusk knew, from his years of field research saying the wrong things to women, this had been both the wrong question and the wrong volume to ask it.

"What do you care?" Carrie shouted back. "Your name wasn't mentioned. Mine was."

"I don't need trouble from your husband," Tusk said, quieter.

"My husband," Carrie said, grabbing his laptop and shaking it, "doesn't watch this dog-ass show. You know who watches this dog-ass show? Do you know? See those," she looked at the screen, "forty-six stupid screen names in the chat box? Those forty-six stupid names represent forty-six dipshits who are friends with my brother, which means they know me."

"Well, one of them is me," Tusk said.

"I'm most definitely fucking counting you as one of the forty-six dipshits," Carrie yelled.

Tusk put his hands up like he had seen a hundred perps do. "I'm just worried is all," he said. "Like if next time you come back someone sees you—"

Carrie cut him off with a short, loud laugh. "You don't understand," she said, tossing the laptop back onto the bed. "That won't happen."

"How do you know that?"

She closed the laptop. "I'm not coming back." Carrie picked up her phone from the nightstand, turned, and went through the door and down the stairs.

Chapter 3

JP stubbed out his cigarette and lit a joint. He tapped at the wireless keyboard in his lap, flipping through show cues, clips, and notes on the large screen mounted above the fireplace. He had fitted the fireplace with its own screen that played a video of a fire on a continuous loop. An alarm pinged on a third monitor on his coffee table where his feet were propped. Two minutes till his pre-show live stream for his premium fan club members. He pulled out the decanter and ice bucket along with the crystal highball glass. The decanter was filled with water and food coloring to turn it a rich, bourbony brown. He rarely drank at all now—or at least he was trying to rarely drink at all—and never before a show. Not anymore. The marijuana was fake, too, just a hand rolled cigarette.

JP had started the pre-show live streams as a lark back when he drank before the shows, and before everything else too. The original format was nothing but him drinking and mumbling a rehearsal to himself, often ranting and riffing directly to the audience. The pre-shows started getting enough views that he put time into giving them a format, developing bits and segments. The drinking and smoking were important to his audience according to all his analytics, so he kept up the appearance now. He was definitely quitting for good this time.

One minute until the live stream. He checked his phone and saw a message from Dex. "Professor cut us loose early. Leaving now. Definitely be at the show tonight." *Awesome,* JP thought, *baby brother will be there tonight*. Dex was the most enthusiastic about JP's moderate success, though his family was all supportive. Not his father, of course, but what else was new? He decided that was how he would open the pre-show, thirty seconds to air now. He'd announce his younger brother would be at the show then comment about his family being supportive except for his dad—though, truth be outed, Carrie's husband Morgan was a bit of an eye-roller, but he didn't come right out and dog him, which was appreciated—and then how his dad only supported the Seahawks, Myrtle Beach's high school football team. Then what? He needed a line after the Seahawks thing to complete the joke. All his dad supported were the Seahawks and—ten seconds to the live stream. *C'mon, JP*, he said to himself, *what else does that miserable old bastard support?* All he supports are the Seahawks and...BANG, there it was. He had it. Three, two, one—show time. He clicked his laptop and the three webcams went live and his viewers' screen names filled the chat box on his screen.

"Righty-o, Cassidians, JP-Nuts, and, more generally, devoted viewers," he said. "This is JP Cassidy giving you the Big Welcome." He tapped the keyboard and a giant "WELCOME" in a white font filled his viewers' screens. The Big Welcome was one of his hallmarks. "Thanks for buying tickets to the show tonight at Big Lock's and thanks for joining the pre-show. I'm here at casa de JP as *un*usual, no Holiday Inn Express for a change. Tonight is a hometown show. The Kittyfat is..." JP muted his microphone and crinkled the bag of cat treats. Walnut, his enormously fat cat leapt onto the back of the couch on cue, right above JP's shoulder and perfectly into the shot. JP unmuted the microphone. "Right here, by my side as always when I'm home. My friend and compatriot and personal *bête noire*." Walnut stuffed his face between the cushions to dig out the treats JP had taught him to find there. "Shy as always," JP said.

"I'm excited for the show tonight. I have some fun stuff I'm pumped to do for you all plus my baby brother Dex texted me right before this to say he had been let out of his last class before fall break early—big thanks to whatever slacker professor at the U. of South Carolina let him go—and that he was already on the road and would be at Big Lock's for the gig tonight." Dex was a fan favorite, both on JP's show and in general life. Dex was enthusiastic and he was generous with his enthusiasm. He had the ability to be excited for other people, for their successes, their presence at an event, news about their personal lives.

"I'm thrilled to have him there. That means the full Cassidy clan will be in attendance tonight. They're all really supportive except, of course, for Butch, my dad, who isn't supportive of anything except our local high school football team the Seahawks and wearing incredibly white sneakers with his socks pulled up." JP sat up and put on a commercial voice-over tone. "Over sixty shoe fashion, brought to you by Father Time and Skechers. You'll never lose Dad in the dark with Skechers' ultra-ultra-white sneakers. Ergonomically designed for low speed and high visibility." He dropped back into his normal voice. "Actually, I'm being a little dishonest. Mom can't make the show tonight either because she has to stay home and cook Dex every food he ever hinted at enjoying. So just the siblings for—" His phone rang. He took a long drink from his pretend bourbon. "Let's see if this is my brother calling from the road in his saggin' wagon." Dex drove the family's old minivan. A gift for his high school graduation. That is, if you considered an eighteen-year-old Toyota Previa that every child of the Cassidy clan had vomited, fought, spilled food, and made out with high school sweethearts in, a gift and not a punishment.

"Nope, it's my sister, Sailor. Calling from her Honda P.O.S. I presume." JP glanced at the activity in the live chat.

"Answer it! 😊"

"I <3 Sailor. Answer it!"

"My sound isn't working. Should there be sound?"

JP said, "Seems like a strong consensus to answer it and say hello to Sailor. And could someone in the live chat tell fitzybitzy12 that yes, there should be sound. Why the fuck wouldn't there be sound? Do you see a lot of soundless live streams where a person sits here speaking, their lips obviously moving to form words and there's not supposed to be sound? Their speakers are probably muted." JP made a quick decision not to tell Sailor she was on the pre-show. If he got something funny out of the call, he could play it tonight at the actual show. It would be twice as funny because Sailor would be in the audience and wouldn't know she had been on the pre-show. Plus doing that bit live would be a good plug for the pre-show itself. JP answered the call and put it on speaker for his digital audience. "Sailor, what's crappenin'?" he said.

"Hey. Yeah, can you tell Mr. Papaioannou here that taking a picture on his computer does not automatically post the picture to the Internet? You're on speaker by the way," Sailor said.

"Mr. who? What's this now?" JP asked.

"The computer is connected to the Internet. With Wi-Fi," an accented voice said.

"Yeah, man," Sailor said. "But that doesn't mean everything that happens on the computer goes to the Internet. The Internet isn't like a defined place where things just land. Would you tell him, JP? The guy is missing out on sending pics back and forth to his grandson in Dayton."

"Who's missing out? Where are you? Are you calling me from inside a fever dream?" JP asked.

"Mr. Papaioannou called this morning for a problem with his AC but then asked me about his computer, and now I'm trying to explain to him that it's okay to FaceTime with his grandson. I told him you could confirm all this because you were a celebrity on the Internet."

This is why you answer when you're on the air and Sailor calls, JP thought. She always had something going on, some little tidbit. It might be dumb, but it was content.

"So obviously I lied a little," Sailor said.

"Lies?" the other voice, obviously Mr. Papaioannou, said. "These are lies about the FaceTime?"

"No, no," Sailor said. "I'm saying it's a lie about him being a celebrity on the Internet. But like as a joke. It's my brother. Do you have brothers? You gotta mess with them some, you know?"

"Break the balls," Mr. Papaioannou said.

"Dude, yes, exactly. Breaking his balls, that's it."

The chat thread was losing its mind. This was great.

"I'm ded. Mr. Papi is adorable." Followed by a dozen heart emojis.

"Yoooo, Sailor rolled in and just started doing IT support."

"Dick move not telling her she's on the air."

The last comment was from someone named HopAlongBaller19. JP recognized the name. They had started logging in recently and throwing shade at him in the comments. Nothing over the top, but they were always pissy. JP didn't get it. The person was paying money to watch someone they clearly didn't like. But cash was cash and viewers were viewers, so if the weirdo wanted to waste their time, fine by JP.

"Mr. Papaioannou, this is JP. I'm Sailor's brother. And first of all, I want you to know that I'm very, very famous on the Internet. Second of all, FaceTime with your grandson is totally safe and you won't end up on the Internet in whatever scary fashion you imagine happening."

"See," Sailor said. "It's safe. You're going to be happy you get to see the little guy. And he'll like it."

"Your brother is like this Kardashian? Is influencer?" Mr. Papaioannou said.

"Well no, they're like, actually famous," Sailor said.

"The Kardashians are," Mr. Papaioannou said followed by a sound JP couldn't quite place: *twah twah*.

"Did he just spit?" JP asked.

"Are you spitting?" Sailor said at the same time. "Dude, that's your floor."

"They are very bad. Malaka."

"What's *malaka*?"

"Word in my country. Is masturbator. Like person who masturbates but not really, just as personality. You know this?"

"Like a jerkoff? Calling someone a jerkoff?"

"Is close enough, yes. Like jerkoff."

"Okay, then yeah, I'll say my brother is like the Kardashians."

"Hey!" JP said.

Twah. Mr. Papaioannou spit again.

"Oh my God, just call your grandson," Sailor said.

"Did you fix his AC?" JP asked.

"Yeah, the drainage hose was clogged. It's fine now," Sailor said. "Hey listen, guess what? Jug is back. I saw him last night. Did you know?"

JP choked a little on the fake joint he had just hit and coughed. "Back? Back where? Here?" he hacked out.

"Dude, you alright? Yeah, back in town. I thought he might have hit you up."

JP got his coughing under control. "How long has he been back?"

"I don't know. A few days, I guess. I was half in the bag when I saw him. Didn't ask a ton of questions."

"Why is that the second thing?" JP nearly yelled.

"What?"

"Why is that the second thing you're telling me? Why wouldn't you lead with that?"

"I don't know," Sailor said, confused. "That's just the order it came out in. You guys were buds, I thought you'd want to know. I didn't realize the extra minute Mr. Papaioannou's issue took was going to throw your Jug's-back timetable out of whack. You need to rush out and get a haircut or something in case he swings by? Calm down."

JP stared at the phone in his hand. Jug was back. Fuck, that meant. Wait, double fuck, he was still streaming. He glanced at the chat log.

"Yo, I think homeboy blew a gasket. He's just frozen."

"Jug? Y'all know people with the dumbest names."

"It's obviously a nickname, dickface." HopAlongBaller19 again, chiming in.

JP gathered his thoughts and tried to get cool. "No, it's fine. Just surprising news is all," he said to Sailor.

"If you say so. Oh, I also wanted to ask you something. Like obviously don't say anything to her about it, but do you think Carrie is having an affair? Lately she's been—"

JP hung up the phone. "Whoops, seems like we lost Sailor," he said for his viewers. He cleared his mind, looking for his rhythm. He would have to process the Jug news after the broadcast and figure out what to do. Same with the question about Carrie having an affair. He didn't know what prompted Sailor to ask that. Carrie was the kind of person who cleaned her oven on a monthly schedule. She semi-regularly reminded JP that he'd need to get a colonoscopy at forty-five, an appointment more than fifteen years away. He couldn't picture someone like that having an affair. Carrie was going to be furious if she found out he live streamed something like that. Maybe he'd hung up in time and no one had caught it. He looked at the chat again.

"We all heard the part about the affair, right?"

"Boy you better call her back and get the deets on this affair. I'm invested now."

"Told you he was a dick for not telling her she was on air." HopAlongBaller19 again.

JP reached down under the coffee table where the real bottle of bourbon was—only for emergencies, he had told himself, though what kind of emergency required bourbon? "Need a little refill," he said, hoping he sounded cool and unaffected. He opened the bottle and poured about two fingers worth straight into his mouth.

"Here he goes," HopAlongBaller19 said. "This should be a beautiful disaster."

•••

Sailor was in Mr. Papaioannou's living room talking to JP when the call dropped. She tried calling him back but it went straight to his voicemail. She stared at her phone, remembering her texts to Carrie the night before, texts she didn't really remember sending. She thumbed into her messages and saw one with just a number, no name. She opened and saw the message, "This is Lula's number." She had responded with just, "Sailor." So they *had* exchanged numbers. Lula might text her at any moment. Sailor wasn't sure if she did or didn't want that to happen, but now that she knew it was a possibility she couldn't take it hanging over her head. Sailor didn't know how to go on a date, or how to not be someone Harper described as "incapable of growing the seed of respect in your partner that's necessary to sustain a maturing relationship beyond the infatuation stage." It would be easiest if the woman just went back to Florence and never spoke to her again. Sailor turned off her phone. She would call JP later, once her hangover fully subsided and the mystery woman's theoretical text message felt less daunting. She wanted a second opinion on her theory about Carrie. Sailor had idly suspected Carrie was seeing someone for a while. Her usually reliable schedule had dark spots that couldn't be accounted for, times she didn't text back or answer her phone. Plus, Sailor was familiar with her older sister's sense of retribution. When they were young, Sailor had given Carrie's dolls hacked-up haircuts with kitchen scissors and Carrie, in turn, cut the hair of Sailor's dolls. But she gave them neat bobs and layered styles with feathered bangs as if demonstrating to Sailor the right way to do things. They actually looked better. Carrie favored mimicry that drifted toward correction over one-upmanship. Sailor imagined Carrie having an affair like that—an illicit paramour with good financial sense and a clean kitchen. All this made Sailor impatient to meet Isaac and get his camera so she could start tailing Morgan and Nina. The excitement floated the little bottom-feeding thoughts she'd had about her sister's fidelity to the surface.

Almost a year earlier, Carrie and Sailor had been out together at Big Lock's one night when Dex was home from college on break. A friend of Dex's and JP's—a member of the gaggle that always encircled their brothers—was there playing pool. Tusk. It was short for something longer that Sailor couldn't remember. Sailor had met Tusk several times by that point. She liked him. He was quieter than the others, who always seemed to be competing to break from their role in the chorus and get a three-minute solo off some story or joke.

"Do we know that one?" Carrie had asked Sailor, nodding toward Tusk.

Sailor looked up from her phone where she was badgering her weed dealer. "Chrome dome over there?" she said. "That's Tusk. He transferred in part way through JP's senior year but then he moved to Florida. Jupiter or Neptune, one of the planet places down there. But then he came back again. He's around sometimes now. Cop I think."

"And you're texting your drug dealer to come here?"

"Should Parker not come in wearing his *I'm a Drug Dealer* hat, firing bags of weed from a T-shirt cannon?"

"Does he date one of the seagulls?" Carrie asked. That was their name for the pack of girls who hung around their brothers' friends who, with a few exceptions, Carrie and Sailor thought of mostly as a human garbage dump.

Sailor caught something in her sister's tone, or maybe something in the question itself. She looked over at Tusk and then back. "Are you into him or something? Like to get back at Morgan?"

"Lower your voice," Carrie hissed. She had confided only in Sailor at that point. Sailor was very nearly moved to violence by the news of the affair. It was the angriest Sailor could ever remember being. A true rage that made her realize any fury she felt in the past was actually something else—mere frustration, or impatience, or even good old-fashioned self-righteousness. Hearing that someone had, unprovoked, so thoroughly hurt and betrayed her sister, highlighted how much Sailor took Carrie's graciousness for granted. That was a younger sibling's privilege, earned through years of getting hand-me-down bikes with broken pedals and being given video game controllers that weren't even plugged in, and it enraged her that some outsider, some interloper, would betray that. When Carrie told her, Sailor pulled out one of her stun guns and announced she was going to go put a couple thousand volts across Morgan's balls and then a few thousand more up Nina Capaldi's cooch. Carrie calmed her down and make her promise not to do anything or tell anyone until she figured out what she was going to do. Sailor stared at her hard when she said that.

"What do you mean *figure out what to do*? You leave his cheating ass. Or, you know," Sailor sparked the stun gun a couple times.

"No, please," Carrie had said. "I need time to think."

That night at Big Lock's, Sailor kept on her hunch. "You are, aren't you? Wondering if you could sleep with him to get back at Morgan."

"What I'm wondering is if I can get you to stop looking at your phone and talk to me," Carrie snapped.

Sailor's phone lit up with an incoming text from Parker right then and she said, "Fucking finally, he's outside. I'll be right back." She hopped off her chair and charged out the door and forgot about Carrie's uncharacteristic questions about Tusk.

The conversation came back to her now as she went into the kitchen to find Mr. Papaioannou. He was at the counter loading baklava into Tupperware. "For you," he said, gesturing to the baklava.

"You don't have to—"

"Oh po po po, stop. You be too polite. Take food. Enjoy. You nice girl. Not like Kardashians." Mr. Papaioannou closed the lid on the Tupperware and started to hand it to Sailor until something out the kitchen window caught his eye. "What is this now?"

It was Isaac pulling up out front in his work truck. Sailor had asked him to meet her here. "It's my friend," Sailor said. "He's lending me his camera."

"Is construction worker?"

"Yeah, he's doing the house a couple streets over."

"Tell him stop leaving truck in road."

"He leaves his truck in the road?"

"Not this truck. Another truck. By the construction house. I take walk at night, see this truck. They leave all night. Not safe in the dark. Someone will hit it." He placed a hand on Sailor's shoulder. "I call my grandson on the FaceTime. You smart girl. Know to fix things. If my wife still alive she like you, say to fatten you up. She always want to make fat the people she likes." He put the baklava in her hands. "You eat this. Get fat for my wife, okay?"

"It's usually Air Down There's policy for employees not to eat entire Tupperwares of dessert at the behest of the deceased wives of our customers but."

"But you make exception for me, right?" Mr. Papaioannou said, winking at her. "Smartypants."

Sailor met Isaac by his truck. He handed over his camera. Sailor declined the tripod and remote control packed neatly in a black case on his backseat. His surfboard was strapped to his over-cab rack.

"Going out on your lunch breaks these days?" she asked, nodding at the board.

"No time," Isaac said. "Got to make that money while the sun's up, you know? They ain't going to be building this fast and this much forever. Bunch of us been going out at night."

"Well that's not at all stupid," Sailor said. "Y'all have a few beers first to really prove your intelligence? Chum the waters so you can fish for sharks at the same time?"

"So hilarious," Issac said. "How's it your brother's making a run at a comedy career and not you? You know that new Starlight Sands hotel they built at 74th?"

"We haven't been formally introduced, but I know the name."

"They got a bunch of their floodlights pointing at the beach and the ocean at night till about ten. Trying to encourage evening beach walks for the offseason tourists or something. They'll have to shut them down when the turtle's nesting season starts, but for now that's our night spot."

"Be careful doing that dumb shit, would you?" Sailor said. "I don't want the responsibility of taking care of this thing if you make it an orphan." She held up the camera. "You get sucked out into the dark on a riptide or something."

Isaac smiled and pulled a fifty pack of glow sticks out of the truck. "We're lit up out there like the damn fourth of July," he said. "Keep everyone accounted for."

Sailor drove back to her apartment, rolled a few joints, and filled a bottle with water. She changed out of her Air Down There shirt and jeans and into a reasonably clean pair of yoga pants and a sleek designer top Carrie had found at TJ Maxx but didn't like and passed along to her. She completed her outfit with her ten-year-old work boots.

The towel was still in the same place it had landed when she tossed it on the bed that morning. Lula must have opted to take a shower back at whatever hotel hosted high school volleyball coaches in town for tournaments. Presumably something by the convention center.

Sailor opened the dresser drawer where she kept her weaponry and considered the second stun gun—the other one she had worn to her call earlier was still in the car—and her Hellcat Compact nine millimeter. If she was going to be spying on people it might be best not to have the gun on her if she was caught. That could look murdery. In the end, though, she decided she would rather look murdery than murdered if she had to follow Nina or Morgan to somewhere shady. She was specifically thinking of that run-down bar Morgan liked.

Sailor slipped the gun and holster into her waistband and left the second stun gun in the drawer. She looked at her bed where one of the pillows still held a dent from Lula the volleyball coach's head creasing it. She had been standing next to the ghost of her relationship with Harper for a long time. Now she felt she had taken at least one large step past it.

"First steps," she said to the empty room. "Hey presto, just like that."

•••

Bevel had been to jail before, but never in his own cell. "Earned yourself a VIP room, asshole. Thanks for embarrassing me," his cousin Craig said as he shoved him into the small room.

"You're the embarrassment," Bevel snapped. "Arresting your own cousin."

"You think I want you here around my job? I'd rather arrest some decent folks. Instead, I get a call for breaking and entering and it's my own family? Can't even leave you sitting on a bench for two minutes. The hell was that all about?"

"None of your damn business. And I ain't broke or entered a damn thing neither."

"What're you doing up on those people's front porch then?"

"A man can't be up on somebody's front porch? The Constitution says I got the freedom to be wherever I want. It's called pursuit of happiness and if being up on a front porch makes me happy then the Constitution says I can do that."

"Bevel, you've never read one goddamn word of the Constitution."

"You don't know that."

"I know that the pursuit of happiness is from the Declaration of Independence, not the Constitution. So I'm declaring you've never read either one."

"They're the same thing. Call my momma."

"Your momma doesn't know the Constitution from prostitution. Though I'll admit she the people forms imperfect unions that insure domestic non-tranquility and promotes herself on welfare."

"I ain't entirely sure what that last bit means, but I know when someone's calling my momma a whore. You're going to be sorry you said that shit."

"You don't know what it means 'cause you've never read one goddamn word of the Constitution you sweaty stick of grease."

"I get a call. Call my momma."

"I'm not calling your momma or your sister, and we both know I'm not calling your daddy 'cause no one knows who he is or anything about him except that he was most definitely a meth head." Craig slammed the cell door, turned, and left.

Bevel paced in his small cell while he thought of a bunch of good comebacks to the litany of insults against his mother, but Craig didn't come back. He set those aside and thought about the more interesting thing that had happened: seeing that piece of shit Jug. He reacted stupidly, he knew that. He no doubt added time to how long it would be before he got out of incarceration and could do anything meaningful to Jug. As soon as he recognized him, though, it was like the bullet in his leg had sent a pulse to his brain telling him to take revenge for the permanent limp he had now. That limp was the only reason a slob like his cousin Craig even had a chance of catching him when he took off from that house. He honestly wasn't trying to break into it, at least not at that moment. That would come later. A neighbor called the cops. Bevel heard Craig's partner say so when he was talking to dispatch in the police car. According to Craig's partner, the neighbor reported "a real sketchy looking guy creeping around the neighborhood... No, 'sketchy' is my word, the guy was Greek or something. He said, 'Man who is sinister' and 'Looks as if drugs. Very stringy.' We stopped by his house and got a statement." When did people become so untrusting? What did he ever do to the Greeks? It was a shame. He managed to hit three houses before his arrest. Bevel had fortunately hidden his baggie of crystal in his waistband. They hadn't found it in his pat down. He would have to be careful with that, really dole it out since he didn't know how long he would be in here.

He fished out the baggie of crystal. He could have just a little right now, he decided. He would carefully parcel out the rest. He opened the baggie and scooped the granular powder onto his pinky nail, then raised the fingernail to his nose and snorted it back. His engine revved and his energy coalesced. He felt himself drop smoothly into gear. That was better. And there was still a lot left. He could have a little more. He scooped and snorted. That was it. Now he was rocking and rolling. He would keep it real cool and get through this and get out of here and find Jug and snap his leg for him real good which wasn't exactly the same as taking a bullet to the femur but close enough for revenge and then he would snap his neck but only after he had some time to live with the snapped leg and feel the throbbing pain of it then he'd kick Jug in his broken leg while he lay—

"Hey!" A voice slammed an unwanted period onto Bevel's thought stream. He stuffed the baggie back into his waistband and swung around to face the door of his cell. An officer was peering at him through the wire glass. Bevel could see a white AirPod in each ear. "I said put your hands through the slot. I'm not telling you again," the cop said.

Keep it cool keep it cool keep it cool, Bevel thought, putting his hands through the slot in the door. "Sorry," he said, as normally as he could manage.

The cop at the door snapped handcuffs around Bevel's wrists and said, "Whatever man, stand back." Bevel stepped back and the door opened. "Step out of the room," the cop said. Bevel stepped into the hallway. "Walk straight ahead. Stop at the white door on the left. Let's go," the cop instructed.

They went down the hall and through the white door. Bevel found himself back in bookings and release. Across the white and gray tile floor he could see into the lobby of the police station where a row of glass doors led outside. The cop with the AirPods walked Bevel to a small room with a table bolted to the back wall. He closed the door behind them and removed Bevel's handcuffs.

"Place your hands on the wall and spread your legs," the cop said.

"What's going on?" Bevel asked.

"Place your hands on the wall and spread your legs," the cop said again. "That's what's going on."

Bevel did what he was told, saying, "Man, I know my rights."

"Okay, list them," the cop said.

"What?"

"You say you know your rights. Go ahead and list them for me while your hands are against the wall and your legs are spread." Bevel was stumped. It was like you needed a law degree just to be arrested these days. "That's what I thought," the AirPod cop said, standing behind Bevel and running his hands around his waistband. "Dumbasses come in here every day telling me they know their rights and every one of them, to a man, clams up the minute I ask them to name them. Y'all are just saying shit you heard on TV instead of—" His right hand found the lump in Bevel's waistband

and felt around inside the band for the opening. He pulled out the baggie of crystal. "Look here what officers Daniels and Schmitt missed. Fuckin' Knight called it."

Bevel was flying from the crystal. Arms up on the wall, peering around his armpit, he saw AirPod cop place the baggie on the table and felt him go back into his waistband, checking for anything more. Bevel felt his opportunity coming and formulated a plan. His thoughts were moving so fast that what he was about to do felt like it was already done, like it had already happened. His body just needed to catch up with his mind.

AirPod cop wriggled around inside Bevel's waistband. Bevel spun from the wall, grabbing the officer by the neck and dropping to his knees, using his full body weight to slam the cop's head into the metal table. AirPod cop fell back onto the floor, blood running down the side of his face, his mouth opening and closing silently. Bevel snatched the bag of crystal off the table. He cracked the door to the small room and peered out into the processing area. No one looked up. Bevel looked at the doorway that led to the lobby. He knew from experience it was locked and had to be buzzed open from behind the desk. The only other way into the lobby was to go over the desk itself and through the small opening in the bullet proof glass. He looked back into the room. The cop was still on the floor, mouth working soundlessly. Buzzing with confidence from his high, Bevel made his call. It wasn't like someone was going to unlock the door for him.

"Help," he shouted into the processing area, opening the door all the way. The room quieted and heads snapped up to look at him, like feeding animals at the approach of a predator. "He's having a fit or something," Bevel yelled, pointing back into the small room. "I don't know what happened. He started jerking and fell down. Better get you an ambulance or a doctor or something. Someone help him."

Two officers came around the desk and ran into the room. Bevel backed away to give them space. A third cop was still behind the desk, leaning over, straining to see inside the room while speaking into her walkie talkie, requesting an ambulance. This was as good as it was going to get, Bevel reasoned. He darted behind the desk and scurried to the section that faced the lobby. There was bullet proof glass over the desk here, but a two foot by two foot window opened in the middle of this for transactions. It stood open now. Bevel dove through it headfirst, hearing the cop with the radio behind him yelling, "Hey! Shit! Stop!"

Bevel hit the lobby floor face-first, but he couldn't feel a thing at the moment. He scrambled to his feet, bolted through the front doors, and took off sprinting nearly as fast as his feverish thoughts.

•••

Nina Capaldi threw abuse and invective the way other women might throw shoes. Though, she threw those too. She should have worked as a baggage handler at the airport as much as she liked throwing shit, Morgan thought bitterly. He was standing in her condo, listening as she called him a "special breed of pathetic that went beyond dickless."

"No," Nina said, "You know what? It's a baby dick, that's what you have. Being a dickless man would at least be interesting. You just have a little baby-sized dick. And your gay wife sucks it like a Tic Tac."

She was angry he didn't respond to the texts she sent earlier in the day. She was almost always angry with him. Her expectations of his time and attention did not, in his opinion, match the realistic abilities of a married man having an affair. "There's no call to bring my wife into it," Morgan said. "How would that make her gay anyway? Sucking my dick?"

"One of them's gay, aren't they?" Nina said. She stood in the living room of her condo, arms crossed, staring him down across the room where he was hovering by the door. "I just assumed it was your wife. And that it's probably your fault she turned gay." Nina knew perfectly well it was Carrie's sister, Sailor, who was gay, but she liked to pretend not to remember details in order to demonstrate how little people meant to her. Particularly when it came to Morgan's wife's family. She liked to act as though so many of them were gay she couldn't be expected to remember which ones specifically. Nina enjoyed feigning ignorance about things in a way that allowed her to exaggerate and suggest rumors, to be meaner than she could within the bounds of the truth.

Nina was briefly Morgan's chief source of joy. Their affair was the embodiment of what he saw as his success. She had been an expensive endeavor since the first night he met her at Ruth's Chris. It was a dinner that Hector Simpatico, the primary investor and advisor for his property development, invited him to. He lied to Carrie about the dinner—"It's strictly business, not social. No one's bringing guests."—because he wanted to stretch the wings of his recent wealth and ascendency without his wife there to remind him and everyone else that there were limits on where the night could take him. Nina was one of several women there who didn't appear to be attached to anyone in particular. As soon as Morgan saw her he felt the unrestrained gallop of possibility he was looking for. She was blond, slender and busty like someone from a movie or an overly photoshopped Instagram page. She wore bright red lipstick and dark eyeliner, makeup meant to pull your eyes away from whoever was speaking and have them settle on her impassive face, unbothered by blatant staring. Nina was cool and aloof during the informal introductions made before the meal. Her face made no expression as Hector introduced her to the various men he had invited, and their dates if they had one, until he got to Morgan. She smiled at Morgan, her teeth bright white against her red lips, her head lowered slightly, looking up at him with her soft almond eyes.

Morgan felt good. He was wearing an off-the-rack suit but he'd had it tailored. He thought it did a solid job of hiding his gut, which was expanding ever since the money from Hector's investment came in and restaurants started featuring more heavily in his diet. He was drinking more too, going out more often. Enjoying the spoils of his efforts was how he saw it. The guys he rolled with more and more these days lived fast. Work hard, party harder was the creed. The cocaine he dabbled in now should have cut his weight. Wasn't that how it always happened in movies? He figured it must just take a little time to work. He was clean-shaven, no tie, pressed white shirt opened one extra button, hair meticulously styled to look rakishly brushed back. That way it drew attention from how his cheeks, puffed up with the weight gain, had started sagging a bit. Whatever. The coke would thin that out soon enough.

He didn't manage to sit by Nina at dinner, but afterwards, when the party had moved to the bar, he approached her and asked if he could order her a drink.

"Dom Pérignon," she said. "Get the bottle. I might want a second glass."

Morgan raised his eyebrows. The Dom was four hundred dollars a bottle. He knew because he had lain in bed the previous night reading the restaurant's menu on his phone after Carrie had fallen asleep, in awe at the prices of basic things like potatoes and salads, amazed he would be ordering simple food that cost so much. A four-hundred-dollar bottle of champagne for a woman who was not his wife on a night that was not an occasion besides it being a Thursday, made his blood rush. He reminded himself that he was limitless.

"What if I suggested something cheaper?" Morgan asked, trying to sound flirtatious, humorous.

"Then you'd have to find someone cheap to drink it with you," Nina said.

"That won't work," Morgan said. "You've got to have a drink. We're celebrating."

"Are we? What are we celebrating?" Nina cocked her head, looking at him with more interest now.

"The night we first met, of course." Morgan gestured to the bartender who rushed over with the obsequiousness of a butler. "A bottle of Dom Pérignon for the lady," Morgan told him. "I'll have a Macallan 15, neat." The bartender got to work and Morgan turned back to Nina. He had her full attention now. He pushed the price tag of that attention out of his mind. He could afford it. He was a developer now, he could afford all sorts of things.

"I'm Nina," she said, taking the glass the bartender poured for her.

"I'm Morgan," he said, holding out his tumbler with its obscenely stingy pour of Macallan. "A toast to the night we first met."

"Be brave," she said. "Save the toast for the morning we first woke up together."

It all happened so fast he couldn't have controlled it even if he actually knew what he was doing. It came so easily he felt it would have been ungrateful to stop it. Morgan didn't tell Nina he was married until their third date. He was sick the whole day leading up to it. He tried to imagine any kind of scenario where he could somehow get away with not telling her but the only one that presented itself was never seeing or speaking to her again. He couldn't imagine that either. He prepared for her to be enraged when he came clean, but instead she nodded and said, "I figured." Morgan was relieved, believing he had fallen into the perfect affair. Within a week she was using his marriage against him to get what she wanted. Dinners, jewelry, gifts, his time—anything he resisted that she wanted was met with the threat to tell his wife about them. He was a hostage in their relationship. What was worse was he had orchestrated his kidnapping himself.

"I'm sorry I didn't call," Morgan tried now. "I have stuff going on with work and home and—"

"Oh, just shut up," Nina said, flopping down on her couch and staring at the TV, which was muted, showing something from Bravo. "You always have some shit excuse. You had time for your wife didn't you? Who you don't even fuck? I shouldn't even have let you in. Get out."

Morgan figured this was a win. He had been ripping lines of coke all day and he was anxious and irritable. He didn't want to be there anyway. He turned to leave.

"That's it?" Nina yelled, seeing him go. "You're just going to walk out of here after the shit you pulled? That's classic you, Morgan. A hick who can't hack it." She stood and held up her phone. "Maybe I'll just give your wife a call and say, 'Hey, don't worry, he's running on home to you now. I'm done with your hick-who-can't-hack-it husband and you can have him back.' How 'bout I do that?"

It was a routine threat. Nina made it all the time when she wanted to pull his strings. Morgan knew he should go. Just walk out, get through the next day, and never speak to Nina again, but as he was reaching for the doorknob while she threatened to call Carrie something occurred to him. He could turn this around for once. She had been threatening him for most of their relationship. Now, he could finally get the upper hand, crawl out from under the power her unattached life afforded her over his life of lies. "Go ahead and call her," he said, turning away from the door and coming toward her.

"You think I won't?"

"Do it. Call her now while I stand here," Morgan said, crossing his arms.

"Oh, you're a tough guy now? Is that it?" Nina said.

"The fuck does that even mean?" Morgan snapped. "I said call my wife. Now." Morgan's heart was going faster, his blood was up. He had never yelled at Nina. He was always cajoling, pleading. Now it didn't matter. Nina only had the house number and Carrie was gone for the day, stormed off somewhere because he wasn't going to that idiot JP's mixed-media stand-up comedy show or whatever the hell it was he did. "You're not dialing," he said, pointing to Nina's cell phone, ever present in one hand.

Nina wasn't backing down, but Morgan could see she knew something was wrong, that something had shifted, that he was serious. "I'll call her right now," Nina said, her voice flat, her volume normal. She punched at the screen with her thumb and put the phone to her ear, staring at Morgan. The dull thrum of the ring reached Morgan where he stood. Nina let it ring three times then hung up and said, "There's no answer. What the fuck is going on?"

"Call back and leave a message," Morgan said, calm, cool.

"Enough, Morgan. What is this?"

"Did you see my last text?"

"I stopped reading your pathetic texts."

Morgan suspected this was a lie, just some move she was pulling, like not being able to remember which Cassidy was which. He laughed, short and loud and derisive. "You don't get it, do you?" he said. He didn't really know what he meant by this, but it was the kind of thing she was always saying to him to get under his skin. He felt like a god saying it to her now as he turned and started to leave.

Morgan was flying, ready to take his performance in this final conflict—because he was now definitively finished with Nina—and carry it with him to the Range Rover for another bump of coke like a new best friend. Then it got better. As he reached the door Nina called out, "Wait. Morgan, wait." He stopped. He couldn't remember being this happy since the day they broke ground on Palmetto Glades. "Fine, I read the text, okay? You have big news? Is this... What's your news?"

Morgan was stalling when he wrote that. She had been pummeling his phone with text messages, a brigade tactic she used regularly, and he had replied, *Big news, I'll call later, get excited* in a performative attempt to get her to stop. He didn't expect it to work. It hadn't. She wrote back, *Call me right now you fucking pedophile.* He figured he would tell her he sold a house or something when he finally saw her, but this had worked out so much better. "I left her," Morgan said. "My wife. I left her. Like we talked about." This was untrue, but that didn't matter, it ought to level her some, knock the arrogant condescension out of her tone at least.

"Like you talked about," Nina replied too quickly, her expression neutral. She stared off into the corner, distracted.

"Like I—" Morgan's soaring high faltered. If he thought about it, sure, he was technically the one who was always saying he was going to leave Carrie, but obviously he said it for Nina's benefit. Why was she getting specific about it? He hadn't meant it anyway, it was just something you said when you needed to appease your angry mistress. "Like I always said when we were talking, yeah," Morgan said. "Like we talked about." He waited for Nina to be overcome with embarrassment at how she had treated him now that she thought he had left his wife for her.

Nina crossed her arms. "You don't want to stay here, do you?"

"What?"

"I mean, you can for like a night, I guess. But you can't like, *stay here* stay here."

"I don't need to stay here," Morgan said, deflating.

"Thank God. I couldn't have you like, in my space all the time," Nina said, going back into the living room and sitting down on the couch.

Morgan followed her away from the door, into the room in a slight daze, replaying the last few seconds in his head. "I said I left my wife," he repeated, just in case he misspoke the first time and actually said something else that warranted this blasé response.

"Yeah, I heard you. So?" Nina said. "Was it like a scene or something? Oh! Do you think she told her family already? The cute brother is doing his streaming thing today." She took her laptop from the coffee table and opened it. "Do you think he'll talk about it? Do you think he'll talk a bunch of shit about you? He works for you, right? You have to fire him now that you left his sister. I bet he talks a bunch of shit about you." She was navigating to whatever site JP hosted his nonsense on. Morgan reached over and gently tried to close the laptop. Nina jerked the computer away from him and fixed him with an angry look. "What do you think you're doing?"

"Can we talk about this?" Morgan said. "I don't want to watch JP's stupid show."

"I don't give a shit what you want to watch," Nina said. "I can't believe you just tried to slam my laptop closed on my hands. That's so inappropriate."

"Nina—"

"Do you even have any idea how unhinged what you just did is? Do you?" Nina opened the site with JP's show, already in progress, and held her finger down on the volume key until JP's voice was blaring, tinny and sharp, from the mediocre speaker.

"Did you fix his AC?" JP was saying.

"Yeah, the drainage hose was clogged. It's fine now," a second voice said. "Hey listen, guess what? Jug is back. I saw him last night. Did you know?" Morgan turned his attention fully to the show at the mention of Jug's name. Jug was the dirtbag guy Carrie had a thing for when she was younger. He was still creeping around when Morgan met her and started giving her a taste of what a decent guy was like. Then Jug vanished. The Cassidy family took this harder than was really warranted. Morgan understood there was a history there. The guy had grown up next door, there was an abandoned puppy quality to the whole dynamic, but Jug was just another local loser. Myrtle Beach hadn't suffered the loss of a great mind when he took off for wherever.

"Back? Back where? Here?" JP was saying through a coughing fit. Fucking stoner, Morgan thought. Asshole was supposed to be sober.

The second voice sounded like Sailor. Morgan squinted at the screen. Sailor wasn't on the video. It looked like JP was on the phone with her on speaker, having their conversation out loud for the audience. Morgan wondered if Sailor knew their conversation was being broadcast.

Nina was observing, unhappily, Morgan's sudden attention to the show. She only put it on because she thought it would annoy him. "This is stupid," she said suddenly, and began to close the laptop herself. Morgan, who had not wanted to watch at all, now felt a spiteful compulsion to continue watching in response to Nina's blatant antagonism. He snatched the computer off her lap and held it up to his face, making a show of listening intently. "Oh my God," Nina said, "I can't believe you just did that. You just slammed into me and—"

"Shut the fuck up!" Morgan screamed, leaning over to pour as much volume as he could directly into her face. Nina recoiled from him, mouth still open but silent now. Morgan turned back to the laptop.

"No, it's fine. Just surprising news is all," JP was saying to Sailor.

"If you say so. Oh, I also wanted to ask you something. Like obviously don't say anything to her about it, but do you think Carrie is having an affair? Lately she's been—" and then Sailor's voice cut out.

"Whoops, seems like we lost Sailor," JP said, having clearly hung up on her.

JP started rambling on and Morgan sat back on the couch. Carrie was having an affair? Really Sailor had only asked whether JP thought Carrie was having an affair, but Sailor read people and situations with remarkable clarity sometimes. Carrie always commented on it, ironically. Jug was back and Sailor thought Carrie was having an affair. Morgan was furious. How could she? He was out every day trying to get a major real estate development off the ground—way harder than it looked, it turned out—and she was off fucking someone else. Morgan realized, somewhat distantly, that he was also fucking someone else, but Carrie didn't know that so it didn't do anything to lessen her betrayal. He glanced over at Nina who looked to be getting some of her wind back after hearing the part about Carrie and the affair.

"You piece of shit," Nina snarled. "How dare you talk to me that way in my own house. Do you even—"

"Oh fucking what am I even doing?" Morgan said, getting up. He started for the door.

"Excuse me?" Nina yelled. "And don't think I missed that your wife is cheating on you. Did she even notice that you left her? Did she seem excited when you told her?" Morgan threw her laptop on the floor as he went. "You're paying for that."

Morgan stopped walking to the door and came back. "This laptop?" he said, picking up the computer from the floor. "I'm paying for this?" He intended to throw it against the wall and smash it, make some kind of clever scene, but he was suddenly just too tired of Nina and all her shit to even care. He realized, as the urge to smash leached from him, that indifference was the cruelest thing he could inflict on her. He had gone about this all wrong since the beginning. He tucked the laptop under his arm. "Guess if I'm paying for it that makes it mine," he said. "Bill me."

He turned and walked out the door and drove to Big Lock's where he knew he would find his wife.

Chapter 4

Sailor watched the door to Nina Capaldi's condo from the front seat of her Honda in the parking lot and played with Isaac's camera. If she pulled her knees up into her shirt and stuck them out the neck hole and got the angle just right with the camera, it looked like she had massive boobs. She snapped a handful of these shots and looked at them on the camera's little screen. "Bet those would destroy my lower back," she said to herself. She was bored. She had been in the parking lot for a couple hours watching Nina pass by her living room and kitchen windows, mostly looking at her phone and dragging on a vape pen. Carrie told Sailor not to play private detective, but she would change her tune when Sailor got the photo evidence she needed.

Nina's condo was on the second floor. Sailor saw a sliding glass door through the kitchen window that led to a balcony on the oceanfront side of the building. She was watching from her car hoping to catch Morgan coming into the parking lot, but after the boredom of the past two hours she got out, slung the camera over her shoulder, and walked around to the back. The ocean announced itself as always, the breaking waves like a small battle taking place in the distance. The moon was up, hanging full and glowing over the sea. It illuminated the ocean-facing side of Nina's condo. It was fancy digs for a woman with no discernible employment, Sailor thought. She saw a lit window that must be Nina's bedroom and another door to the balcony. The unit below Nina's was dark, either empty or no one home. Sailor approached that unit's deck rail. She was wondering if she could climb it someway, maybe hoist herself quietly onto Nina's balcony, when the balcony door above her opened and Nina stepped outside. Sailor froze. Nina was directly above her. If she came to the rail and looked down, there was no way to miss the woman in the bright green designer top, even in the dark. There was the sound of a chair creaking slightly as she sat, then a quiet blowing sound that Sailor guessed was Nina exhaling. A moment later Sailor smelled the tropical scent of whatever flavor vape Nina preferred.

"Answer your goddamn phone," Nina muttered to herself. There was the buzzing sound of a phone vibrating, the person calling her back, Sailor figured, then Nina was cooing, "Hey Daddy." Sailor made a face. Gross. Was that Morgan?

Sailor quietly removed her own phone from the thigh pocket of her yoga pants, turned it back on, and activated the voice memo's recording function. She held it up over her head trying to get it as close to the balcony above her as she could without the screen-glow being visible.

"He's gone and won't be back. That loose end is snipped," Nina said. "Okay, fine, he's not a loose end, whatever. The point is, it's done. When can I come over?" Sailor heard the thin sound of whoever was replying but she couldn't make anything out over the steady shush of the ocean fifty yards away. "That wife of his might be having an affair, by the way," Nina said. "Or he thinks she might be at any rate."

Sailor perked up. Nina was talking *about* Morgan, not *to* him. It sounded like they had split up. So much for her pictures. Maybe Nina had a new guy already. One with a dysfunctional concept of father-daughter dynamics.

Sailor was surprised to hear Morgan thought Carrie was having an affair too. She always thought Morgan was about as observant as an eyeless potato. She wondered how he had caught on. Carrie was low-key, undramatic, and careful. Sailor had only a vague suspicion, she was surprised Morgan had noticed anything at all.

"The sister said it on the brother's live stream today randomly," Nina said to her caller. "He didn't take it well." Sailor was confused for a moment, then she realized what had happened. Fucking JP, that rat. She had forgotten about his live stream when she called him from Mr. Papaioannou's house. Shit, Mr. Papaioannou. She was hit with a second dose of guilt. She specifically promised the old man he wouldn't end up on the Internet unexpectedly. Her phone call to JP had done exactly that. JP was going to get it. She tilted her phone a little to see the time, wondering if she could still make it to his gig tonight and ruin it in some way.

"Wait, what? But you said I could be done with him," Nina said now. She listened for a moment then said, "You said *one more day* a day ago." Her tone was angry. "I'm done. I finished it." The caller said something and Nina replied, "Sorry, Daddy," in the same cooing voice she had used when she first answered. Sailor rolled her eyes. She didn't know who Nina was talking to, but she was confident it wasn't her father. "He probably won't answer his phone but I can find him. He's probably at the brother's dumb show or on the b—" Nina listened a moment then snapped, "I said yes. I'll find him." She sighed. "Shepherd him through to completion, I got it." A pause. "Thank you, Daddy." Then the call must have ended because the next thing Sailor heard her say was, "You withered piece of dry dog shit. Fucking hell. Dragging my ass out to goddamn Big Lock's like some low-class buffet-eater with a—" The balcony door opened and closed and the rest of her rant was cut off.

Sailor came out from under the balcony. She looked up to the bedroom window where Nina was yanking off her top and shorts and pulling a cocktail dress over her head. Sailor doubted Morgan was at JP's show. *The brother's dumb show or on the...* On the what? Nina had been cut off by whoever was on the phone. Sailor didn't know what to make of the call. Someone not only knew about Morgan and Nina but it sounded like they were orchestrating the relationship. She checked her phone, making sure the recording was saved then hustled back around the building. She would tail Nina, find out what this was all about. If Nina was going to find Morgan, she could still get Carrie's pictures. She would get to her car, snap some pics of Nina coming out of her place. Document the whole sequence of events. Her phone buzzed in her hand as she came to the corner of the parking lot and she stopped to look. "Hey. It's Lula from last night. So I'm sticking around for a few days if you want to hang out again?" That was unexpected. Sailor stared at the message, unmoving, as if reacting might somehow alert Lula she had seen it. That's when she became aware of the sound of an engine idling. She looked up from her phone. There was a white van in the parking lot. The barn doors on the back were open, the lights off. No one seemed to be around. That was weird.

A door opened and closed with a bang, Nina on her way out. Sailor would have to wait to get to her own car. She pulled the camera around and snapped pictures as Nina came down the stairs. Through the viewfinder, Sailor saw her pass from the dimness of the stairwell into the illumination of the building's spotlights, mounted up on the third floor and pointed out into the parking lot. A man Sailor hadn't seen stepped from a shadowed corner of the building, across from the bottom of the stairs, and came up behind Nina as she paused to stare into her purse for a moment before extracting her car keys. Nina turned at the sound of his approach. The man, short and slim and never breaking his stride, punched her flat in her mouth with quick, professional efficiency.

Nina fell like her power had been cut, limp and unresisting. Sailor dropped the camera. The man's startling appearance and swift violence doused her in awareness of her own vulnerability with such force it felt like its own punch. She reached in her waistband for the Hellcat. The man was hoisting the stunned Nina and dragging her toward the van. Homewrecker or not, Sailor wasn't going to stand by while the woman got assaulted and abducted. She took her panic and fear and pushed it outwards to force herself into motion. She charged.

"Hey!" Sailor shouted, running toward the man, arms extended, elbows locked like she practiced at the range. "No you don't you fucking pr—" A second man stepped out of the same shadows and clotheslined her. Her head smacked against the asphalt when she fell. Sailor saw a blurry figure loom over her. He said something that sounded like "Loco" before his fist came down and laid her out.

•••

JP leaned against the back wall of Big Lock's. He was outside by the dumpster and the permanent puddles of kitchen-wet that got slopped out the back door. He lit a new cigarette off the one he was already smoking and tossed the butt into one of the puddles that never seemed to dry. He had put in years of smoking joints out behind this bar. The puddles were always there.

JP was drunk. He knew he should be making efforts to sober up before he got on stage in half an hour, but instead he pulled out his flask and swallowed a mouthful of bourbon. There was nothing worse he could have been drinking right then. Whatever, he could do a show drunk, it wouldn't be the first time. Hadn't he done shows drunk all the time when he started out? Granted, he wasn't any good and no one enjoyed his work, but his whole act was better now and he had some legitimate fans. It followed, he felt, that he would be better at doing a show drunk, and that the evening would go well enough. Sure, that made sense, he thought as he took a second pull from the silver flask Carrie had gifted him a couple Christmases ago.

JP heard footsteps coming across the bar's back lot. JP knew who it was before he saw him, had known this encounter was coming ever since he spoke with Sailor, even knew it was likely to happen just like this if he chose to stand out back here smoking like he had a thousand times before. The guy looking for him knew him well enough to find him here, but he knew him well enough to find him pretty much anywhere so it didn't matter.

Jug came into view around the dumpster, saw JP, and stopped. "Figured you'd be back here," Jug said. "Kind of hoped you wouldn't be but...I knew you would."

JP took him in. Flip-flops and jeans, a long sleeve shirt covered by a zip-up fleece vest. JP knew without seeing it that the shirt had some kind of surf logo on the front, some graphic representation of the surfing lifestyle on the back, waves or a board silhouetted by the sun or some such thing. The flip-flops made him smile. "Christ, just wear shoes, man. It's almost Thanksgiving," JP said. He looked at Jug, who smiled. "It's good to see you," JP said.

"It's good to be home," Jug said.

They stood grinning at each other. JP's heart was racing. He didn't know how to have the conversation that this reunion required but he knew for certain that he didn't want to have it. He was not going to be on the honorable side of things. But he was relieved to see his friend, the other brother who had shared most of his life. It triggered a wave of nostalgia. Here in this stupidly familiar place, this dumb nowhere behind a bar in Myrtle Beach that, through poor habits and low ambition, was somehow a recognizable setting in their lives.

JP found himself moving toward Jug and hugging him. Jug hugged him back, squeezing him tighter than he expected and realizing he also had Jug in a bear grip. "I missed you, man," JP said.

"Yeah, I missed you too, man," Jug said, squeezing. "Now get the fuck off me."

Jug let go and shoved JP back. He staggered and fell, partially landing in one of the puddles. JP scrambled ungracefully to his feet, wary, but Jug wasn't coming in for more. He stood a few feet away, fishing cigarettes and a lighter from a vest pocket. "That feels like a fair reaction," JP said.

"Randy," Jug said.

"I didn't think he'd do it," JP said, looking away from Jug and down into the puddle. Randy had been dead for three years now, but his name still knocked the kickstand out from under JP when he heard it. The ever-startling reality that Randy was dead and JP was responsible. *Partially responsible* was how he used to say it to himself, but his own phrasing disgusted him. He was the origin of Randy's death. It didn't matter who else was involved.

"You put him up to it," Jug said.

"No," JP said, hearing how defensive he sounded. "We were just hanging out, talking shit, and I said it. We were doing blow, running our mouths. You know how it gets. How it got. I just said it and he...he went and did it." JP remembered the night in pieces and bursts that felt hot across his memory. Randy wasn't a close friend, but he was around sometimes. He materialized at some point after high school and drifted in and out of their group of friends. They called him Randy the Random behind his back. He was around more than usual that summer three years earlier when JP and Jug started making money with Jumper, a quietly intense bar owner who used to fight MMA, so the story went. Jumper sold cocaine out of his bar, a drug everyone was suddenly very casual about. JP had never even seen it before the first night he did some. Going over to Jumper's to pick up coke put JP and Jug into a scene that was dingy and boring up close, but felt glamorously edgy in the retelling when they came back to their friends with the night's party supplies. The dingy and boring part made them complacent. JP and Jug were drinking beer at Jumper's one evening, waiting for the bartender to retrieve the eight-ball they had paid for and slip it to them in a stack of bar napkins as usual when Jumper opened the door next to the bar. It was unconfirmed whether Jumper really fought mixed martial arts professionally in the past, mostly due to his size making it very easy to believe he had, without needing to look it up. He was six-two or three and jacked, with bright red hair, curly on top and shaved close on the sides and back. He had the pale skin that often accompanied that hair color, tanned only by the universe of freckles peppering him. JP always wondered how he maintained the pale while living in subtropical Myrtle Beach.

Jumper asked them to come to his office and talk to him for a minute. They walked back to Jumper's clean, nearly empty office where he said, "Your bag is gratis and I'll add a hundred bucks each if you drop something off for me. One of my regular employees is indisposed this evening."

"Gratis?" Jug had said.

"Free, dude," JP told him. "What is it you want us to drop off?"

Jug gave him a look. Jumper saw this and smiled, sort of. Jumper smiled the way a traveller in a foreign land might bow, like he understood it was a custom but didn't usually practice it himself. "It's a bag," he said. "One you don't need to open. Just deliver."

And that was how they started doing runs and drop-offs for Jumper. It didn't seem like a particularly great idea, but the glamor-free scene at the bar, the boring small-business feel of the whole thing, made the risk seem minimal. They were both working for JP's dad, Butch, at the time doing HVAC service calls and the extra money was nice. It all quietly escalated. They met Bevel when the drop-offs became exchanges. Suddenly, they were riding out to dark parts of the county with Bevel, dropping off a bag and collecting another with five grand in it, then eight grand, then ten. But it paid. They were making money.

"Dude, we're straight up drug dealers," Jug said one night in his Tacoma as they were leaving Jumper's.

They saw Bevel crossing the parking lot, walking to wherever he holed up when they weren't making runs. "That guy's such a fucking creep," JP said, as they drove past. "And we're not dealers. We're couriers."

"Do you think that matters when it comes to sentencing?" Jug snapped. "Do you think the judge goes, 'Well, since you were just couriers I won't put you in prison. Instead you'll do community service tutoring kids in semantics, your obvious specialty.' Fucking couriers. Are you kidding me?"

"You want to quit?"

Jug kept silent for a minute before saying, "The money is nice."

"Shit yeah the money's nice. Butch doesn't pay all that great."

"Still. I just..."

"Just what?"

"I don't know how to quit something like this if I wanted to. Does running large amounts of cocaine around town seem like the kind of gig where you put in two week's notice? Can you just quit being an accessory to a criminal enterprise? We what? Tell Jumper we don't want to do it anymore and he says, 'Oh, no problem, just go live your lives knowing all about my illegal business'?"

JP had been annoyed. He thought Jug was taking it all too seriously. "Stop, dude. You're overthinking it. You want to quit then we just quit. Unless you want to go out one-big-score style and rob ourselves."

"Rob ourselves? What does that mean?" Jug said. They were back on Kings Highway now, heading north to Pine Lakes Tavern where people were meeting them.

"Like one night when it's just one of us and Bevel, the other one robs us after we've made the drop and picked up the money. Then, we tell Jumper this shit is too dangerous and we're out. Gives quitting a little weight, you know, plus we split the money." Jug turned and stared at JP. "Watch the road," JP said.

"You just thought of that?" Jug said quietly.

"Actually, I thought of it on the drive back tonight while I was trying to tune out that fucking tweaker rambling on about cutting a stash pocket into his waistband and how he used to catch and sell catfish to squatters and whatever all the fuck else he was talking about. I was thinking how I'd almost rather we crashed than have to listen to him anymore. And that made me wonder what we'd do with the money if we crashed. Like, would we have to hide it? And what if we crashed and you and I were fucked up just badly enough we couldn't get up right away—Bevel hopefully would be dead—and someone came along and robbed us in our disadvantaged state. How would we explain that to Jumper? And that's what made me start thinking we didn't even really need to crash. Someone could just rob us on the road out in the sticks like we were. Pull a truck across the road to stop us or throw spiked boards in front of us to blow our tires. What would we do about it? And then I thought, shit, we could just rob ourselves and probably get away with it," JP said. "Pretty clever, right?"

"Dude, tell me you're not serious," Jug said, staring at JP again.

"Watch the damn road, I don't feel like crashing if Bevel's not in the car to get hurt."

"Dude—"

"No, I'm not fucking serious," JP yelled. "Would you relax? Jumper doesn't give a shit about us, okay? If we quit he walks out to the bar and finds two more broke idiots who want a free eight-ball."

"The robbery—"

"Dude, it's not a serious idea. I don't know how to do a fucking robbery."

"We're committing real crimes here, man. I don't want to fuck around and end up at J. Reuben with a mug shot online that everyone texts around to everyone else. Can't get a job the rest of my life that isn't part of some church program," Jug said.

"I get it, man. You think I want an online mugshot and a church job? It's just a thing I thought of. I was just messing with you. Relax."

"Yeah?"

"Promise," JP had said.

The promise was real enough. JP didn't intend to rob anything. Later that night though, Jug disappeared off somewhere. JP and Randy the Random ended up back at JP's, finishing the last of the cocaine and drinking beers. Randy was asking questions about Jumper's and calling JP a "bona fide desperado" and JP couldn't help himself. He was telling Randy about their run earlier that evening, embellishing both because of the coke and because it wasn't really much of a story without the embellishment, just him and Jug and a tweaker on a two-hour round trip to bumblefuck. Somewhere in his jabbering he ended up telling Randy the whole idea, how they just drive back with all this money in the truck and no way to stop anyone with the right plan from taking it off them. JP forgot all about it by the next day.

He told Jug this now, standing by the dumpsters behind Big Lock's, puddle water soaking through the ass of his jeans. Jug sighed and dragged on his cigarette. "Fucking Randy," he said.

"You have to know I wouldn't have really done that. And I wouldn't have told Randy to do it." JP pulled his flask back out. "Not that it matters what I would have done or not I guess. He's fucking dead now." He took a drink. He felt almost sober at that moment, though he knew he wasn't. "I still don't even really know what happened."

"Got himself shot is what happened," Jug said. "Bevel shot him. I grabbed Bevel's gun, tried to wrestle it away from him. And when I did that, I guess I shot Bevel."

"Not well enough. That's how you know it wasn't really my plan," JP said. "Bevel lived."

Jug snorted a laugh. "That's fucked up."

"Yeah, well," JP said. "He put it in Jumper's ear I was in on it. Jumper came after me for that ten grand. So I don't exactly feel super charitable toward that walking shitflap."

Jug stared at him. "I didn't know that."

"How would you? You were gone." JP held up his left hand. "He broke the pinky and the ring finger before he believed me. Clean breaks for what it's worth. They healed mostly straight. I told Butch they got caught in a motor shaft on an installation. He was actually real nice about it. I think he was relieved I hadn't lost them outright. He even gave me extra hours."

"You picked up extra hours with two broken fingers?"

"Had ten thousand dollars to pay back."

Jug's cigarette stopped halfway to his mouth. "But...you said he believed you weren't in on it."

"He did. Still wanted his ten g's back. Randy was dead, you were gone. That left me."

"You should have—"

"Dude, shut up," JP cut him off. "You ever have a former MMA fighter break your fingers while his fry cook holds a box cutter to your throat? No? I didn't think so. So maybe spare me your shoulda, woulda, fucking coulda's. I paid him back. I got sober." He looked at the flask in his hand. "Kind of sober anyway. There have been stretches where I was sober. And I moved on." They stood in silence for a minute. "Why are you back?" JP finally said. "That ten grand run out?"

Jug shook his head. "I didn't take his money."

"Well he certainly thinks you did."

"What about Bevel?"

"What about him?"

"Randy had taken the money before...before everything happened. Didn't Bevel like, retrieve it? I only shot him in the leg."

"You know something, dude, in the midst of my fingers snapping and the threats on my life, I plumb forgot to ask. But seeing as how I had to spend a year and a half on a payment plan to that psychopath Jumper, I would venture a guess that he fucking didn't. Maybe the cops who found Randy took it. Who knows?"

"Did you go to his funeral?" Jug asked.

JP shook his head. "If there was one, it wasn't here. I don't know anything about his family or where he was from. Just that Bevel shot him. Just that he died. Just that I gave him the idea. That's all I know. It wasn't even in the news as far as I saw." He shook his flask, feeling for any remaining bourbon, but it was empty now. He shoved it in his pocket. "So why are you back?"

Jug shrugged and flicked his cigarette into one of the puddles. "Can't stay gone forever. And it turns out there's nothing out there." He waved his hand aimlessly, gesturing to the world at large. "Except fucking Florida. And that ain't much."

"That's where you've been? Florida?"

"Some of the time, yeah. I got around."

"Randy got dead, Bevel got shot, I got my fingers broken, you went to Florida. Maybe Florida ain't much, but on the whole I'd say it's the top prize of the bunch. The new car of the Showcase Showdown." He flicked his cigarette into the puddle alongside Jug's. "So now what?"

The shrug again. "I don't know." He turned. "I'm done for now. Talking with you. You should try to sober up before your show." Jug started to leave.

"Where you headed?"

"Nowhere in particular," Jug said, going back around the building, out of JP's sight. "Just going to hop along," he heard him say.

Just going to hop along, JP thought. He felt an internal chime push through the booze. Why did that stand out? *Hop along*, he thought. That was a weird phrase. Why did he think he had heard it recently?

"Oh," he said quietly to himself.

•••

Carrie sat at the bar in Big Lock's and said, "Like fine, I get it, you're observant, but keep your fucking mouth shut, you know? She doesn't have to go around fucking telling everyone the shit she notices."

Her friend Tayto, cracking open Budweiser bottles behind the bar, said, "She didn't know. It's your dipshit brother you should be mad at."

"I am mad at my dipshit brother. I'm just also mad at my idiot-savant sister," Carrie said.

Tayto handed off the two Buds to a customer down the bar and came back. "You talk to Chess this morning?" she asked.

"Yeah," Carrie said. It felt like years since she had her conversation with Chester. It had only been that morning.

"And?" Tayto put her hands on her hips and looked at Carrie meaningfully. "What'd he say? You taking that scumbag to the cleaners? Open and shut case, right?"

"You know it's not called a case? TV lied to us."

"Oh Christ, did Chess give you that shit? He did the same thing to me when I went to him about my car accident. I said, 'Chess, the reason law talk on TV is different is because real legal talk is boring and it don't make sense and you can only be one of those things and have people give a shit. You can be boring if you make sense. And you can make no sense if you're entertaining. But you can't be both and the legal system is both. So talk to me like you're on TV or I'm taking my business elsewhere.' Like I give a shit about voir dire or whatever."

"Tay, how're you going to tell the guy doing free legal work for you that you're going to take your business elsewhere?"

"I didn't mean my legal business, this was back when we were kind of seeing each other. I meant sexy business. You want me to keep touching your weiner you better make like Matlock and explain this in a way I understand."

Carrie laughed. "How'd he take that?"

"We don't see each other anymore. On the other hand I won my claim so it kind of netted out." She thought for a moment. "Little fucking nerd," she said affectionately.

Haines, one of her brothers' friends, came up to the bar beside Carrie. "Coors Light?" he said to Tayto. The bar was filling up. There were already forty or so people there for the show and more trickling in. "What's shaking?" Haines said to Carrie.

"Just my ass these days," Carrie said.

"Well I heard you were getting some, so I guess it's working for you," Haines said.

"Fuck off," Tayto said, slamming his beer down and splashing him some.

"Get fucked, Haines," Carrie told him.

"You're buying us shots for that," Tayto said. "I'm putting them on your card."

"That's illegal," Haines protested.

"Call the cops, dick," Carrie said.

"Well *got*-damn," Haines said. "If you're going to get mad at a guy who just says your shaky ass is helping you get laid, then fine." He sulked away back near the stage. Tayto started pouring something into a shaker. She plopped two plastic shot cups in front of Carrie.

"I don't want a shot. Pour mine out and charge him anyway," Carrie said. "I already drank more than I should."

"Don't be a baby," Tayto said, pouring the shots. "It's a promo bottle, anyway. It's free. Some company pushing their new bourbon. Called it Dirty Myrtle. Name's kind of funny, I guess." They both picked up a cup and tipped them back.

"Holy shitfire," Tayto gasped, her eyes watering. "It's all heat... no taste...just burn."

Carrie's eyes, mouth, and nose all seemed to clamp down, her whole face puckering. "That was exactly what I don't need," she said. "It's like the sun spit in my mouth." She turned her head to burp and there by the door, after three years, was Jug. She laughed. Her old childhood crush, in the flesh. "Hey baby blues!" she called out to him drunkenly. It was her old nickname for him and the blue eyes she loved as a girl. Jug looked around for the voice that had shouted at him and saw Carrie. He smiled.

"Yeah, our boy is back," Tayto said. "Saw him last night."

"I'm a go say hello," Carrie mumbled.

As she made her way, she saw JP tripping and nearly falling as he took the stage. She heard a voice she was pretty sure was Tayto's yell, "Booooo. Judas!" somewhere behind her. JP struggled with the microphone and produced some screeching feedback before slurring out, "Hoooo-kay. It's only a couple feet off the ground but it feels a lot higher for some reason. Falling down on my way up. Let's see if I can't stick the landing though, huh?"

Chapter 5

Tusk was next door to Big Lock's Bar and Grill in the parking lot of a boutique. The bar and boutique both sat along Kings Highway, the six-lane artery that ran parallel between Ocean Boulevard and the bypass. He was in his own car rather than a police cruiser since Captain Lewis made it clear that following Judson "Jug" Shaw was unofficial business. *Jug. Dumbass name*, Tusk thought, but you couldn't say much when your legal handle was Tuscaloosa. His mom saddled him with that one. "It's where your granddaddy was from," she told him. "That doesn't make it a name for a person," Tusk always replied.

After Carrie stormed out, Tusk had decided he was definitely taking himself to the beach. Then he would go again the next day, making two visits in the same week. Then he would buy a bike and ride to the beach every day. He made it as far as the couch downstairs. He just sat down for a minute to check his phone and the next thing he knew he was waking up nearly three hours later. He realized that if he was going to find Jug and keep an eye on him for Captain Lewis, the best place to start was Big Lock's where his friends would all be gathered.

Now he was sitting in his car, staring at a bar he would rather be in than staking out. His friend JP had a show, his other friends were all inside drinking and watching, along with the woman he was seeing—he assumed anyway, her car was out front. A lot of things he wanted were inside that bar—except for a promotion.

That, for whatever reason, was to be found inside his Cadillac CT5, waiting to spot Judson "Jug" Shaw.

Tusk took notes with the voice-to-text function on his phone. He looked over what he had so far. He had seen Morgan arrive. He was a little ashamed he knew the man's car by sight, but it was just common sense that if you were sleeping with a guy's wife you should know what he drives and what he looks like. You needed to be able to see him coming if things got weird. Carrie never explained much about her husband, but Tusk's job was like eighty percent observation. From what he had observed, Morgan was cheating first and Tusk was payback. If this wasn't enough to justify the infidelity for Tusk, his first look at Morgan filled in the remainder. A smarmy preppy who looked like he took collared shirts very seriously.

Also in Tusk's notes was a guy in a beat-to-shit work van parked at the side of the bar. The roof rack on top was stacked with ladders, two orange and two silver. Probably just some guy with a job to do, but like Tusk, the guy was sitting in his vehicle not going anywhere. Tusk copied the plate number, but he couldn't do anything with that until he was either back on the clock or he could raise someone who would do him a favor. He had already called Jamie half a dozen times and got no answer. Jamie was the only guy Tusk was certain was both on-shift, and who he trusted not to ask a ton of questions about him running a plate off duty. He must have been tied up with something. Or maybe someone in authority finally saw him with those AirPods in and confiscated them along with his phone. There were a couple of staff sergeants who kept it real grade school with shit like that.

Tusk swiped out of his notes and into the messaging app. Should he text Carrie? Something neutral and deescalating? He did the mental math on how long she had been in Big Lock's drinking since he arrived, plus however long she might have been there before he showed up. He put his phone back down. There was apt to be a whole lot of drunken anger on the other end of that text. Plus her husband was with her. Texting her in that predicament would be a shitty move. Though, come to think of it, he hadn't actually seen Morgan go into the bar.

He looked back up and there, standing out front as though he had teleported, was Jug. Tusk jerked upright, startled. Where had he come from? He hadn't pulled up in a car. Did he walk? "Eight twenty-one p.m.," Tusk said into his phone. "Jusdon Shaw, aka Jug, arrives, apparently on foot. No vehicle spotted. Standing out in front of the bar smoking a cigarette, staring up at the bar sign like a weirdo. Tosses the cigarette on the ground. Littering. Enters the bar."

The morose feeling of sitting on the outside while everything good was going on inside dried up, replaced by the rush that came with getting a lead, making progress. Tusk transformed from sad sack back into a cop. He had located Jug. Now he just needed to keep tabs on him.

Tusk didn't love the idea of putting Carrie in the position of having her husband and side piece in the same bar, but he wasn't going to lose his man. He was going in. He would just avoid them as best he could. He was putting his phone in his pocket when he remembered—he hadn't seen Morgan go inside. The sketchy work van caught his eye again. It was moving, headlights off, pulling slowly toward the back of the bar. It stopped with just the front pulled past the back wall, like the driver was trying to peek around the back through the front passenger window. Tusk leaned to the side, straining to get a glimpse of the driver.

"That's weird," he said.

•••

Carrie pushed through the back door of Big Lock's, pulling Jug along by the hand. JP's amplified voice followed them into the night, then winked out like a candle flame as the door closed behind them. A muffled white noise lingered like the trail of smoke from a wick until it was lost in the hum of passing cars and chirping night bugs. It was just the two of them in the quiet.

Carrie laughed, throwing her arms around Jug's neck. She was drunk and happy to see him. The feel of him, his smell of cigarettes and cheap cologne, took her back to their high school days. Jug and JP were juniors when she was a freshman—skinny, scrawny, and scared. Her brother hadn't paid her any attention, but Jug, unannounced, waited outside her classroom to walk her to the cafeteria for lunch on her first day. He casually popped up like that her whole first week. The presence of an upperclassman in her orbit greased social wheels and warned off certain bullies. He drifted back into his own circle the second week but his work had been done. Of course Carrie, who already had a bit of a crush on her older brother's friend, was absolutely flattened, totally in love. She grew out of that but never stopped admiring the sweet boy who spared a little time for her unasked, expecting nothing in return. Compared to her current situation, Jug smelled like happier days, he felt like a simpler time.

"Where have you been?" Carrie asked as she released him.

"Here and there," Jug said.

Carrie laughed again. "Here and there," she said in a deep mongoloid voice, imitating him. "Don't be like that after three years away, man. No one thinks you were secretly recruited by the CIA. If you try to be enigmatic people are just going to assume it was something super lame."

"Maybe that's what I'd prefer they assume."

Carrie drunkenly hopped into a karate stance and chopped him across the chest yelling, "Hi-yah!"

Jug laughed. "Ow, damn. I'm just messing with you. I was in Charleston some. Florida mostly. Workin' and twerkin', you know."

"Laboring all day and dancing all night?"

"Obviously. You know me."

"I do. I expect there was more twerkin' than workin'," Carrie started to say, but stopped when the quiet was broken by the sound of a car door slamming shut and someone shouting.

•••

"I fucking caught you!" Morgan shouted. He had been sulking in his Range Rover, doing bumps of coke, telling himself over and over that he would leave in ten more minutes. Then Carrie and Jug came out the back door of the bar. He saw them embrace and watched them talking intensely.

"I caught you," he yelled again. His wife and that dumb beach rat who used to hang around. They were both frozen, watching him approach.

Jug looked from the yelling man to Carrie. "Is that... You ended up with Morgan?"

"What are you doing here?" Carrie asked. "I thought you had a dinner."

"Exactly what you were supposed to think," Morgan crowed. He was flying from the coke and the thrill of having the upper hand. He hated how Carrie drove into his failing development every day, past the empty lots. Every day seeing his failure and struggle manifest in the half-built houses that were never consistently being worked on. Now he had her. Caught in an act of her own moral failing. "You cheating whore," he said.

"Whoa. Hey. None of that," Jug said, stepping toward Morgan. "What's wrong with you?"

"You stepping to me, tough guy?" Morgan said. He was vaguely aware a conflict wasn't in his best interest with the handful of broken fingers, but he was too fired up for the thought to really take hold. "Talking shit to me when you're cheating with my whore wife by some dumpsters behind a bar?"

"Morgan I'm not—" Carrie said, but then Jug stepped closer and shoved Morgan. "Jug. Stop!" she said.

"I said don't call her that," Jug said.

Morgan stumbled. His mind went hot white, blank with heat and rage. "I'll fucking kill you," he yelled, rushing Jug and tackling him around the waist. They went down. Morgan felt Jug punching him in his back and sides, but he had landed on top of the scrawnier man. He disentangled himself enough to get in a few useless swipes with his good hand. Jug swung at him blindly from his back. For a moment they were a jumble of flailing arms. Morgan scrambled to his feet and got his arm around Jug's neck from behind. He squeezed, tightening his grip around Jug's throat. He had him. Morgan felt Carrie's hands yanking on him with no effect. He heard her yelling that he was killing him but he kept squeezing, lying on his back under Jug, cinching his throat closed to any new air he was trying to pull into his lungs, Jug kicking and rocking and trying to break free and breathe. Dimly, Morgan sensed the severity of what he was doing, but his rage told him it was acceptable, that he was in the right, that he was limitless. Then Jug stopped fighting and Morgan knew it was coming, he was going to win. He had him, he thought. Suddenly, unexpectedly, there was a fire in Morgan's side, a tearing fire and the sickening feeling of a foreign object inside of him. He let go of Jug to clutch at his side, just below his ribs. He felt slick wetness and knew it was blood, but he didn't know how or why.

Morgan saw Jug roll to his knees, coughing and heaving for breath, one hand at his throat, the other holding a knife. "You fuck," he yelled. "You stabbed me, you goddamn hick." Morgan looked at his hand where he had been holding his side. It was red and dripping. "Oh shit," he said. He tried to get up but the pain in his side was brutal, like it was eating up any other energy he might have used. Jug dropped the knife and put his other hand to his throat as well.

Carrie helped Jug to his feet. She looked down at Morgan who moaned at her. "Stabbed," was all he managed.

"Go," Carrie said to Jug. "You need to go." Jug tried to say something but it came out a wheezy mess. Morgan took a small pleasure in this through his pain. "I'll take care of him, just go," Carrie said. Jug staggered away into the night.

Carrie retrieved the knife from the ground. Maybe an inch showed blood in the thin light. Not good, but it could be worse, the folding knife had a nearly four inch blade. She closed it and dropped it into her right boot. She knelt by Morgan and tried to examine his wound, but Morgan wouldn't move his hands. Couldn't move them, it felt like. "Morgan, please. Let me see it. I need to stop the bleeding and get you to the hospital."

"Cheating," Morgan hissed.

"That's not important right now," Carrie said.

"To who?" Morgan managed to say.

"Move your hands. Please."

Like hell it wasn't important, Morgan thought. He gathered his strength and rolled over onto his knees. It was still important, he thought through the haze of pain. Who was she to tell him what was important or not? He got to his feet and managed a couple steps.

"Morgan, stop. You need to lie down and get your feet up. You're going into shock," Carrie said.

Yeah, the shock of finding you here with Jughead, Morgan thought. It was suddenly very bright. He squinted into the brightness and saw the outline of a van. Then the van hit him, and he went down again.

•••

Tusk stared at the van parked along the side of the bar. Observation: otherwise known as driving around, walking around, or sitting around and staring at the world. It was tedious when you first joined the force, but after a while you became good at noticing things that weren't quite right. Like how your eye will go to a crooked picture on the wall.

The van was the crooked picture on the wall.

Tusk stood by his car with the door open. He pulled his cell phone out to call and ask for a patrol car to come over just in case when he heard shouting from behind the bar. The van's headlights came on and it rolled forward and made the turn around the back, out of sight. Something was up. The parking lot he was in was separated from the Big Lock's lot by a divider he couldn't drive over. He would lose too much time in his car. He started running. He heard more yelling and slamming van doors as he approached the back of the bar. The driver's side door of the van was closing as Tusk rounded the corner. He saw the brake lights flare as the driver took it from park to drive and rolled forward. Someone was lying on the ground beside the van.

"Stop! Police!" Tusk yelled. The driver hit the gas. No one ever stopped when they yelled that, Tusk reflected. He might as well shout *Run*. Tusk skidded to a stop by the person on the ground. He was startled to see it was Morgan, who was conscious but clearly injured. He stared back at Tusk with no recognition at all. He was alive, that was good. Tusk looked down at Morgan's side. Blood was weeping from what he took to be a stab wound since he hadn't heard any shots. In his periphery, Tusk could still see the van. It wasn't getting away all that quickly, navigating between the parked cars and the giant dumpsters.

"I'll be right back," he said to Morgan, placing the man's hands on his wound. "Keep pressure on it." He stood and ran like hell.

The van rounded the corner of the bar just as Tusk reached it. He grabbed the back door handle. It was unlocked and swung open, but the driver had gotten through the narrow part of the lot now. Tusk had an awkward grip on the handle and part of the interior door frame. He was dragged off his feet as the van picked up speed. All he could see was a close-up of the back door and the bumper, then the van took a hard right in front of the bar. Tusk lost his grip and was sent rolling across the lot and into Kings Highway. The back of a passing car tire scraped his head as he hit the outer lane of the highway. He heard a horn but didn't take the time to look, just threw himself back up onto the sidewalk as a pickup skidded by, hard on the brakes but not enough to have stopped in time if Tusk had still been on the road. The van pulled onto the highway ahead of the same skidding truck, eliciting another blast of the horn, and accelerated hard and fast, getting away.

Tusk laid on the sidewalk and felt his head where the car tire had gotten him. There was a serious scrape and blood, but he could live with that. Literally, it was an outcome that allowed him to live.

Shit, he thought. *Morgan.* Tusk got to his feet, shaking but not showing it too much he thought, and limp-ran back around the bar. There was no one there. He looked around, confused, and went to where he remembered Morgan being. Tusk turned a circle thinking maybe he'd crawled off somewhere but no. He was gone. There were just the dumpsters and stacks of flattened boxes and weeds and gravel and a dark blotch of blood on the ground to go along with all the other puddles winking in the light burning over the bar's back door.

•••

Sailor came to on the ground in the parking lot. The Hellcat was gone and her head was thick with a toxic fog that made her want to vomit. She sat up and the fog won. She threw up on the black asphalt. She remembered what had happened, but the blow to her head made it difficult to think about anything linearly, so she focused on the immediate, rising slowly to her feet and shuffling to her car. The windows were still down. Her wallet was open on the driver's seat. Her license was next to it but everything in it, including the lone twenty dollar bill, was still there. She slipped it back into her pocket and was about to climb into the front seat when she saw her tires. They weren't merely slashed, they had been gutted. A long jagged arc crossed the top half of each one like a black rainbow.

Sailor felt ill again and steadied herself against her hood while she vomited some more. She was concussed. Her phone and gun were gone, her car was out of commission, and she couldn't really think too long about any one thing without needing to be sick. She heard the incessant sea behind her. Sailor thought for a few moments about where she was and quickly formulated a plan before she could be ill again. She started walking to the beach. Leaving the parking lot, she saw Isaac's camera poking out from under a bush and retrieved it, slinging it around her neck. It appeared unscathed, but she didn't have the bandwidth to inspect it too closely. She made her way to the hard sand, close to the water's edge, and began walking north, the ocean on her right.

Sailor trudged, letting her chopped and stuttering thoughts reel in and out like the waves. Nina had been snatched right in front of her. That was real. She had seen it. The phone call. Whoever Nina was talking to knew about Morgan, wanted Nina to go to him for some reason. That's where she had been headed when she got yanked into that van.

She was lost in the swirl of her aching and abused brain until a brightness loomed in front of her. The Starlight Sands. The hotel's exterior lights were all pointed at the beach, just like Isaac had said. Sailor looked out at the water and saw small green stars, kinetic constellations in the dark water, bobbing gently or moving along the face of a wave, rotating to their own cycles beneath their counterparts in the sky—Isaac and his surfing buddies. Sailor held the camera up and fired off several rapid shots, the flash blinking out at the surfers. Then she dropped to her knees and vomited again in the sand.

•••

Carrie wasn't blindfolded at first, but there was nothing to see except the four walls of the van where she was sure she would die. There was a piece of plywood bolted in, separating her from the driver and anyone else who might be up front.

The van had roared through the bar's back parking lot and hit Morgan like a punch, jerking to a stop after impact. Carrie was so shocked she froze mid-step. The driver, a stringy fellow whose clothes hung off him like they were wet, exited the van, ignored Morgan completely, and grabbed her, slapping a filthy hand over her mouth that she could smell—cigarettes and cat piss. That foul-smelling hand touching her mouth snapped her out of her shock. She fought then, kicking and reaching over her head searching for the eyes of whoever was behind her to dig one out with a thumb. Her assailant had the drop on her though, and the advantage. He reached up and chopped her throat, leaving her coughing and gasping, then bashed her head against the side of the van so hard she nearly blacked out. She was tossed into the back and the van started moving. Carrie was dazed, still choking a little. One of the back doors flew open briefly, headlights from Kings Highway pouring into the dark van. Then there was a sharp turn, a jolt, and the door slammed shut leaving her in total darkness.

She felt around inside the van but there was nothing. The two windows on the back doors were painted over. The ride was dark.

Finally, they slowed and came to a stop. Carrie's head throbbed still, but she pushed through that and got in position. She had thought about her next steps during the ride. She lay on her back, her butt a foot or so from the back doors and her legs bent, knees up to her chest. She heard the front door of the van open and close, footsteps around to the back.

Someone farther away said, "Wait for us."

Right outside the door, her kidnapper's voice said, "Ain't necessary, she's alright." Then the door cracked open.

It was the door to Carrie's left. She slammed her boot into it as hard as she could. She felt resistance and a thump as it swung into the face of whoever was on the other side. She rolled and slid out of the opening onto her feet and started sprinting, trying to take in where she was, get her bearings. She knew she was no distance runner. She needed to get away quickly and hide. Later, Carrie would estimate she got about three strides in before her body locked up and she pitched forward onto her face, frozen on the ground while fifty thousand volts from a Taser ran through her muscles.

Carrie sensed someone kneeling down beside her, but she couldn't see. A thick cloth slipped over her eyes and cinched behind her head. Now she was blindfolded. The urgent and unforgiving hands of two men grabbed her and hoisted her by her legs and torso.

Carrie was hauled aboard and shoved through a narrow hatchway, then tied to what she was pretty sure was a table's center support pole. Despite the blindfold, she knew she was on a boat as much from the awkwardness of the men dragging her around as from the never ceasing movement beneath her feet. She could hear it too, the sound of a hundred kittens drinking milk, the gentle lapping against the sides of the craft.

Her face burned, badly scraped along the right side where she had fallen after the Taser hit her. The men who brought her down into the hold of the boat didn't talk. They were not gentle with her but merely efficient. She was cargo.

The two men tied her to the table and left. A moment later Carrie heard steps down into the hold again. A man's voice, deep but unremarkable.

"No talking," the man said. "No screaming."

There was a sob from somewhere across the room and Carrie realized she was not the only captive. There was at least one other person being held on this boat.

"Quietly crying is fine," the man said, in response to the sobbing. "But keep it quiet. I want you both to think deeply about your situation. Especially you, Miss Runny." Carrie felt the man's foot kick lightly at her leg. "This is obviously serious. This is obviously dangerous. You're not superheroes or special agents. You're not getting out of here. The only thing you can accomplish in this situation is making us angry. And if we get angry enough, this will begin to feel inconvenient. This will start to feel like it's not worth it. We won't even hurt you. What I'll do is, I will empty a gun straight through the floor of this boat and let it sink with you two inside. And then we'll leave. Simple as that. It's not my boat. I don't care about it. And you're not something of mine either." His footsteps retreated up the couple of steps. There was the sound of a door or hatch closing.

Carrie could hear the other woman sniffling. Small whimpers. She was scared. Carrie was scared. "Hey," Carrie whispered. "Are you alright?"

"I'm tied up." The woman took a deep audible breath, trying to calm down. "My face hurts. They hit me."

"Do you know who they are?"

The woman was quiet for a bit before she said, "No."

Carrie thought about that. It was easy to misunderstand a situation with a blindfold over your face, tied to what felt like a breakfast table on a boat. Still, that pause before the woman said "no" felt too long. "Sounds like you had to think about that," Carrie said.

"I don't know who they are," the woman insisted. "But I think I know where we are. We're on a boat."

They've thrown me down here with a moron, Carrie thought. *Maybe they're kidnapping imbeciles and it turns out I'm one too and this is how I find out.* She flashed to a memory from sixth grade when they split the class up for math. Carrie had looked around at the other kids in her half of the class and realized they were the kids who always had their assignments handed back face down. She was in the dumb class.

"We're on the waterway up toward Atlantic Beach," the woman continued. "In a marina that isn't built yet. There's a temporary slip. Just one boat."

Maybe she's the one stuck with a moron, Carrie thought, hearing all this. "How do you know all that?" she said.

"I think it's my boyfriend's boat. He burned a pizza in here last week and the smell hasn't totally gone away."

Now that she mentioned it, Carrie could pick out the faint underlying odor of burned food in the cabin. "Who's your boyfriend?" she asked.

The woman sighed. "This idiot named Morgan Childress."

Chapter 6

Sailor woke in her bed with a start. She felt for a body next to her but there was no one there. Lula. That was yesterday. Why did she feel like someone was here? And what was that knocking sound? She got out of bed and followed the knocking to her front door. She opened it. Lula was on the other side holding a take-out tray with two coffees and a wax paper bag that looked to hold baked goods.

"Hey," Lula said. "So, is this weird? It's weird, I don't know why I asked out loud. I know it's weird. And when you didn't text me back I should have just..." she trailed off.

"Should have just what?" Sailor asked. The night was coming back to her, though there were gaps. She needed to think and to do that she needed to find a joint and a cup of coffee. Happily, a cup of coffee had just knocked on her door, so while she agreed with Lula that her showing up there was weird, she was willing to roll with it.

"Your face...I didn't...you have company, I shouldn't..." Lula stuttered, her eyes looking at something over Sailor's shoulder.

"I have what?" Sailor asked, turning to follow Lula's gaze. She saw a figure lurching up from the couch in her darkened living room, coming her way. Tall. A man. Sailor shouted, "Out of my house!" She grabbed one of the coffees and chucked it at the figure, hitting him square in the face.

"Owww! Shit!" the man yelled, dropping to one knee and wiping frantically at his face. Lula stepped into the doorway and threw the second coffee, hitting the man again, this time on the top of his head. "Shit!" he screamed again. "Stop!"

Lula fumbled out her keys and got the pepper spray dangling from the ring. "Should I spray him?" she shouted.

"Light him up!" Sailor yelled.

"Sailor, please! Fuck, stop," the man yelled. He had fallen onto his back with his hands in front of his face. "Sailor, it's me. It's me!" the man yelled.

The voice cut through her adrenaline and Sailor put a hand over the pepper spray, saying, "Wait. Isaac?"

"Yes!"

"Oh no," Sailor said, rushing over to him. She knelt beside him and wiped at the hot coffee with the hem of her shirt. She turned back to Lula. "Get the towel, quick. Run it in cold water." Lula ran into the bathroom and Sailor heard the shower run. Lula ran back out a moment later and handed the wet towel to Sailor who applied it to Isaac's face. "Issac, I'm sorry," Sailor said. "I didn't know you were here. You just..." *Scared me*, she thought. She had been terrified. She felt the residual fear from the other side of it now. Seeing Issac had been an echo of seeing the man who took her out back at Nina's. She didn't much feel like admitting that, though, so she just said, "You caught me off guard."

"This towel smells bad," Isaac said, getting to his feet. He gently touched the skin under his eyes and on his forehead, red from the hot coffee. "Is that from the Starbucks on 82nd?" he asked Lula.

"No, I didn't know there was one up here. It's from the one on 30th," she said.

"That's lucky. Guess it had a little time to cool. I think it'll be okay," Isaac said.

"What are you doing here?" Sailor asked.

"I brought you here," Isaac said. "I found you on the beach, vomiting with your face all busted. You refused to go to the hospital. I stayed on your couch so I could check on you during the night. You were obviously concussed."

The pieces clicked for Sailor. They were fuzzy, but she remembered. Isaac and the guys helping her to Isaac's truck. The guys talking about finding whoever did this. What was that part? Then she remembered her story. "I got robbed," she said aloud to Isaac and Lula. She had invented this, thinking she was protecting Carrie's privacy. Her head had been too screwed up to think about the fact she was stalking her brother-in-law's mistress. If she could just get home she could get to a phone somehow and call the cops. So she said she got robbed. The guys had heard this and gone right into impotent hostility, wanting revenge on her behalf. Sweet boys. She would bring coffee and treats to one of their morning surf sessions this winter.

"You got robbed, but they left my camera," Isaac said flatly.

"They weren't the kind of robbers who like photography," Sailor said. "Philistines. A lot of thieves are, you know? Not the British of course, they'll take the art first even, but—"

"Yeah, alright, I'm already hours late for work and my face hurts," Isaac said, cutting her off. "And all you have for me is a towel that smells like low tide." He tossed the damp towel onto the couch where he had spent the night. He turned to Lula. "Whoever you are, it was not nice meeting you. Decent arm, though."

"Thanks," Lula said.

He turned for the door. "Isaac, wait," Sailor said, grabbing his shirt. "Thank you."

Isaac nodded and gestured at her face. "I filled your ice cube trays. You should have ice now. Put some in that gross towel and put it on your face for the swelling." He shut the door. From inside, Sailor heard the chirp of his truck unlocking.

Sailor turned and there was Lula, smiling, saying, "So, yeah, this is definitely weird but now it feels like it's not all me. So that's nice."

•••

Tusk read through the notes in his phone hoping something new would jump out at him. Nothing did. He didn't call in the incident with the van and Morgan the previous night. What was there to say? *Officer in need of assistance. A suspicious van drove away from the scene of what I think was a stabbing. No victim. Yes, you heard that right, there was a stabbing but there is no victim. Send as many units as you can to the bar where I'm stalking a civilian.*

After losing the van and Morgan, Tusk went back to his car and tended to his cuts and scrapes with fast food napkins from his glove compartment. When JP's show ended, he saw JP's younger brother, Dex, and Haines carrying a passed out JP from the bar. Tusk got out of his car and caught up with them. Dex saw him coming and smiled. He had lifted his unconscious brother's head and made a faux-ventriloquist voice out of the side of his mouth, saying, "Here comes Officer Tusk. Say, do you know why cops smell so bad? Because they're *on duty*."

"What happened to him?" Tusk asked, pointing to JP, slumped between the two men.

"Beats me," Dex said. "He was already in fourth gear when I got here. His lesser nature got the better of him, I guess."

"How was the show?" Tusk asked.

"It was a show, alright," Dex said, amiably. "Wasn't a very good show, but it was certainly a show."

"He started out okay," said Haines, propping up JP from the other side. "But at some point, he started rambling that vengeance was coming for him and things just never got coherent again after that. Plus Tayto kept heckling the shit out of him."

"Why?"

"Girl-code," Dex said. "My brother made some unwise choices earlier concerning both my sisters and their privacy. Though, hell, you know him, he could've also pissed off Tay independent of that."

Dex and Haines loaded JP into Dex's minivan. Tusk had hung around the parking lot for a while longer before going home and crashing. That morning, he checked in at the station and got a cruiser. He drove back to Big Lock's and pulled around back. Now he was reading his notes and trying not to think about Carrie's car still being parked out front, which meant she had been drunk enough to need a ride home.

So Morgan is just sitting back here in his car and then what? The guy in the van knifes him and drives off? That didn't make any sense. Did he even know if Morgan had been knifed? He was confident enough to move forward with it, he decided. Tusk had only gotten the quickest glance at Morgan's injury, but he knew a knife wound when he saw one.

Tusk paced a circle around the backlot. Obviously anyone could be walking around with a knife on them, but there was one guy Tusk knew for certain carried a knife because he had seen it only the morning before: Jug. Tusk was certain Jug was at the bar last night, and Tusk hadn't seen him pull up in a vehicle. Tusk had looked up and suddenly there he was. Almost like he had gotten out of a car that was already there. A car or maybe a van. A van parked at the side of the bar.

Tusk widened the circle he was pacing to walk through the staff parking area. It was the only place to park back here. JP's car was still there, backed against the chain link fence. Dex must not have brought him back to pick it up yet. It had been there when Tusk searched the area the night before, looking for Morgan, wondering if he had crawled off somewhere and maybe passed out. There was no Range Rover then and there was no Range Rover now either. Tusk walked back to the dark spot where gravel and dirt had absorbed Morgan's blood and crouched there, thinking. Maybe Morgan drove himself out of here, or maybe someone picked him up, or maybe Tusk had everything wrong.

What he did know: Morgan had been stabbed and left lying next to a van that fled with Tusk hanging off the back door. It was possible Jug arrived in that van still carrying the knife Tusk saw him slip into his pocket that morning.

What he didn't know: where to find Jug. But he knew someone who had seen him recently. Tusk climbed back into his cruiser and put it in gear. He pointed the car toward Sailor Cassidy's apartment. It was a start.

•••

The sounds of the house broke through JP's dreams before his hangover did. Half-heard voices rising and falling like waves, doors opening and closing with their metal click, the refrigerator tearing open, condiments rattling in the door trays, a toilet flush whooshing before pulling away to the thin whine of the tank refilling, muttered curses from somewhere in the back, the hiss of the sink coming on, drawers that opened with the squeal of an engine running bad bearings. There was shouting then talking then shouting then talking—the ululations of a crowded house as he'd always known it. He believed it was a Saturday from his youth for an instant before the headache announced itself. It thrummed, pulsing, the rhythm so steady and unyielding that it triggered an existential panic at the possibility that this headache was eternal, unending.

JP was on the couch in his parents' living room. He sat up slowly as someone in the kitchen, Dex he thought, said, "She isn't answering her cell. I left messages." JP rubbed his eyes and took a deep breath, trying to get mellow enough that the hangover wouldn't bother him, a process that never worked but desperation kept him trying. There were no atheists in foxholes, the saying went. He would try praying next, as long as he was making his way through guaranteed failures. The tone of the voices he was hearing snagged his passing thoughts—something was wrong. He heard his mother say, "We're not calling the police with my daughter's life on the line."

"Who are these people?" His father's voice but sewn through with despair, like a sob was waiting in the wings to come on stage. All wrong. Like waking up to see a giant crack through the middle of the mountain that had loomed outside your window your whole life.

"Just criminals," a third voice replied. "Scumbag criminals who don't want to work so they wreck the lives of others." It took JP a moment to place the speaker. "This country is going to hell." It was Morgan.

A burning smell reached JP's nostrils. It did nothing to help his hangover. The smoke detector went off a second later, ripping his skull in half. He got to his feet and made his way into the kitchen. Through the noise he heard his mother. "Oh my God, the bacon," she said.

"Ma, stop, I got it," Dex was saying.

"I'm so sorry, I just...I just..."

"Mom, it's okay, let go. Please. I got it."

JP came to the doorway and saw his father slumped at the kitchen table, his eyes red from crying. His mother stood by the sink looking dazed, holding a smoking frying pan. Dex was alternating between trying to coax it out of her hands and flapping a dish towel at the screaming smoke detector on the ceiling. Morgan sat at the kitchen table with Butch. He looked pale with dark circles under his eyes, like he might faint at any moment. Morgan looked up at JP as he came into the kitchen.

"JP," he said. "I'm sorry, but I have some really terrible news."

•••

JP, Dex, and their mother and father sat at the kitchen table. Morgan was out front in the driveway "collecting himself" as he put it. JP had to admit he did look terrible. You obviously don't expect a guy to look great when his wife doesn't come home one night and he wakes up to a text message saying she's been kidnapped and he has to scrounge up a hundred grand to get her back, but Morgan was wearing it especially hard. The guy looked like he had survived a vampire attack.

"The farmland?" JP asked his dad.

"He says it'll be collateral against a loan. Says along with the value of Palmetto Glades he can go get the money from the bank today," his father said. Butch was red-eyed and tight, frozen in his seat, eyes on the table. JP looked over at Dex who was also watching their father with concern. This helplessness, the stillness as though the hot wire that drove him had been snipped, was something they hadn't seen before. It made it feel like Carrie was lost forever.

"That's it?" JP asked. "He takes the deed to the old farmland and they hand over a hundred grand, just like that?"

"He has a relationship with the bank," Butch said. "He was prepping a loan anyway. The farmland will increase the value of the collateral he's putting up and he says he can get the whole thing closed today if we get over there quick."

"She's not answering. Why isn't she answering?" their mother, Pam, asked. She was clutching her cell phone, dialing Sailor's number over and over and holding it up to her ear, then putting it on speaker, then holding it to Dex's ear saying, "Is it connecting? Do you think maybe my phone's just not connecting the call and that's— Oh, no, there's her voicemail."

"Mom," Dex said, trying and failing to get the phone away from her. "Mom, it's okay. She's just asleep and her phone died. She's fine."

"They might have gotten her too," Pam said, dialing again, this time on speaker. They all listened to Sailor's voicemail message announce, "What's up? It's Sailor. Do not leave me a voicemail. Do you understand? No. Voicemail. I will never listen to it. Ever. I don't understand why phones even still have this option. Text me like a normal person." Pam didn't leave a message this time.

"I didn't think that land was worth anything," JP said, not wanting to look at the sad sight of his mother helplessly squeezing her cell phone. He knew she was going to get up and try the old landline on the kitchen wall in a minute. "Just in case there's something wrong with my cell," she was going to say.

"I guess everything's worth something to a bank," Butch said. "But it's a family decision. He wants to just pay them. I agree. But maybe you all want to call the police. Wouldn't be able to stop you so let's just get it out there."

"Well, I guess—" JP started to say.

"You guess what?" his mother cut him off, raising her voice. JP shut up. Pam turned to her husband. "A family decision? What in the hell are you talking about? I'm not sitting here waiting for a cop to ask me stupid questions. Go get our daughter. Sell this goddamn house if you have to." She pulled her wedding and engagement rings off her finger and slapped them onto the table. "How much can you get for those? How much can you get for my car? We're going to sit here and what? Vote? This isn't a vote." She turned and looked at her sons. "You don't get a vote." She pivoted back to her husband. "Butch, I swear to God if you're not out of that chair and in Morgan's car with the deed to that dog-ass farmland in the next ten seconds I will knock your ass out and sell you to science as a corpse. And when you come to, I'll do it again, and I'll keep doing it until I have enough money to ransom my child. And you two," she turned back to JP and Dex as Butch rose from his chair and went to the cabinet in the living room where they kept their important papers. "You better go find Sailor and bring her back to this house where I can see her or I will rip this town down to the nails." She got up from the table and went to the kitchen phone on the wall.

"I've never even seen that old farmland anyway," Dex said. He stood up and slapped his older brother on the shoulder. "I'll drive."

•••

Sailor held the towel full of ice to her face while the coffee brewed. The post-concussion was worse than the hangover the day before. The scene with Isaac in the living room had left her shaken. She had gone back to her room and found her second stun gun, slipped it into its holster with the other one, and strapped it around her middle over a tank top. She pulled a baggy Hawaiian shirt over the whole thing and felt better. Comfort weaponry, comfort clothes. *That's how you push through fear*, she told herself, fighting the flashes of anxiety from the night before strobing through her like club lights.

Lula worked the coffee maker, glancing nervously over at Sailor from time to time. "Should we take you to the hospital?" she asked.

"Not unless the hospital has coffee," Sailor said.

Lula stopped what she was doing. "Is that a yes, then?"

"What?"

"There's always coffee machines in hospitals. Might even be a Starbucks."

Sailor considered this. "You caught me a little bit on my back foot this morning, Lula. I don't want to go to the hospital." She rummaged through the ashtray on her coffee table until she found a roach that looked like it might have a hit or two left in it. *Hey presto*. She lit it and sat down at the counter between her living room and kitchen, looking at Lula and smoking. "No offense, but what are you doing here?"

Lula leaned against the counter, watching the coffee drip. "I should go."

"That's not what I said."

"I texted you last night and you didn't write back. This was the wrong move."

"I didn't get a chance to write you back because of the," Sailor gestured at her face with the towel of ice. "The fists in my face. My stolen phone. Things came up, you know?"

"They stole your phone?"

"Stole my phone, slashed my tires." Sailor thought for a moment. "I was probably going to write back."

"Probably?" Lula brightened a little.

"I don't know. I don't really do this. Or I haven't really done this. What we did, you know? Or, I mean—" Sailor's head hurt. She didn't want to mess up this conversation, but she wasn't in any condition to get it right. "I've done the sex part. The meeting someone out at a bar and bringing them home part, I haven't really done that. I had like one girlfriend. For kind of a long time. You're the next person I've met since her. So like, I don't know. I've never met the next person I was going to meet after a breakup before. But I think I would have written you back. Except..."

"The fists and the phone."

"Right, those."

"I don't do this either."

"So much for walking me through it then." They both watched the coffee maker for a moment. "Let's go somewhere," Sailor said. "That thing makes really shitty coffee."

"I know. I had it yesterday."

Sailor got up and shuffled toward the door. "There's a hotel down the block on the beach that does breakfast. They make a decent cup of coffee."

"Are you okay to go out?"

"I'm alright. This isn't usual either, by the way. I promise I'm usually drama free," Sailor said, opening the door. Standing on the other side with his fist raised, about to knock, was a uniformed cop. The cloud of weed smoke hanging in the apartment rushed out the open door into his face. Sailor turned back to Lula. "Usually," she said. "But not today."

•••

Tusk was about to knock when the door opened and a cloud of weed smoke blew into his face. *Definitely the right apartment*, he thought. Sailor stood in the open door looking startled and beaten to shit. Her face was swollen. Purple and black bruising spread across it like a raccoon mask. Sailor held a towel to her face, filled with what Tusk assumed to be ice.

"Shit, you alright?" Tusk asked. "What happened?" The smell of weed wafted at him again and he said, "Can you come out here and close the door maybe? I—"

"Oh no you don't," a voice called from inside the apartment. A woman Tusk didn't know appeared behind Sailor, pulled her inside, then stepped into the doorway in her place. "My client doesn't have to leave her place of residence and you have no probable cause to come inside."

"Your client?" Tusk asked.

"Yes. I'm her attorney," the woman said.

"Did you get busted with weed again?" Tusk asked Sailor over the woman's head.

"You have priors?" the woman asked, turning to Sailor.

"You're a lawyer?" Sailor asked the woman. "I thought you coached volleyball."

"Not as a career. I'm a lawyer. And he has no probable cause," the woman said.

"It smells like a bong hit came to life and took another bong hit coming out of this doorway," Tusk said. "Which would be more than enough reason for me to come inside."

"How would a cop know what a bong hit smells like?" the woman said, crossing her arms and staring at him like she had just played her trump card.

"Because I've sat next to Smokey Joe here at the bar when she hasn't done her shirt laundry," Tusk said.

"Lula, it's okay, really. I know him," Sailor said.

"Why do you want her to step outside so badly?" the woman, Lula apparently, asked Tusk.

"Because I need to talk to her and I don't want to sit in there and marinate in secondhand pot smoke when I have to go out and be a cop the rest of the day. It's bad for my vibe to show up smelling like a dorm room on four twenty. Also, I'd rather not put myself in the position of seeing a bunch of half-smoked joints scattered all over the place and feel like I need to do something about it."

"You see them as half smoked, I see them as half left," Sailor said, stepping around Lula.

"Glad to know you're a pipe-is-half-full kind of stoner," Tusk said. "But I'd rather not see them at all."

"You're really a lawyer?" Sailor said again to Lula.

"Civil cases only but—"

"I knew it! With that dog-ass probable cause nonsense," Tusk said.

"Two of them were against police officers for wrongful arrest and detention," Lula finished.

Tusk considered this. "So you fucked up a cop or two in court," he said. "You probably beat toddlers at Scrabble too. Good for you. Do you mind if Sailor and I chat privately for a minute?"

"Not when my client has a head injury."

"Are you really her client?" Tusk asked Sailor. "What happened to your head anyway?"

"I got laid out after I saw a kidnapping," Sailor said. "What happened to your own head?" Sailor reached out and took Tusk's chin, gently turning his head to see the scrape the passing truck tire had left.

"Did you really see a kidnapping or is that the head injury talking?" Tusk asked.

"I'm sorry, you saw a what? You said you got robbed," Lula said.

"I need to report the kidnapping," Sailor said, taking the ice from her face and turning back to her apartment. "And I need to do it sitting down, I think. That *is* the head injury talking."

Lula followed her inside saying, "Who got kidnapped?"

Tusk sighed and started after them. He was going to smell like weed the rest of the day.

•••

Sailor explained the previous night the best she could while Lula ran around her apartment hiding ashtrays and paraphernalia and turning on the ceiling fans. Tusk did his best to keep his eyes on Sailor and off any contraband he would feel conflicted about.

"Why didn't you report this last night?" Tusk asked when she finished.

"Yeah," Lula chimed in. "Or first thing this morning?"

"Thank you, counselor," Tusk said, rolling his eyes.

"Y'all, I'm like, pretty concussed," Sailor said.

"We were about to have a coffee date!" Lula said.

"Probably would have ruined it when I got my thoughts straight and remembered to call the cops in the middle of things," Sailor said. "It's lucky Tusk showed up."

"Thank you," Tusk said. He made a face at Lula as if to say, *So there.* Sailor saw his eyes go to the coffee stains streaked across the carpet from earlier. "Is that coffee all over the floor?" he said, rubbing his fingers on the damp carpet. "Oh. Wait. Is 'coffee date' like a sex thing I haven't heard of?" Lula opened her mouth, preparing a vehement protest Sailor assumed, but Tusk held up a hand. "Actually don't tell me. It doesn't matter." He took an antiseptic wipe from a pouch on his belt and started cleaning the hand that had touched the coffee. "You'll have to make a statement at the station so we can start knocking on doors of the complex to ascertain the possible victim's name and—"

"It's Nina Capaldi," Sailor said.

Tusk dropped the antiseptic wipe into an ashtray. "You know the victim's name? I thought you were just there checking the building's compressors."

"I recognized her. We went to high school together," Sailor said. It would probably come out that she was lying, but she couldn't let the woman's abduction go unreported any longer than it already had. Carrie's embarrassment wasn't worth Nina's life. "I think she works over at Grand Strand Bank. We see each other around town, say hi, that kind of thing."

Tusk nodded and started talking into the comm unit velcroed to his chest, calling in a wellness check on Nina at her apartment.

"You're not going to start looking for her?" Lula asked.

"We have to determine that she's definitely missing first," Tusk said.

"She just told you she was dragged into a van!"

Tusk sighed. "No, she *thinks* she was being dragged into a van. Then she got knocked out. Then she met up with a bunch of surfers on the beach who brought her home. Then she started to have a 'coffee date,' or whatever you two were about to do, and *then* she remembered to tell a passing cop that she witnessed an abduction. And now she's concussed and, I presume, high." He turned to Sailor. "You high?"

"Don't answer that!" Lula said.

"I'm pretty high," Sailor admitted.

"Sailor!"

"Listen, I believe her, but we need to determine that Ms. Capaldi is definitely missing before Sailor here comes in and tells her wild-ass story, alright? While we wait for that, Sailor, I need you to tell me if you know where Judson Shaw is."

"Jug? Why?"

"Because I also have a story about a van," Tusk said.

•••

JP slumped in the front seat while Dex drove. He checked his account balance on his phone. Nine hundred and thirty-five dollars and fifty-eight cents.

"What's that?" Dex asked, leaning over to look at JP's phone.

"Watch the road," JP said, pulling his phone away too late.

"Just ninety-nine thousand more and we're in the clear," Dex said. "Check the ashtray for change as long as you're looking."

"Hilarious," JP said, but he opened the ashtray anyway and found a roach. He lit it and cracked the window. His hangover considered the new substance entering the arena. It didn't abate, but it stopped kicking up as much fuss.

"So rehab obviously went really well," Dex said.

"It's your weed," JP snapped. "You drive around with this shit in your ashtray just asking to get busted if some cop pulls you over. Waste your whole—" The hangover flexed a little as if spurred on by his hypocrisy. "Just stay in school and study," he ended weakly, tossing the last of the roach out the window.

"Yeah, well, no worries now that I've seen what kind of money comedians make."

"Did you bring me to the house last night?"

"Yeah, you were super fun about it too," Dex said. "Incoherent and mostly dead weight. It was a great first night back."

"You couldn't have tossed me anywhere else but on their couch? Into traffic or off one of the piers maybe? Or, here's a crazy thought, my own apartment?"

"Oh right, your apartment, why didn't I think of that? Hey, why don't you show me the keys I would have used to get you into your place?"

JP felt in the pockets of the pants he had slept in, then grabbed his jacket off the floor where it had slid from his lap and rifled through those pockets. "Where are my keys?" he asked.

"That's an excellent question, and one I wish you'd figured out before Haines and I hauled your ass up a flight of stairs to your door. Damn Walnut crying from the other side. Did you leave him any food? Not that he couldn't stand to skip a meal."

"He's got plenty of food. Why didn't you at least put me in our room?" JP asked.

"My whole damn life you and I shared a room, and Jug half the time. Then I went to college and I got a roommate. I was looking forward to coming home and sleeping in a room that didn't have someone else in it for a change. I didn't feel like giving that up because your drunk ass lost your keys."

They were quiet for a moment. Then JP said, "He's back. Did you know that? Jug."

"The hell you say. When did that happen? How's he doing? Where'd he go?"

"I saw him last night. Briefly. He said Florida some. Just around really, job hopping. You know, I didn't really go to rehab." He didn't realize he was going to say the last part until it was out of his mouth.

"I'd sure as shit hope not," Dex said. "Would be an awful bad referral for the place the way you carry on. What'd you tell us all you went to rehab for? Mom and Dad paid for that. Didn't Carrie and Morgan kick in too?"

"I paid them back. I got in some trouble and needed money."

"You couldn't think of a better way to ask for a loan than pretending to go to rehab?"

It was half a wish at the time. JP had to pay Jumper back and rehab was the only thing he could think of that his family would produce money for quickly. It was a lie he wished was true. He imagined disappearing into a facility for two months and coming out normal, happy and new. Instead he spent two months pretending to be in a facility in northern Georgia.

"No," JP said in answer to his brother's question. "What else would anyone have lent me money for back then?"

Dex chewed that over. "Fair point I guess. Where'd you go for two months?"

"That's the thing. I was out at the house on the family land." He had holed up out there, not knowing where else to go and knowing no one from his family ever went there. The house had a roof and walls, but it wasn't livable for decent people. Their great grandparents had lived in it, but it was essentially abandoned now. A rural clapboard two-bedroom left to fend for itself off a two-land road lined with fields of cotton, tobacco, and weeds. JP meant for it to be temporary until he cleared his head and figured things out a little. One night, with nothing else to do, he started practicing jokes for a five-minute stand-up set. He liked stand-up comedy and would have watched some, except his phone was dead, and the old house didn't have electricity. He didn't have enough gas in his car to justify running it while his phone charged. Two hours later he was pacing around the small circle of candlelight he had in the dark, doing bits out loud to see how they sounded.

That started it. He stayed in the house for two months, writing jokes and occasionally driving down the road for lousy groceries from a country gas station. When he came back to Myrtle Beach, he had half an hour of well-rehearsed, albeit untested, material.

"That's what I don't understand," JP continued. "You've never been out there and who knows the last time Mom and Dad saw it but, Dex, there's no way in hell that place is worth anything. Not unless Morgan knows something the rest of us don't."

Chapter 7

Tusk didn't want to explain all about Sailor's brother-in-law, and all the other pieces that didn't add up. He didn't want to explain because he couldn't. He had no victim, no evidence, and no idea what had become of Morgan.

"Judson was spotted at the scene of a potential crime last night," Tusk told Sailor. "I'm looking for someone who fled the police in a white van." That was the best he could give her to explain why he was looking for him.

"Just call him Jug. No one calls him Judson except Nana Jean. He drives a Tacoma anyway. Not a van," Sailor said.

"Great, then *Jug* can explain all that to me when I find him. Look, Sailor, the police are looking for him," Tusk lied. "He's already spent a night in jail. It'll be better if I can find him and talk to him than if someone else pulls him over and drags him in."

"This is bullshit," Lula said. "Whenever a cop tells you it will be better if you just do what he wants, it's bullshit."

"He's probably at his grandma's," Sailor said.

"Nope. Not last night and not today. I've checked," Tusk said. "He's staying somewhere in town but we don't know where."

Sailor got a strange look on her face, like she suddenly understood something, but it was hard for Tusk to tell if it was the weed and concussion or an actual realization. "I'll show you," she said.

"Just tell me and I'll go. Law and Order over here can take you to a hospital until I call you about Nina," Tusk countered.

"Tell me what you think Jug did."

"I can't disclose the details of an ongoing investigation."

"And I can't disclose the details of the ongoing knowledge I have of the whereabouts of a suspect in your investigation. Your totally real investigation."

They stared at each other.

"Fine," Tusk finally said. "Get in the fucking car. And change your shirt. Do you have one that smells less like a California grow house?"

"Ha!" Lula cackled. "I knew it was bullshit. My girl's on to you."

"Be less thirsty," Tusk hissed at her as he went outside to wait while Sailor changed.

He was secretly pleased when it worked out that Lula had to ride in the back like a perp. "Why can't Sailor and I take my car?" she asked.

"Because I'm not caravaning all around Myrtle Beach following your Subaru. This isn't the Oregon Trail. Ride in the back or don't come," he said.

She pouted but got in. Neither of them knew where they were going. Sailor wouldn't say and Tusk wasn't in a position to argue.

Before Sailor took them wherever she was taking them, though, they pulled up to the Hi-Fi Coffee Bar. Lula sulked in the back and Tusk rode the small pleasure available in that. Sailor pushed some bills through the bars to Lula. "Would you mind going in and getting the drinks?" she said. "My head is still a little swimmy."

"What about him?" Lula said, gesturing to Tusk.

"Cold brew, no sweetener," Tusk said. "Thanks."

"I mean why can't you go get the coffee?"

"He can't leave us sitting here in his cop car. He could get in trouble," Sailor said, before Tusk could answer. Tusk raised an eyebrow at this but didn't say anything, just nodded. He let Lula out of the back. She looked a little hurt, like a kid being left out of a game, but she went inside and Tusk got back in the driver's seat.

"You've been screwing my sister," Sailor said before he had closed the door.

"What? No. I'm not. Why would you say some shit like that?" Tusk said. He heard how obviously guilty he sounded. He was so shocked by the accusation he couldn't think of what a person not sleeping with her sister might say.

"Dude, you're not in trouble," Sailor said. "*I'm* not the cops."

"Myrtle Beach P.D. doesn't really have jurisdiction over things like that."

"No, but one of their officers hunting down his married lover's childhood friend and using her sister with a head injury to help would probably make the news. You, as an employee, are definitely in their jurisdiction."

"I'm not 'hunting him down.'"

"You even enlisted me as your tracker."

"You're concussed."

"I'm still right. Two things can be true at the same time."

"That's what you think this is? That I'm looking for Jug 'cause of some connection to your sister?"

"You won't explain what this is about. But Jug is like a brother to me. You? You're cuckolding someone who's literally a brother to me. Through marriage anyway."

"Why are you in the car then?"

"I don't particularly like my brother-in-law."

You would be happy to know he might have been well and truly stabbed then, Tusk thought, but he didn't want to play that card yet. "I don't think your sister likes him much either," Tusk said.

"There's not much to recommend him," Sailor admitted. "Jug, on the other hand, is a real Cassidy family fan favorite."

Tusk sighed. What was it with this goober? Captain Lewis wanted tabs kept on him. The Cassidy family was all in on him. Meth heads at the station were clamoring for a piece of him. He was a run-of-the-mill white guy with no dress sense. Sometimes people just liked something, or someone, specifically because it *wasn't* special, he guessed. Reassuringly plain and unchallenging. Maybe that was Jug's appeal. He wasn't even threatening enough to keep in jail more than a night to sleep off a case of the stupids. Come to think of it, he legitimately was not interesting enough to be a person of interest. Tusk wasn't going to arrest him. He had no victim, no proof—just a hunch and a favor to do for the captain. He could afford to make some promises.

"Listen," Tusk said. "Help me find this guy and I promise you I'm not going to arrest him or charge him with anything. Not today anyway. He does something dumb in the future, I might arrest him. Today I just need to talk with him. No connection with your sister."

"Who you're definitely sleeping with," Sailor said.

Tusk was saved from having to fumble through a denial again by the radio. It was the station desk following up about Nina. "No response at her home," said the voice over the radio. "No vehicle in her name so we can't check the lot."

"She has a vehicle," Sailor said. "It's a white BMW five series." She told him the license plate number.

Tusk stared at her while he told the station desk the make, model, and plate number then asked to have the responding officers check the lot. "Treating this as a potential abduction," Tusk told dispatch. "I'm talking to a witness now who says she saw it. We're coming in shortly." Sailor looked out the window.

"You just happened to recognize a kidnap victim in the parking lot of her complex while you were servicing their HVAC unit and you just happen to know where she works and you just happen to know her license plate number?" Tusk asked.

"Why? Is that weird?" Sailor said. "I'm observant. You could pick up a few pointers from me. It'll help with your cop work. For instance, look out your window."

Tusk turned and saw Lula standing at the window with a tray of coffees. He rolled down the window and accepted his and Sailor's drink and thanked her, in what he hoped was a sincere tone. Things were ratcheting up. He could feel it. Better to play nice with everyone and reduce any antagonism.

"What'd I miss?" Lula said, sliding into the backseat.

"Nina's not home. The officers on site are checking the lot for her car. And Sailor is about to take us to find Jug," Tusk said. "Right?" He directed this last part to Sailor.

"Three stops," Sailor said. "Give me three stops and we'll find him."

First, Sailor directed them to a house under construction in a neighborhood west of the bypass. Workers popped in and out of the house's various openings—windows, doorways, the garage. Tusk always found construction sites very bee-like.

"We're not getting out. Just pull up," Sailor said. She rolled down her window. "Yo, Pez," she yelled. A thin Hispanic guy with a big head looked up and took a few steps toward them, stopping at talking range. He ducked his head to look in at Tusk and Lula in the back. "Calm down, dude," Sailor said. "Everything's alright."

"Did you arrest that lady back there?" Pez asked, edging a little closer.

"Yeah, I became a cop since you saw me last night. I arrested that lady for acting shady when she saw the police car pull up. You're next."

"I am not arrested," Lula called from the back. "I just have to ride back here."

"She is not arrested," Tusk confirmed.

"Oh look, y'all agree now," Sailor said. Then to Pez, "Stop acting like you've ever done anything cops care about. You paint *Lord of the Rings* figurines when there's no waves. Get over here."

Pez crossed his arms. "You said that to be hurtful. You know damn well they're *Dune* figurines. I don't go in for that dork-ass Tolkien shit."

"I'm just winding you up," Sailor said. "Did Isaac find a bunch of old cigarettes and trash again this morning?"

"No, thank God," Pez said. "I'm sick of hearing him fuss about it. How's your face?"

"Hurts like a motherfucker."

"Makes you look tough, anyway."

"I don't feel tough."

"Don't matter if you feel tough. You just are tough, baby."

"Thanks, Pez."

"See ya. Stay out of trouble."

"Go on," Sailor said to Tusk, who drove them back toward the main road. "Wait," Sailor said, suddenly. "Pull over there."

An older man stood on a small front lawn, looking into the narrow space between two houses. "This isn't one of the three stops," Sailor said. Then she shouted out the window, "Hey, Mr. Papaioannou!" The old man turned and squinted at Tusk's cruiser.

"Is Sailor?" he asked.

"Yeah, it's me. Did you FaceTime with your grandson?"

"Yes!" the old man yelled. "It's good. It's good." He smiled and came to the car. "He waves camera all around. I say, 'Hold still or Papou will be sick!' He just waves more. Ha! Zouzouni mou." The man's face grew stern as he took in Tusk and the police cruiser.

"But what is this? You arrested?" He looked at Tusk. "She is good girl. Why you arrest?"

"No, no, Mr. Papaioannou. I'm not arrested," Sailor said. "He's my friend. I'm just helping him out. You told me you see a truck parked at that house being built down the road, when you walk in the evening. Is it a Toyota Tacoma?"

"I tell them they should not park their truck there overnight. Is just on side of the road. Is not nice for the neighborhood, you know?"

"You told who that? The guys working at the site?"

"Yes. They pretend not to know. But I say *twah twah.* Is disrespectful to neighborhood."

"Did he just spit?" Lula asked from the back.

"Last night, truck is not there. Maybe they finally listen. Who knows?"

"How's the system?" Sailor asked, nodding to the compressor between the two houses.

Tusk squeezed his eyes shut and took a steadying breath like they'd taught him in training. *Remain calm,* he thought. *Remain cool.* This was a bad idea. Sailor was chatting up some spitting old fool, wasting time, getting nowhere. He was in the middle of it now, though, and it felt too late to stop things. Three places, Sailor had told him. He tried to ignore the term "sunk-cost fallacy" floating through his mind and listen in case there was something worthwhile in all this.

"I catch neighbor lady at my drain hose," Mr. Papaioannou said. "She say it floods grass and gets to her foundation. *Twah, twah.*"

"This guy spits a lot," Tusk said quietly so Mr. Papaioannou, who was glaring at his neighbor's house now, couldn't hear.

"It's kind of his thing," Sailor said.

"Now I watch," Mr. Papaioannou said, eyeing the house. Tusk saw movement at the front curtain. "I watch you!" Mr. Papaioannou yelled at the impassive front door. "And now police are here. You see? They watch you too. They know about you!" He turned back to the car and leaned on the window. "This is good. She see police. She not come to my hose again. Thank you, Sailor. You are very good repairman." He pointed at Tusk. "Make sure you not arrest this one. Okay?"

"It's repair woman," Lula said through the grate. "Or really, repair person would be preferable."

Mr. Papaioannou looked at Lula for a moment, then turned back to Tusk. "I don't know that one," he said. "You probably right to arrest." He turned and walked to his front door.

Sailor had them drive to another house being built, but she told Tusk not to bother stopping when she saw the workers on site. She gave him directions to the next stop.

"I don't think whatever this is, is working," Tusk said.

"One more," Sailor said.

"Is there another client of yours who'll be spitting like a llama and using my cruiser to intimidate his neighbor? 'Cause if so, I'm fine skipping it." This was a dead end. Following up with Sailor had been a reasonable idea based on the information he had, but Sailor was not a reasonable person—a concussion, being high, an overnight guest or girlfriend or something hanging around, living room hosed down with coffee for who knew what reason, construction sites and spitting old men. Tusk wanted to bail.

"There's an email account for Air Down There," Sailor said. "It's where the job orders come in. We all have access to it. Any job we get, the address is in there. There's nothing financial tied to it, and the whole business is essentially family or people close enough to be like family, so we're pretty lax about the password."

"What a great story," Tusk said. The generosity of spirit that had taken him at the coffee shop was gone. "Tell it again. Tell it again," he chanted.

"I thought it was good," Lula said.

"Did you finish your coffee, Lula?" Tusk asked. "Or are you still *thirsty*."

"We don't change the password when someone stops working for us, is what I'm getting at," Sailor said. "Someone like Jug. Isaac told me yesterday he's been finding stuff on his sites in the morning. Like someone's hanging out in the places at night. The sites he told me about are all places I'm doing the HVAC installs. The job orders are in that email account."

Tusk thought about this. "You think Jug is finding the addresses of half-built houses in the email account from his old job and overnighting in them?"

"I do. He's really clever about dumb shit like that. The kind of guy who knows how to get a boot off his car without paying the fine."

"They record the vehicle information when they boot a car. It's not like you drive away and they don't know who you are. You just get a warrant if you do that."

"He doesn't consider that part of things. Like I said, he's only clever about the dumb shit. Make a left here."

Tusk was familiar with the type. Local jails did ninety percent of their business on people who were only clever about the dumb shit. Tusk thought of them as short-term solution experts. Jug fit the bill—pissing in a parking lot rather than walking two minutes back to the bar he had just come out of. That didn't mean he was holed up in one of the random places the Cassidys were contracted on, though. There were hundreds of other possibilities where the guy could be crashing, all of them a lot more pleasant and less exposed to the elements. Myrtle Beach was filled with motels and it was the offseason. He shouldn't have given his time to Sailor's three-places-he-might-be game. Tusk thought she was going to swing them by some of his friends' houses, or ex-girlfriends' maybe. The kind of places people actually went.

"That's thin, Sailor," he said. "Real thin. I mean, the odds of him not having some other place he could stay—"

"He doesn't."

"—and then thinking of that exact plan with the email account and all that—"

"He did."

" —are so slim that it's—"

"There's his truck."

"What?"

"Right there."

Tusk looked where Sailor was pointing. There was the same Toyota Tacoma he had arrested Jug beside two nights earlier.

"And he's inside that house," Sailor said, pointing to the yellow wooden skeleton of a beach house across the road from the truck. "Work's paused on this one until after Thanksgiving when the electrician gets back from Des Moines. Jug must have moved last night."

Tusk stared at the incomplete beach house. A three-story insurance claim waiting for a hurricane. He thought of what Carrie said the last time she had spoken to him, just before she stormed out of his place.

Sailor just knew things.

•••

Carrie slept somehow. Disorienting sleep, with dreams that mirrored her real life predicament and were indistinguishable from being tied to a table on a boat until, in the dream, she stood or broke her hands free. Then she would jerk awake and find herself in the same uncomfortable position. She could hear Nina whimpering a few feet away, going through something similar no doubt.

Nina.

Carrie wanted to hate her, but it was hard to hate someone suffering at the hands of the same sons of bitches as you. She hated Nina before she found herself on this boat, and she would hate her after she got off the boat. For now, she hated whoever the assholes were who had tied her to this miserable table.

Carrie heard the birds coming to life outside, song and song-reply, the first tentative screeches of the seagulls. Dawn pushed through the fibers of the blindfold. Morning had come. Her ankle hurt, but that was the one ache Carrie didn't mind. Jug's Buck knife was still in her boot. Its painful weight digging into the bone of her ankle was the single advantage she might have to help her get free. She wasn't sure how exactly, but the possibility was important. She didn't have any illusions about stabbing her way out of this mess, but she might be able to cut herself free and slip away. Assuming there was even a way to sneak off Morgan's boat.

The fact that Morgan owned a boat kept circling inside her head, never quite landing in her brain. She knew it was something relevant to her—more of Morgan's lies and an expensive lie at that—but it was hard to find the boat interesting when she was tied to it. It was just a problem. Not unlike Morgan himself, actually.

The door at the front of the cabin opened and someone dropped heavily down the few steps. Nina startled her with an outburst.

"Just call Hector, okay?" Nina said. "He'll fix this. Whatever it is...I mean, it's money right? Of course it's money. Call Hector, okay. He'll want us back."

Carrie thought, *Us?* She wondered who Nina thought she was. They hadn't spoken much after Nina revealed they were captive on Morgan's boat. What was there to discuss? *How are you enjoying being kidnapped, beaten up, and tied to a boat?*

It sucks, how about you?

Oh wow, yeah, same for me, it sucks ass.

"We haven't seen your faces," Nina went on. "He'll take care of it." She sniffled. "Please," she added, saying the word like it was foreign.

"Hector," the man who had come down the steps said. Carrie was pretty sure it was the same voice that told them he would sink the boat with them in it the night before. There was a rustling sound and the man said, "What's the passcode for this phone?"

Nina told him. "Um, he's...he's under—"

"There's no Hector," the man's voice said.

"He's under 'Daddy,'" Nina said quietly.

Ew, Carrie thought to herself.

"Ew," the man said.

"It's part of the job," Carrie thought she heard Nina mumble.

"What?" the man said.

"It's what he likes to be called," Nina said louder, the scared and pleading tone back in her voice. "He can get you money for us. If this has something to do with Morgan then you should go kidnap his wife, not us. Just let us go. We know how things work. We won't go to the police. I'll even tell you her address."

Carrie listened as Nina rattled off her home address.

"His wife," the man said flatly. "Hmmm." There was the sound of feet ascending the few steps and then the closing of the door to the cabin.

"Hector better pay this jerkoff and get me the fuck out of here," Nina said when the door closed. All the fear-performance was gone from her voice. "Does Hector have you working some chump right now? Can we send them after his wife instead of us? 'Cause sister, let me tell you, if they collect the human grain sack Morgan's married to, they're going to have a hell of a time getting any money. That white trash family makes fuck-all. One of them's a goddamn podcaster or some stupid shit, and the rest of them do some gross manual labor."

Carried changed her mind. There was no need to wait until later, she had plenty of capacity to hate Nina right here and now.

•••

Sailor's head was clearing. There was an otherworldliness to the morning's proceedings that she couldn't entirely shake, but she couldn't say how much of that was due to her head injury or Lula's presence and riding around in a cop car searching for a guy she hadn't seen in three years.

Sailor and Lula left Tusk in what would eventually be the carport beneath the beach house. The house sat atop pylons to save it from the inevitable flooding and provide a covered place to park. Then they went up the stairs.

"How did you know where he'd be?" Lula asked quietly as they climbed the unrailed wooden steps.

"I don't know how to explain it," Sailor said. "It's not magic or anything. And I'm not always right. I kind of just see how people behave and it becomes really clear what things they'll think about and do. Weirdly, I usually can't tell what I'm going to do next, though." She thought about that a little. "In fact, I don't think I ever know."

"That sounds scary," Lula said.

"It is. Sometimes."

Lula reached up and took Sailor's hand. Sailor stopped walking and looked down at her. Harper hadn't been the holding hands type. She disdained public displays of affection, and Sailor had gone along with that in the thoughtless bandwagoning of Harper's opinions that she always hoped would gain her approval and bless their union. Feeling the warm pressure of Lula's hand, she decided she liked it. Sailor gave Lula's hand a squeeze and they reached the third floor.

Jug was on the floor in a sleeping bag like a red and gray caterpillar who had attempted a cocoon out of empty cans of Coors Light, which were scattered all around him. He raised his head sleepily when he heard them.

"Sailor?" Jug asked. "What are you...are you on a date?"

Sailor looked at Lula and smiled. "Hell yeah," she said to Jug. "Now crawl your ass out of that sleeping bag and look alive. The fuzz is downstairs and wants to talk to you."

•••

Jug was bawling when Tusk came up the stairs.

"It's okay," Sailor was saying. "He just needs to talk with you." Jug was smoking a cigarette so fast it looked like he was burning diesel. "Dude, did you do something?" Sailor asked.

"Did I kill him?" Jug asked through his tears. "I fucking killed him, didn't I?"

"Killed who?" Sailor asked.

"Yeah, killed who?" Tusk echoed, not wanting to lead him into any of his own theories.

"Do not answer that," Lula said to Jug. She turned to Tusk. "As this man's attorney—"

"I'm going to stop you right there," Tusk said. "I know you think I'm an idiot because I'm wearing this badge, but I know damn well you can't go around declaring yourself random people's attorney. So save it." He turned to Jug. "Who do you think you might have killed?"

"Carrie's husband. What's-his-face," Jug blubbered. "Sailor, I'm sorry. He was choking me. I couldn't breathe and I—"

"You didn't kill him," Tusk said.

"Are you talking about Morgan? You told me this didn't involve my sister," she said to Tusk.

"It doesn't."

"Is she alright?" Jug asked. "I left her there with Morgan. He's alright too?"

"You left who there with Morgan?" Tusk asked. "Carrie?"

"You lied to me," Sailor said.

"No I didn't, I don't know what he's talking about," Tusk said.

"I stabbed Morgan because he strangled me when I told him to stop calling Carrie a whore. Then I left him and Carrie behind Big Lock's near the dumpsters," Jug said by way of explanation.

Sailor stopped arguing with Tusk and turned to Jug. "You did what?"

"Yeah, same question from me," Tusk said.

"Alright, let's all calm down," Lula said. "Jug, I know you don't really know me."

"Were you at the bar the other night?" Jug asked.

"Neither here nor there," Lula said. "I think it's clear that no one is quite sure what went on with you last night. And you do not have to tell the police anything if you don't—"

"Ah hell, I don't care about telling him. I just want to know everyone's okay," Jug said. "I didn't want to kill no one." Jug laid out his whole story. He went all the way to the beginning, starting with him and JP being invited into the back room at Jumper's.

There was a lot for Tusk to process when Jug finished: drug running, a murder, blackmail. All of it was hearsay, none of it was provable, and there was essentially nothing he could do about any of it except maybe charge Jug with trespassing, but even that required someone to press charges. A grand string of crimes had been laid before Tusk, and the only thing he could harvest from it was to maybe get this dipshit to go to his grandma's house and stay there so he could tell his captain he had gotten the guy settled in somewhere.

"Who was in the van?" Tusk asked. "The one that pulled around to the back of the bar where you were fighting?"

"I didn't see any van," Jug said. "Once I could breathe again I just ran away like Carrie told me to. Like a coward," he added.

Tusk didn't see any reason to argue with that last part. Maybe the van was just some terrified random citizen who pulled up on a stabbing and took off when Tusk came charging around the back. Had Carrie gone to get Morgan's car to drive him to the hospital and they just missed seeing one another? It was all a little wild, but it made some sense. It would explain why Morgan's Range Rover was gone and Carrie's car was still at the bar. It would certainly explain why Morgan himself was gone. Between chasing the van down and rolling around Kings Highway, Tusk could have easily missed the Range Rover pulling out of the parking lot.

Sailor said, "Not that I'm not happy to see you and all, but why did you come back?"

"I finally saved ten grand. I thought I could talk to Jumper. Pay him back. I figured Randy's death...that would probably be solved by now, or settled at least. I didn't kill him anyway. That was Bevel. Though it don't seem like Bevel got hung up for that, since I saw him yesterday morning in jail. I thought I could buy my way back home but it takes a while to save ten g's. It's a lot of money. Then the whole thing with Morgan...I thought I killed him and just..." He leaned back against the exposed studs of a wall. "I'm just so tired. I don't want to figure things out anymore." He looked up at Tusk. "You want to arrest me?"

"Not especially," Tusk said. "You don't have any outstanding warrants. I don't have a body or an assault report from Morgan. What I do want is for you to stop trespassing in this beach house and go home. And I want to be able to find you there later if we need to get in touch with you."

"It's not safe for my Nana, especially since Bevel knows I'm back. Jumper probably knows by now too," Jug said.

"I can have a patrol car watch the house," Tusk said.

"You don't know Jumper, man."

"Let me ask you this," Tusk said. "Do you feel like you're doing a good job staying out of trouble and off Jumper's radar the way you're currently going? In two days you've been to jail, been seen by your former co-conspirator, and stabbed a guy."

"That's a fair point," Jug conceded.

"Clean this shit up and go home," Tusk said. "We'll watch the house. Bevel should be in J. Reuben Correctional by now." He looked over at Sailor who, for the first time the whole crazy morning, looked truly worried. "What's with you?" he asked.

"I don't have a phone. Carrie must have called me a thousand times by now" Sailor said. "I have to call her. Can I borrow your phone?"

Tusk thought about Carrie sitting in a hospital next to her stabbed husband, getting a call from his number. "If you want her to answer it, you better use Lula's phone," he said.

Chapter 8

Sailor helped Jug collect his sleeping bag, clean up his empties, and haul it all down to his old Tacoma before she called her sister. Tusk didn't want her to use his phone to call Carrie. His reluctance reminded Sailor she had unintentionally told JP's entire audience that Carrie was probably having an affair. Tusk was a part of that audience, which meant Carrie had probably heard by now. Sailor didn't want to ask Tusk about all this in front of Lula and Jug, so she picked up some empty Coors Light cans and thought about the best ways to apologize to Carrie while she followed Jug down the wood stairs and out to his truck.

Sailor gave him a hug before he climbed into the driver's seat. "Welcome home, dipshit," she said.

"Thanks."

"Nana Jean's been through it with you disappearing."

"I called her a few times."

"Well, if she'd only looked after you a few times instead of your whole stupid life I guess that would have been enough," Sailor said. "And don't think Butch and Pam aren't going to give you hell too."

Jug drove off. They were on the south end, less than a mile from his grandmother's house. Sailor borrowed Lula's phone and punched in Carrie's number from memory. She texted first, knowing Carrie wouldn't recognize the number. The text message bounced back, displaying a red exclamation mark beside it and the word "Undelivered." She tried again. The message didn't go through. She called. It didn't ring. A three note chime and an automated voice told her the number could not be completed as dialed. She read over what she had dialed, mouthing the numbers to herself. It was correct. She tried again. Same automated message.

"No answer?" Lula asked.

"I don't get it. It's not even going to voicemail," Sailor said, dialing Carrie's number a third time. Same result. She held up the phone with the number typed in, showing it to Tusk.

"What am I supposed to do with that?" he said.

"Check it against your phone and tell me it's right."

Tusk thumbed through his phone for a minute then looked back and forth between the two screens. "You got it right."

Sailor called again and got the same result.

"Maybe it's off because she's in the hospital?" Tusk said, lowering himself into his cruiser and pulling out the radio handset. "Doesn't some of the equipment like, interfere with cell phones or something? Try one of your brothers." He started speaking into the radio.

Sailor didn't much feel like communicating with JP right then in anything but loud declarative name-calling, but she was worried about Carrie. She punched his number into Lula's phone, texting first like she had done with Carrie. This time it went through. When she called, though, it went to his voicemail. She had never understood how people got so worked up they smashed a phone, but now she was beginning to get it. Then Lula's phone buzzed in her hand with JP's number. She answered. "Hey, where are you?" she asked. "Have you talked to Carrie today?" JP didn't respond. There was noise and shouting in the background. "JP? You there? Have you seen Carrie? She's not answering her phone."

"Hang on," JP finally said. "I got to call you back, Mom's got the shotgun."

The line went dead. Sailor stared at Lula's phone. She felt her circle of concern widening.

"You okay?" Lula asked.

"I can't reach Carrie. JP hung up on me. And my mom is apparently stomping around out there somewhere with a shotgun," she said.

"She's got a shotgun? It's barely after breakfast."

"I'd call Dex," Sailor said, "but I'm legitimately worried I'll find out he's in the middle of holding up a liquor store or giving his debit card number to a Nigerian prince or something."

"You know that BMW five series with the license plate number you happen to have memorized because you're observant?" Tusk said, standing up out of his cruiser, still clutching the radio handset. "They found it in the parking lot at Nina Capaldi's residence."

"Great, can someone start looking for that poor woman now, please?" Sailor said.

"They ran the plates. It's not registered to Nina. Guess who it's registered to."

"Is it someone I can call who might give a shit that she was kidnapped?"

"Maybe so," Tusk said. "It's your brother-in-law, Morgan Childress."

•••

JP and Dex let themselves into Sailor's apartment. "Well, she was here at some point this morning," JP said, sniffing the air. "It smells like a Colorado ski slope in here. That's a good sign."

"She made coffee too," Dex said from the kitchen. JP looked in and saw Dex turn off the burner on the coffee pot. "It looks like she didn't drink any though," Dex said.

"Probably for the best. That thing makes really shitty coffee."

When they got back home, their mother was on them at the door. "Did you find her?" she asked.

"No, but she was definitely there this morning, Ma," Dex said. "She had made coffee and there were other…signs."

"Dishes and stuff," JP said, jumping in. "She's alright."

"Why isn't she answering her phone?" their mother demanded. "If she's alright, why isn't she answering?"

"I don't know, Ma. Maybe she lost her phone," JP said.

"I'm going to go try her from the bedroom phone," his mother said. "Maybe the kitchen phone is messed up. You two get back out there and keep looking."

"Ma, she could be anywhere—" Dex started to say, but their mother wasn't hearing it.

"Then go everywhere and look!" she screamed. "Check her job sites, check the restaurants. Check whatever store sells those ugly Hawaiian shirts she likes. Look. Everywhere." She turned and went to her bedroom.

"I'm still wearing what I slept in last night," Dex said. "I'm going to change and I'll meet you out front."

"You want a to-go coffee for the car?" JP asked, heading into the kitchen.

"Milk and sugar," Dex hollered from their room.

JP pulled travel mugs out of the cabinet by the sink. His phone buzzed in his pocket with an incoming text then buzzed some more with the slightly different pattern of a call. He pulled it out and looked. A text on the homescreen read, "Dudeface, it's Sailor. I'm using a friend's phone. Pick up when I call." The incoming call was from the same number as the text.

"Oh shit," he said to himself. "Ma! I got her! She's calling me," he shouted. Right then he heard screaming from outside. He stopped to listen and his phone stopped buzzing. "Crap," he said.

He thumbed his way into the phone and called the number back. There was another scream from outside. It sounded like it was coming from next door, at Nana Jean's house. "Did you all hear that?" he called to the back of the house.

Sailor answered on the first ring. "Hey, where are you?" she asked. "Have you talked to Carrie today?"

Before he could respond, JP heard the back door open and slam and what sounded like his mother's voice yelling, "No more! Not today! Not. To. Day!" He looked out the window above the kitchen sink and saw his mother marching next door to Nana Jean's house, still in her robe and slippers, holding the shotgun their father kept in the bedroom closet.

Sailor was saying, "JP? You there? Have you seen Carrie? She's not answering her phone."

JP only vaguely registered this and blurted over her, "Hang on, I got to call you back, Mom's got the shotgun." He hung up and ran to the back door yelling, "Dex!"

Dex was in the bedroom doorway asking, "What's going on? Did you hear that yelling? Did Mom just leave?"

"She's armed!" JP yelled, rushing out the door. Dex fell in behind him.

They ran up Nana Jean's front steps and through the door after their mother. There, they found the source of the yelling. Nana Jean was sobbing. Hysterically. She had her thin old arms around Jug, her face buried in his chest, wailing loudly. Jug had his hands raised, like a thief who had just been caught, because JP's mother was still holding the shotgun on him with a shocked look across her face.

"Mom," JP said gently, not wanting to touch her in case she startled and the gun went off.

Nana Jean turned her red, wet, face toward them at the sound of JP's voice. She didn't take her arms from around Jug. "Oh hell, Pam, don't shoot him," she said. "I just got my boy back. My boy just came home."

•••

"Welcome home, I guess," Dex said to Jug. JP watched him ease the shotgun away from their mom.

"Thanks, Dexxy. It's been kind of a rough re-entry."

"You can put your hands down," JP said. Jug lowered them and put them around Nana Jean, who was still blubbering into his shirt.

JP and Dex led their mother back home. She was a little dazed. "Jug's home," was all she said as they crossed the small distance between the two houses.

"It's been a long morning, Ma," JP said. "Listen, Sailor just called me. She's alright."

"You talked to Sailor?" his mother asked, as they came back into their living room.

"Yeah, for a second anyway, before I saw you marching off across the side yard like Wyatt Earp at the OK Corral. Here, let's call her back." JP tapped the unfamiliar number Sailor's call had come from, then tapped the speakerphone button. The ringing sound trilled hopefully through the living room. Dex sat on the couch removing the shells from the shotgun. The ringing stopped as the call connected. Their mother leaned expectantly toward the phone JP held aloft with his fingertips like a serving tray.

"You dog-ass shitflap," Sailor said, instead of hello. "You absolute dick wagon."

"Hey, um, so you're on speaker," JP said.

"I don't give a cunt hair what I'm on, you ass stain" Sailor yelled.

"On speaker with Mom," JP clarified.

There was a silence from the phone that JP felt was dangerous. Finally Sailor said, "I'm going to fight the shit out of you when I see you." She added, "Hey Mom, sorry about the language."

"I'm just so happy to hear from you," their mother said, bursting into tears and sobbing.

Dex helped her up from the couch and led her toward her room. "Come and lie down, Mom, alright? Just take half an hour and rest."

"JP, can you take me off speaker phone, please, and put me right up to your ear?" Sailor said, sweetly.

"Um....okay," JP clicked her over to the phone and instinctively held it away from his ear. "I'm here," he said into the mouthpiece.

"Dick!" Sailor's screaming voice came through tinny and sharp.

"So, I deserve that," JP said. "But I need to catch you up on some things." He filled Sailor in on the morning so far. There was a long silence when he finished. The weight of their missing sister settled on him heavily now that the initial task he'd been assigned—finding Sailor—was accomplished. That had given him something to do that felt like it was helping, that there was movement toward a resolution. Now it was over. The larger helplessness of the family's position was front and center. "We're all really relieved to hear from you," he said, just to fill the hopeless air with sound, though it was true. Dex came back into the room.

"Where's Morgan now?" Sailor asked.

"He and Dad went to the bank. Dad's got the title to the family land to sign over for collateral or something. I don't really understand banking."

"The family land?" Sailor asked. "You mean that crappy little house?"

•••

Morgan and Butch sat next to each other in two captain's chairs staring at the empty desk in front of them. Morgan tried to keep his breathing steady. The stab wound was in his side, his love handle actually.

At the emergency department the night before, they had wanted to admit him, to keep him for a few days or at least overnight. He lay on the bed with his shattered fingers hanging off the left side while a young attending stood on his right putting twenty stitches into him, saying, "You're one lucky fella."

"That's what they call me," Morgan said, dismally. "Morgan the Magnificent, Luckiest of Them All."

"I'm being serious," the attending said. "You fall on a broken beer bottle and get a gash this deep, it's really lucky nothing vital was hit."

Morgan got up and limped out before a nurse even had a chance to come dress the stitches. It was nearly dawn when he got back to the house. He hadn't waited to get a prescription at the hospital, but there were some Percocet stashed in his closet that he'd bought off Jumper a while back. He wanted the painkiller to actually kill the pain this time, rather than just take him for a trip. He chewed one and chased it with some coffee, then put back a few lines of coke. He didn't want to be sleepy. He cleaned up as best he could and struggled over to the Cassidy's.

He was riding atop the snow of an avalanche and there were no options but to keep riding, maintain balance, and try not to think too much. He had called the whole sliding mountain into motion just a day prior. He'd been dripping sweat in the chilly back room of Jumper's Bar, flaring from the inside out on account of the cocaine. The sweat ran into his eyes as he blinked back into Jumper's steady gaze. The cocaine, as always, made it impossible for him to think of anything but cutting free from his obligations and partying himself insensate. He didn't usually allow himself cocaine until after four o'clock. He was responsible that way. The delicate rationalizations that guided his usual routine hadn't mattered anymore though, since everything had gone to hell. So he'd ripped three lines out in the parking lot under Myrtle Beach's mild November sun and gone into the bar's back office.

Like its owner, the bar was also called Jumper's, though it wasn't in as good shape. Jumper the bar owner was a beast, muscles rippled across him like a wind-blown sea. The bar, by contrast, appeared to have been flooded several times by that same sea, and left to dry without much thought given to ventilation. The place was pickled by grease, smoke, and booze, a lot of it run through a human body before being sweated, vomited, or exhaled back into the establishment.

The office where Jumper and Morgan sat was tidy and sparse. The desk must be pretty old, Morgan figured. There were two holes the size of pencil erasers on the surface. Two chairs sat across from one another, a couch along the back wall, and a coffee table—all of it bare. No computer, no phone charger plugged into the wall, or cords snaking about. Morgan couldn't imagine what Jumper was doing in there before he came in. Push-ups, he guessed.

"You're slam sure, abso-fucking-lutely positive, this is how you want to do this?" Jumper asked Morgan, holding him tight in his gaze.

Morgan blinked and tried to appear poised and assured but, on account of the cocaine-induced sweat, dripping with confidence was the best he could muster. "It's a simple, lucrative plan."

"Lucrative, yeah alright, the money's not bad. But simple? Fuck right off with that. You ever done this before?"

"No," Morgan admitted.

"Then shut up with *simple.*" Jumper said. "And for you, this is seriously personal. So you best be sure." Jumper opened a desk drawer and removed a pack of cigarettes, a lighter, and a clean ashtray. He lit a cigarette. "Ten grand," he said. "It ain't that much. I mean, it's not nothing. Like, if you needed a new roof on your house, that big sucker you live in over in Palmetto Glades, it would cost you about ten grand. That's a heavy layout if it landed on a waiter or a teacher, but you? A real estate hotshot? That ain't much. Shouldn't be, anyway."

Morgan fully caught the indication that Jumper knew where he lived, but didn't want that unpleasantness to interfere with the demeanor he was trying to project, so he ignored it. "Ten grand is enough for you to want it back, isn't it?" Morgan held up his left hand with the black splint supporting four broken fingers and one broken thumb. He resented having to convince the man who smashed up his hand to let him repay him. Wasn't that the whole point of the hand-smashing?

"Open your head and understand something. I don't want it back," Jumper said. "I didn't loan it to you. It's due to me. You owe it." He pointed at Morgan's hand. "You seemed to think the stakes here weren't real, that they wouldn't be enforced. Besides, I only broke your fingers. The thumb is your own bullshit." Morgan unconsciously reached over with his good right hand and gently felt the contours of his thumb splint. He had thought maybe Jumper wouldn't notice when he showed up with the thumb splinted in addition to the fingers, but the man had an exacting eye. "In fact," Jumper continued. "I'm mad you broke your thumb, because I was saving your thumb for the next time you failed to understand how serious I am. Now when you fuck up, I'll have to break the fingers on your other hand, which means when you come crawling around here, I'm going to have to open doors for you and shit. That's going to piss me off and I'll have to break your foot. Then you'll need a wheelchair. And this place ain't exactly wheelchair accessible, unless you want to add another couple grand for me to build you a fucking ramp. So don't wave your whole broke-ass hand at me like you're doing me a favor and throwing the thumb in for free."

Morgan took out his own cigarettes and lit one, flipping the lid on the box with his working hand and pulling the cigarette out with his mouth. The coke was surging on him. He inhaled and steadied his breathing. *You're a salesman*, he said to himself, *sell the deal.* "Well I can't rightly wave any of it since it's broke to shit but yeah, the thumb was a workplace accident," he mumbled. "I didn't mean to imply." Finding his rhythm, he had pressed on, "But my point is, this will square us and then some. Yeah, I have money, but I think in terms of maximizing every dollar, so everything's tied up in investments. I'm not super liquid. If you just want the ten, hey, no problem." He hoisted his broken fingers. "I get that you're serious. I'll go to the bank, move some things around and get the cash. This opportunity, though, it's too good for either of us to pass up. And there's no victim. You make thirty grand. The whole thing takes two business days."

Jumper gave him a look and said, "Twenty grand."

"Twenty?" Morgan said, confused.

"You owe me ten grand. If we do this, I make twenty, not thirty. The first ten makes me whole. What you owe."

Morgan felt the urge to roll his eyes go to war with his desire not to have any more fingers broken. "You make twenty grand. My bad," he said.

Jumper exhaled smoke and cocked his head, studying Morgan. Even his head, with its curly red hair, had muscles, Morgan noticed. They extended up from his neck and were visible through his fade, shorn so close to the scalp you could see through it. Jumper chuckled. "How you figure there's no victim?"

Morgan's throat tightened. He didn't like to dwell on this part of the plan. "Well, Jumper, for thir— sorry, twenty thou, I'm expecting you not to make her an actual victim. We discussed this. Take her somewhere clean, nice. Keep her safe." Jumper smoked and stared at him. "It's not a real kidnapping," Morgan went on. "You just, you know, detain her for a couple days, and then you get paid, and this is all over. She's home in time for Thanksgiving. She's a little traumatized but, you know, since nothing actually traumatic will have happened to her..." Morgan watched Jumper, waiting for him to affirm this understanding. "Right?" he prompted.

"Safe, clean, nothing traumatic," Jumper intoned, stone-faced. "And you're telling me the bank transactions, all of that, only takes two business days?"

Buoyed by the coke and the sense that Jumper was buying this, Morgan plowed ahead. "Two days. I've got the paperwork in place. The bank's all ready to go. They'd love to get it wrapped up before the holiday. You'll get thirty thousand dollars Tuesday night, ten of which you're already owed," Morgan emphasized. "I get the deed to some land. The kidnapee comes home. Big joyous reunion, everyone is safe and sound. The end. Happy Thanksgiving. Simple. Lucrative." Morgan sat back in his chair and blew a cloud of smoke. He waited. This was it. Classic sales technique. Whoever spoke first lost. Morgan couldn't afford to lose. He couldn't afford anything.

Jumper stared at him, adjusting the pack of cigarettes on the desk. Finally, to Morgan's relief, he said, "And we take her tonight? Carrie. Your wife. Tonight?"

With the confidence of a broke man surrounded by pickpockets, Morgan had said, "That's right. Tonight."

Some bits of the plan had gone astray since then, and that was mostly on Morgan. He should not have gone over to Nina's after leaving Jumper's. All he needed to do was hide out on his boat and wait. Instead, he ended up sitting in his car behind Big Lock's watching JP, who stumbled outside after Morgan parked around back, smoking cigarettes by the dumpsters like a real winner.

Morgan had opened Nina's laptop and keyed in the password while JP chainsmoked. Nina typed in her password so slowly, thanks to her long manicured nails, that Morgan had been able to learn it the second time he watched her do it. He tethered it to his phone's internet service. He wanted to listen to JP's livestream again, to the part about Carrie's affair, but apparently the "live" in livestream was literal. He couldn't find a recording. Nina had her phone and laptop synced. Morgan saw from a pulsing telephone icon that she was currently on her cell with someone. He clicked the icon to see who it was. Her father. Labelled, sort of cutely for such an unsentimental and caustic person as Nina, as "Daddy" in her contacts. He called a lot, in Morgan's opinion. He clicked over into the call log and confirmed. Dozens of calls to "Daddy." She must hate her mom, Morgan thought. Like zero phone calls for her. In the call log list on the laptop, the full phone number appeared under the contact name. Morgan noticed it was a local area code. Didn't she say her parents lived in Atlanta? Not only was it a local area code, it seemed familiar. While he pondered this, the call log window collapsed gently and was replaced by the main phone screen saying, "Call ended." He closed the laptop and tossed it in the passenger seat. What the hell was he doing here?

If Carrie was running around on him with Jug though—if Jug was really back in town—he figured they would be at Big Lock's together at some point. *Then what?* Morgan had asked himself, sitting in the Range Rover with Nina's laptop in the passenger seat. *What exactly would you do then?*

For starters, he answered himself back, *I'd tell her I made up the client dinner specifically so I could catch her in the act. Make her think I was on to her all this time and was only skipping this stupid night to catch her breaking my heart.* That would teach her to yell at him about going to a client dinner.

That doesn't make sense, Morgan told himself. *None of that makes sense. Carrie was angry you weren't coming tonight. She's not meeting someone here. She thought she was coming here with you until today.*

Morgan leaned back in his seat and closed his eyes. *What am I doing here?* he thought. *There's a very delicate plan in place and I'm jeopardizing it with unrealistic jealousy, stirred up by a pothead and a drunk rambling to each other on a shitty livestream. Just start your car, go to your hideaway, and lay low until tomorrow.*

He had almost done that. He had almost gotten himself back on track but when he opened his eyes and reached for the ignition, there was Jug, coming around the bar and suddenly standing between Morgan in his Range Rover and JP by his dumpster. It *was* real.

Morgan had picked up the pre-paid gas station phone he purchased the day before and called the single number programmed into its memory. Jumper picked up on the second ring and said, "Change your mind?"

"I did," Morgan said. "But not about what you think. Remember when I said to take her somewhere nice? Take good care of her? Yeah, you don't have to do that anymore."

And then, of course, he'd gotten himself stabbed and hit by a van.

Now, as he sat beside his father-in-law in an office at Grand Strand Bank, the flunky who was personally assigned to the Cassidy land title chore came in, smoothing the front of his suit and smiling. "Gentlemen, I appreciate you waiting so patiently." The man shook both their hands saying, "Don't get up. I'm Roger Blankley. I'll be facilitating our transaction today." He took his seat behind the desk. "I believe we're doing a title transfer this morning, is that correct?"

"That's right," Morgan croaked. He cleared his throat and steadied himself. "Mr. Cassidy here has all the proper documentation." Morgan took a deep breath he hoped wasn't super obvious and hauled himself to his feet. The Percocet was working but not hard enough. His side throbbed and he swooned a little.

"If you'll just excuse me—" Morgan began.

"Where do you think you're going?" Butch growled.

Morgan decided to take this opportunity to get in a few licks and make up for the open disdain Butch always showed him. "This is a large transaction we're doing here, Butch," he said slowly and with the deliberate patience one would normally reserve for speaking to petulant children. "I know you don't understand, but I have to go speak with some people to get this done. So you just sit here with Roger and he'll help you through the couple of things you'll have to sign, okay? You'll have to write your name on some papers, okay? You understand?"

Butch stared at him with his mouth open, shocked by the visible contempt Morgan was certain he never expected his son-in-law to have the balls to show him. Roger pretended to read something on his computer screen.

"I'll be upstairs with Mr. Simpatico," Morgan said breezily to Roger. He turned back to Butch. "Close your mouth. You're at a bank, not a monster truck rally."

He walked out of the office thinking, happily, that he would never have to see Herbert "Butch" Cassidy again in his entire life. Maybe he was lucky after all.

•••

"Can't you turn the siren and lights on?" Sailor asked Tusk. She reached for the starship's worth of buttons across the cruiser's dash and console. "Which one of these is it?"

"I'm not rocking up to the front of Grand Strand Bank with the full show going like the place is being robbed," Tusk said. He swatted her hand away. "Don't start touching things. Did JP tell you anything else?"

Sailor's mind was flying. She tried to organize the pieces. Morgan and Jug get in a fight, Tusk chasing down a white van, Nina Capaldi's car being in Morgan's name, her near-daily trips to Grand Strand Bank, Morgan and her father at the bank now, the worthless old family lot, Carrie was missing.

Carrie was missing.

She tried to pull everything into a straight line. "He said," she began. "He said...that Carrie..."

"Alright," Tusk said, gently. He put a hand on her shoulder. "Alright."

He reached down and flipped on the lights and siren.

Chapter 9

Almost exactly twenty-four hours earlier, Hector Simpatico asked his secretary to call Chester Hobbes and connect it to his office once Chester was on the line. He never called anyone directly.

"Mr. Hobbes is on line two," Sunny had called from outside his door. The intercom was broken, which annoyed Hector on the grounds of accountability. The IT team couldn't figure out what was wrong with it, but it wasn't slowing him down in any practical way. He didn't mind shouting.

"Chester," Hector bellowed into the phone. "I appreciate you taking the call."

Chester's morning was open after his early meeting with Carrie Cassidy, but he wanted to be solicitous so he said, "Of course, it's not a problem. I appreciate you thinking of me at all. Though, again, Hector, just out of a sense of due diligence I want to point out that contract law isn't my specialty."

Hector Simpatico was a private investor who funded so much local development with Grand Strand Bank that he had his own office in their eight-story building on Grissom Parkway. His relationship with Grand Strand Bank was strengthened, of course, by family relationships. His brother Michael was the bank's Chief Financial Officer. Hector did not appear imposing at first glance. His suits and neatly parted hair drew attention away from his physical stature. The first handshake usually tipped people off, Hector always squeezing harder than was polite and seeming to be making an effort at holding back. As a teenager, he had loaded sacks of gravel at their father's quarry in the summers and after school and thickened into a slab. Michael worked inside doing bottom-rung tasks for the accounting department.

A week earlier, to Chester's great surprise, Hector had called, via his secretary, and asked Chester to work some contract negotiations for a land deal out west of the Intracoastal Waterway. It was mostly redlining and document review. It paid, but Chester already got paid well. The call was exciting because it was Chester's chance to work with some of Myrtle Beach's business elites. It was an important opportunity. At the very least, it would net him some bigger divorce cases.

"Grand Strand Bank is a community bank, Chester," Hector said. "They want to create business ties within the community. They bring in local independents like this all the time. It's a good PR play for them and a good networking opportunity for you. Everybody plays, everybody wins."

Hector gave Chester some information about the deal, some of his own perspective on the wants and needs of the two parties involved, a short monologue on where he, Hector, stood in the whole mix, and ended with a "thousand-foot view on the big picture, what we want to accomplish here." Then he sent the call back to his secretary to get Chester's retainer and send him the paperwork.

Hector replaced the receiver of the phone and watched the lights to ensure his secretary had the line and there was no more connection to his own device. Hector believed security and caution were matters of habit rather than paranoia, so he followed his routines. Having confirmed the connection on the phone was closed, he crossed out *Chester Hobbes, attorney, L.E.* on his yellow legal pad. The yellow legal pad was ever-present. He kept paper notes and burned them at the end of the day. *L.E.* was his shorthand for *Loose End.* That's what Chester Hobbes was, a loose end now neatly snipped.

Morgan Childress had told him how Chester Hobbes worked out Sailor Cassidy's marijuana possession charge a year earlier. Not only did Chester get Sailor off with light community service, he did it pro bono. Morgan said they wouldn't have any trouble with the father, Herbert Cassidy—or Butch as everyone called him—but Morgan was about as reliable as an infomercial product. It might work, though it was just as likely not to, so it better not be your only plan. Better to tie Chester Hobbes up with work that would create a conflict of interest if the Cassidys decided to turn litigious, taking their free legal counsel out of the equation.

The thing that might make them litigious concerned the Cassidy's farmland from two generations back. Herbert Cassidy's grandfather, who was also named Herbert Cassidy, owned approximately two hundred acres of land west of the Intracoastal Waterway. It passed down to his son, another Herbert Cassidy, and then down to the current Cassidy patriarch, Morgan's father-in-law. The land sat unused, the Cassidy's either unwilling or unable to farm it or sell it. Morgan mentioned this land casually back at the beginning of his and Hector's relationship. Hector had pulled the public records mostly just to gauge how full of shit Morgan was. Sure enough, there was a deed, yellowed and thin in the simple typewriter formatting of pre-computer bureaucracy, showing that the original Herbert Cassidy owned two hundred acres of land. Further documentation showed it was willed down to his son and then his grandson.

Having finished with Chester, Hector picked up his personal phone this time and dialed his brother's number. Michael was always in the car at that time of day, showered and dressed after swimming for an hour in the ocean. If it was rough or too cold, he might use the pool at the ocean-front development where he lived, but it had to be mighty cold or dangerously rough. "If you start the day fighting the sea nothing else is hard," he liked to say. He picked up right away. "All good?" Michael asked when he answered.

"Fine. No issues," Hector said.

"You think the kid will actually bring this in?" Michael asked.

"Better than fifty percent chance he gets it over the line," Hector said. "He's a bullshitter, but not untalented. He still sold three houses and got them mostly built. He would have made a go of that place if we had let him. And it's his father-in-law so maybe it's a no-brainer, just coming to him on a platter. A gift for his daughter and son-in-law to grow their lives and family or some other sentimental lever pushing him to turn it over. Or he just wants to push the property tax over to his rich developer son-in-law who can sit on the land until the day it's useful." That day was here, whether Herbert "Butch" Cassidy III knew it or not. There was a new highway being planned that would run within a mile of Butch's land, cross over the Intracoastal with a new bridge, and connect to Grissom Parkway. All the Cassidy acreage was about to go from being forty-five minutes from the beach to ten minutes from the beach. The value was going to soar. Whoever owned that land was going to be able to print money building houses.

"Is the payout actually necessary?" Michael always wanted to know this. His brother's chief means of fiscal conservatism was simply not paying anyone anything. There was a logic to that way of thinking that was almost elegant in its brutal simplicity, but brutal simplicity led to simple brutality when people got mad they had been stiffed, and that part of things always fell to Hector. He preferred to skip the violence if possible. It was taxing. Wasn't the point of money to make things easier? "You already broke some piece of him, didn't you? His thumb? Speaking of levers, is that not a big enough one to get this done without the one-fifty?" Michael asked.

His brother had him there. Morgan had gotten upset—totally understandable, how could he not?—in this very same office as Hector explained that the bank would be foreclosing on Morgan's development, taking over the property, and most likely selling his house. It happened. Usually they just cried, these guys Hector and Michael financed then busted out, but sometimes they got mad. Morgan apparently had a little wire in the blood—he stood up, he shouted. He jabbed Hector in the chest with the index finger on his good hand. The fingers of Morgan's left hand were splinted, something happened on one of his sites he'd said. Hector had calmly picked up his pen, a tortoiseshell red Pelikan Souverän fountain pen, a gift from Michael several years back. The younger man had continued to jab Hector in the chest as he spoke. Morgan was feeling the rush of aggression sweep through him, Hector knew. The anger felt righteous no doubt, appropriate and justified, something he deserved to feel and act out.

"Calm down," Hector told him. He gripped the pen lengthwise in his fist.

"Don't tell me to fucking calm down" Morgan had said. Jabbing Hector's chest on *calm* and *down*. "You're stealing my development out from under me and think I'm just going to take it? "Fuck," *jab*, "that," *jab*. "We're going to court. I'll drag this through the legal system." Hector watched Morgan's injured hand, held out to his side, forgotten, bobbing with the slow over-weighted undulation of a bird landing heavily on a thin branch. The thumb sticking straight up next to the splinted fingers, last man standing. "Let me tell you something," Morgan shouted. But before he could let Hector know whatever was on his mind, Hector reached over and grabbed his thumb, slipping the Pelikan behind it and making a fist. He squeezed and Morgan's thumb snapped against the pen. Hector didn't let go. Morgan's mouth opened and stayed that way, silently though, while his eyes went out of focus. It took a second for the pain to catch up to his brain and then he groaned.

"Sit down," Hector said, not letting go of his thumb. When Morgan continued standing there, Hector squeezed a little. Morgan moaned and grabbed at him. "Keep your hands off me," Hector said, squeezing harder. Morgan dropped his right hand and Hector backed him over to a chair, not letting go. "You owe us quite a lot of money," Hector said. "Me and this bank. So, I'm explaining to you what the next steps are going to be."

Hector and Michael had done this before: provide a loan to an eager and naive entity for development then, through a whisper campaign, make it impossible for him to actually work the development. The naive entity can't get construction crews to show up, licenses and applications for city services take forever, potential buyers are poached through better deals elsewhere. Finally, Hector and Michael would repossess the land, collect insurance on the defaulted loan and write down the loss while heroically turning the development around. It was one of a dozen financial strategies they employed. You needed a lot of irons in the fire—that was how you created wealth. Most people misunderstood that. It didn't happen through a windfall, it happened incrementally.

Hector hadn't explained any of this to Morgan. Instead he said, "Try to remain dignified, okay? You've lost your money, you've lost my money. Hold onto one thing. Maybe you climb out of this mess and try again inland, away from the coast. Somewhere with lower stakes." That was when Hector had remembered the Cassidy land and a rumor he'd recently heard. A rumor that his inquiries were proving to be more than a rumor. A new highway going up for a vote in the city council in the next several weeks. He released

Morgan's hand. The young man slumped in momentary relief. It wouldn't last. Hector had broken enough thumbs to know there was a throbbing pain waiting just down the road when the adrenaline wore off. "Unless you can negotiate like a gentleman," Hector said. "Then, of course, perhaps there's still more to discuss."

Morgan was panting, but he managed to breathe out the single word, "Negotiate?"

"Your family. Specifically your father-in-law. I believe you told me once there's a land interest there. That's worth talking about. There might be something we can do there." Hector dialed a number on his cell phone and said, "My office, please. With your med bag." He put the phone down on his desk. "First let's get you cleaned up."

Edison, long and rangy, muscled like a heavy ship's rope come to life, entered the office in his creased khakis and golf shirt, carrying a rectangular nylon bag. He had looked at Morgan in the chair, taking in his hand, then over at Hector. "You been taking first aid courses, Hector? That's professional looking."

"Morgan here came in with the splint and treatment on his fingers," Hector told him. "But while he was here, he managed to hurt his thumb as well in an accident with his car door."

Edison knelt in front of Morgan and gestured for his hand. Morgan hesitated and Edison nodded reassuringly. Morgan held out his clipped wing. Edison examined his thumb gently and declared, "Fractured. We'll splint it. Got a nice scaffolding right next door to build on." He took tape, gauze, and a splint out of his bag.

"While Edison does that, Morgan, let's negotiate," Hector said. The one hundred and fifty thousand dollars was actually a first and final offer, non-negotiable, but Hector had no doubts at that point that Morgan would understand.

In response to his brother Michael trying to skip the payout one day before Morgan was supposed to show up with his father-in-law and hand over the ticket to a multi-million dollar land deal, Hector had explained "The money keeps the peace. And it legitimizes the deal if anyone looks into it. Just have it sent over today, alright?"

"It just hardly seems like it's worth getting out of bed for, a hundred fifty, much less covering a paper trail," Michael had said.

"You've lost touch. That's life changing money for the average schmo. People in this town don't make that in three years. Have it sent to my office, please."

"Yeah, fine," Michael had said. "When is the title transfer supposed to happen?"

"Tomorrow, he says," Hector told his brother. "They're coming in the morning."

And to Hector's surprise, they were actually here, on time. Roger Blankley had called up when they arrived. The elevator dinged out by Sunny's desk and Morgan slouched into Hector's office.

•••

Tusk turned off the siren and lights before they pulled into the bank parking lot. Sailor sat in the cruiser like Tusk had asked while he went inside to look for Morgan and her father, but it was tough. She wanted to storm into the bank and pull Morgan out physically. To fish-hook her fingers into whatever stab-hole Jug created and drag him outside, demanding to know where her sister was. Tusk, of course, hated that idea. It reminded Sailor of the night Carrie told her about Morgan's cheating. Sailor wanted them to act out. Carrie hated the idea. No wonder she and Tusk ended up together. They were both rationalists, acting like the world gave a damn if you remained calm. She gently ran her fingers along the bruise across her swollen face. Though, maybe she could use a dash of that calmness. A few seconds of consideration and she probably would have seen that second guy lurking in the shadows last night. The one who dropped her and stole her gun.

"I'm really sorry about your sister," Lula said from the backseat. "I know you must be scared for her."

Sailor turned in her seat and faced Lula through the cage separating the front and back of the cruiser. "I'm angry for her. Not scared. I'm mad."

"Right," Lula said. "Sorry."

"Don't be sorry. It's just, you can't be scared. Some people get to be scared. We don't, you know? People like you and me, there's people out there who want us to be scared all the time and we can't give them that. When something's scary, I just turn that into anger. Emotional alchemy."

"Is that healthy? It doesn't sound healthy."

Sailor shrugged. "Maybe not, who knows? Nothing's really healthy when you look at it too close, right? Just being alive is slowly killing all of us." She hooked her fingers through the squares of the prisoner partition. "Thanks for coming along today. I know it's been strange."

"Would a kiss make you feel better?"

"A kiss?"

Lula shrugged. "I got that or a piece of gum from my purse."

Sailor laughed. "I don't chew gum."

Lula leaned forward. "I guess it's a kiss then." She pushed her lips against Sailor's through the bars.

•••

Jumper stood on the simple wooden dock that constituted a slip in the undeveloped lot, smoking and staring at the stern of Morgan's boat where the name "Boatacious" shimmered in sparkling blue letters. Like "bodacious" he figured. He tried to think of what he would name his own boat if he ever bought one, but he couldn't think much past "Boat Milk" which rhymed with oat milk and was a terrible name. He couldn't think past this dumb name because of another name: Hector. The mistress had dropped the name like it was an exclusive credit card. *Here, this should take care of it.*

Jumper lit a new cigarette off the one he was smoking and flicked the old one into the water where it blemished the surface with a short-lived but sinister little hiss. *Far and a Wave* he thought to himself. That was also bad.

He turned and watched Puto up by one of the vans, arranging his folding table with his bottles and cups and saucers. Puto was white but had gotten the ironic honorific "Puto" from some of the Hispanic kitchen staff after he surprised everyone by beating the shit out of Petey "Bullethead" Barasco one night at the bar. Bullethead was one of the world's unfunny men who tried to overcome his affliction with the tried and true method of bullying. Skinny and slow-witted Puto—his real name was James—was an easy target. Bullethead had been torturing James one night, calling out everything from his crooked teeth to his ill-fitting shirt, turning to look up and down the bar for laughs, when he noticed the Mickey Mouse watch James wore.

"What kind of gay-ass watch is that for a man to wear?" Bullethead said, grabbing James's wrist as he placed another seven and seven in front of him. James tried to pull his arm away as Bullethead said, "You got the pajamas to match?" He looked up and down the bar for any laughs he might have scared up. "Fuckin' kids watch. Jumper's got child-labor working behind the bar," he said. That earned a few chuckles, spurring him on. Bullethead tried to work a finger under the watch band. "Give me this fuckin' thing. Let me make a man out of you, get this fuckin' thing off your—" and that's when James smashed a pint glass into his face with his free hand. He came over the bar then, knocking Bullethead backwards off his stool and landing on top of him, swinging wildly and screaming, "Bitch. Get your fucking hands off me you bitch!" over and over. Óscar, the line cook, had to pull James off the bloodied Bullethead. He was still screaming "Bitch" on repeat as Óscar dragged him to the back office to calm down. James had become Puto after that.

"You know it means bitch, right?" Jumper asked him after he heard him replying to the name.

"Yeah, 'cause I whipped that bitch tried to steal my watch," James said.

Fair enough, Jumper figured. James had never been given a nickname for a victory before, only for his defects. If he was happy with it, great, now he was Puto.

Puto was Jumper's most constant companion. Jumper liked Puto's quiet satisfaction over simple tasks. The world moved on simple tasks, if you stacked up enough of them.

After Morgan left his office the previous day, Jumper had taken a stool out at the bar where Puto was cleaning and restocking. Puto poured him a coffee and said, "You want anything in it, boss?"

"What's Mickey say?" Jumper asked, even though the time was displayed at the top of his phone.

"Says it's after twelve."

"Little Sambuca, on the side. And a clean ashtray." Puto poured a shot of Sambuca and swapped out Jumper's ashtray. Jumper tipped half the shot into his mug and looked up from his phone.

"You told Óscar and Ángel to keep an eye on our friend, the real estate mogul?" Jumper had asked.

"He's at a condo on the north end. Grand Dunes. Óscar said a lady let him in. Not his wife."

"A lady?"

"'Peligrosa' Óscar says."

"That's interesting."

"Can I ask something, boss?"

"Go on."

"How come he don't have ten grand? Car like that, house like that. Seems like he should have money, don't it?"

"That's an astute observation," Jumper said. Puto stared at him. "You noticed it doesn't add up," Jumper clarified. Puto smiled, pleased. "It's 'cause he's full of shit," Jumper explained. "He's all debt, no cash. Car's a lease probably. His development isn't developing. He can't move the lots."

"How come?"

"Probably because he's a shitty salesman. The kind who thinks whoever speaks first after an offer is made loses. But it's a dead zone when you drive through. No activity, so no money coming in. And his daddy-in-law's land isn't going to get him any. Not in two business days anyway, even if the old man does sign it over. That's not how things work. He's assuming we're idiots."

The worst thing about Morgan, in Jumper's view, was his seemingly inextinguishable belief that people saw him the way he imagined himself. Jumper had met plenty of guys who were little more than a slick line of bullshit in a golf shirt, but they usually had a sense of their own grift and its limits. Morgan genuinely believed that people accepted the things he told them.

"Why're we taking his wife then?" Puto wanted to know.

"He's putting something together. I don't know what it is, but I know he needs at least two days to get it done and I know he thinks it'll produce serious money."

"That's why he's giving us twenty k more'n he owes us?"

"If he actually gives it to us."

"You think he won't? Even with us havin' his wife and all?"

"According to Óscar's report just now, it sounds like his wife might not be all that important to him."

"We saw his wife that time we cased his house," Puto said, indignant. "She was in nurse clothes or something medical. Nice looking. If I had a wife like that, with a good job and all, I wouldn't let her get kidnapped. Not for no ten grand I owed."

"That's because you're not a piece of shit, Puto," Jumper said. "Morgan, on the other hand, is. But, unfortunately, he's convinced himself that he's just a clever guy who somehow ended up in a tight spot, rather than a piece of shit. He can't face a hard truth about himself. That colors his thinking."

Morgan wasn't the first. Jumper had seen many people waist deep in a degenerate life surprised to find out sharks swim easily in water of that depth. They either didn't believe it was real—that fingers got broken, that people got shot—or they believed the other half of their lives from the waist up protected them. It didn't. That was just the part that got wet next when they were bitten, chewed, and pulled under.

Jumper didn't actually expect Morgan to make good on the thirty grand. Someone had their foot on Morgan's neck besides him. Whoever had broken that thumb. Morgan said it was an accident at one of his construction sites, but a man with four broken fingers wasn't on a job site using his damaged hand. The thumb was the work of another heavy hitter Morgan was into for something. Something, or more specifically some amount, large enough for Morgan to orchestrate his wife's kidnapping and risk giving Jumper that bullshit story about a bank loan in exchange for the deed to his father-in-law's land. Absolute nonsense.

Though, the wife's kidnapping must factor in somehow. Maybe her old man really did have some land. It didn't matter. What mattered was that there was money somewhere in Morgan's stupid scheme, and Jumper intended to stay on top of him until he found it. He was sure he would need to kill Morgan at the end of all this. He didn't especially like going that route, it exposed him to too much heat, but sometimes people simply failed to appreciate an escalating scenario. Jumper was always clear in his intentions. If a man casually breaks your fingers over a debt, the end result of not paying that debt should be obvious, shouldn't it? But people didn't always heed the signs. Like Bullethead.

Jumper knew Bullethead would not be understanding about getting his ass beat by Puto in a bar filled with his acquaintances. He was not the kind of person to analyze how his own actions contributed to an outcome. So Jumper had explained to him that retaliation would not be tolerated. He said it that clearly.

"You got your ass kicked fair and square. Mouthed off to someone and caught the blowback. That's it. That's the end. Retaliation will not be tolerated," he said.

"Who the fuck do you think you are? I don't give a fuck what you say on it," Bullethead shouted. He had been surly even before Jumper asked him to come back to the office, out in the bar telling anyone who would listen how he was going to kill Puto when he caught up with him. Puto was off that night. He was surly still when he saw Óscar sitting on the couch as they came through the office door. And then, sitting across the desk from Jumper, downright hostile. "I catch that little queerbait I'm'a reach up his ass and turn him inside out like a sock's what I'm'a do," he continued. "You ain't got no say in it. And I ain't scared of your wetback fucking kitchen rat henchman sitting back there neither." Bullethead had turned and gestured at Óscar on the couch. "The four-foot stump of—"

Óscar was quiet, fast. He was behind Bullethead in the same instant the man turned back to Jumper, one hand yanking his head back by his hair and the other holding a box cutter to his throat. Bullethead froze, tensed, but kept running his mouth. "You won't do it. There's people out there at the bar who saw me. Know I'm here. Know you had me come back here."

Jumper opened his desk drawer. He took out his cigarettes, an ashtray, a hammer, and two deck nails. "Good people, you think?" Jumper asked, lighting a cigarette. "The ones at the bar? The kind of people who go to the police when the loudmouth piece of shit they all quietly hate goes missing? Is that the impression in your mind of those folks out there at the bar?" Bullethead didn't say anything. "Yeah, it's not my impression of them either," Jumper said. "Give me your hand."

"The fuck for?" Bullethead said.

"Mis alitas de pollo," Óscar said.

"If he takes much longer you can slit his throat," Jumper said. To Bullethead, "Óscar has an order of chicken wings that were placed right when you came in. He'd like to get back to the kitchen. See, we work here. We have things that need to be done. So, if you don't put your fucking hand up here fast enough to keep Óscar from getting his order out late, he's going to just cut your throat and be done with it. Because he takes pride in his work. Because he has respect for his coworkers. His coworkers like, for instance, James. So, do you want to put your goddamn hand up here? Or do you want Óscar to cut your throat to protect his friend and coworker and the punctuality of his chicken wing order?" Bullethead put his hand on the desk, palm down. Jumper took one of the deck nails and held it to the back of Bullethead's hand. He hefted the hammer.

"Wait," Bullethead said. "Hey. C'mon now. You ain't seriously going to—"

Jumper banged the nail through his hand into the desk with the hammer. Bullethead screamed.

"Other hand," Jumper said.

"No. I get it. I won't touch him."

"Óscar," Jumper said, making a dragging gesture across his throat with a finger.

"No. Shit. Okay," Bullethead sobbed, placing his other hand on the desk.

Jumper stood and placed the second deck nail on the back of Bullethead's hand. He brought the hammer down three times hard, driving the nail between the carpal bones of the ring and middle fingers and into the desk's wooden surface. Óscar withdrew the box cutter and released Bullethead's hair. Petey "Bullethead" Bascaro sat gasping and moaning, blood pooling under his palms.

"Do you notice what's not happening right now, Petey?" Jumper said. "None of those people at the bar are rushing back here to see if you're okay. Do you know what that means? It means you were wise not to test whether we'd cut your throat or not. You made a good choice! Now, let's see if you can make another good choice. Remember when I said retaliation will not be tolerated? Do you remember, Petey? Nod if you remember." Bullethead nodded.

"Okay! Because before you didn't seem to be on board with the whole no retaliation plan, and see? I had to take your hands out of the equation. Do you understand now that I'm serious about that? I know verbalizing might be tough so go ahead and nod if you understand." Bullethead nodded again. He was staring at his hands, breathing heavily through his mouth. Jumper reached over and wiggled the top of each nail, loosening them enough to pull free from the desk. Bullethead screamed again.

"Sounds like we get each other now," Jumper said. "Go on and stand up. Stand the fuck up." Bullethead got to his feet holding his gruesome hands in front of him like a T. rex, a nail still staked through each one. Jumper came around the desk and stood before him holding the hammer. "You work construction, right? Day labor, anyway. Why don't you go ahead and keep this." Jumper slipped the handle of the hammer through Bullethead's belt. "A consolation prize for your time with us here today and a reminder. Okay? Okay." He opened the door. "Now get the fuck out of my bar." Bullethead went through the door and turned right, headed for the back door he saw at the end of the hall. "No, no," Jumper said. "Other way. Out through the bar. I've gone to all this trouble, you're going to serve as an example for me. Efficiency, Petey, that's our credo around here. We use every part of the buffalo, you know what I mean?"

Jumper and Óscar watched Bullethead shuffle down the hall and use his shoulder to push through the door to the bar. They heard someone say, "Jesus Christ!" through the open door. There were an assortment of other muffled exclamations they couldn't make out as the door swung closed again.

"Why you give the hammer?" Óscar said.

"Just thought it was a nice finale. Why?"

"Waste a good hammer." Óscar shrugged. "He be back. Maybe get the hammer back then."

"I nailed his hands to the fucking desk, man. He's not coming back. No one comes back after some shit like that."

"Jesus."

"I couldn't name a single thing in common between Bullethead and Jesus if you gave me a week," Jumper said. Óscar blinked at him. "Besides the nails in his hands, you got me on that one."

"Jesus go to the priests' place of business, make a big fight. They tell him stop. He say no. They nail him. He come back." Óscar pointed at the door Bullethead had just lurched through. "That Petey, he come back. You see."

"I'm not a professional theologian, Óscar, but I'm confident that's not what that bible story is meant to convey."

"We make a bet. He comes back, you buy real nice hammer for the bar. I pick it out."

"What if I'm right?"

Óscar hissed at him, something he did when he heard something he thought was stupid. "Then I buy hammer for the bar. What you think? Shit. Mis alitas." He hurried down the hall to the kitchen.

"Alright then," Jumper had said.

Sitting in the bar after Morgan left while Puto stocked glasses and changed out his ashtray, Jumper had figured he would probably have to kill Morgan in the next three or four days. If things got hot enough for him, Morgan's ego would eventually crumble and he would go to the police. No nails for him, not that Jumper had a hammer anymore anyway.

Jumper tossed his phone down on the bar, tossed the rest of the Sambuca into the coffee Puto had just topped up, and lit a new cigarette. "We heard from Bevel lately?"

"Bevel always turns up," Puto said. "Kinda unfortunate, actually. He ain't real pleasant. You want me in the van taking the wife tonight?"

"Maybe," Jumper said. "Not sure how we should play this yet."

"Ain't he said she'll be at Big Lock's at eight? We can get her on the way in or the way out."

"He did tell me that," Jumper confirmed. "Thing is, if a man owes you ten grand he doesn't have, and promises you thirty grand if you show up at a certain time and place and kidnap his wife, it's worth assessing whether or not that's a set up to get out of paying you anything at all."

"You don't want to take her no more?"

"I didn't say that. But we'd be dumber than shit-scented candles if we just showed up where he said to and tried to yank his wife into a van. I need to think. Need more info from Óscar. Need to—" The door to the bar pushed open right then, letting in a blast of autumn sun like a searchlight, highlighting the white trail of smoke threading skyward from the end of Jumper's cigarette. Jumper turned. "Bevel," he said.

"Got an address for you J-man," Bevel said, crossing the room to the bar. "All good. Found you another house. Four one six Pinecrest Dr." Bevel pulled back the left sleeve of his grubby hooded sweatshirt and showed Jumper his inner arm where *416 pinecrest dr* was poorly printed in black marker. "Fifty now and fifty after you scope it right?"

Jumper noticed Bevel wasn't wearing shoes but decided not to comment. What Jumper needed was someone to absorb the risk of yanking Carrie Cassidy into a van at Big Lock's Bar and Grill. "That's awfully good work, Bevel," Jumper said to the shoeless amphetamine junkie twitching in front of him. "And good work like that, it begets more good work. Better paying work too."

"Begets?" Bevel said. "Is that from the Constitution? 'Cause I ain't read up on that as good as I maybe thought."

"It means I got another job for you, Bevel," Jumper told him. "You're being promoted."

So they got the wife and the mistress. In for a penny, in for a pound as far as kidnappings went.

Down in the cabin of the boat now, Morgan's mistress didn't realize she was sharing captivity with Morgan's wife. She seemed to think they were both connected to this Hector and the wife wasn't correcting her, which meant she was smart. He twirled the baby monitor receiver around his finger.

The women were quiet now, but he had heard the mistress say the wife's family didn't have any money. Jumper never believed Morgan was going to get any money from the family, through their land or otherwise. Maybe he was just trying to get Jumper to take his wife off his hands, or maybe he was making some kind of play at this guy Hector who was connected to his mistress. If Morgan thought he could set Jumper up, he was going to be in for a surprise when two dead bodies showed up on his boat. Óscar and Ángel had followed Morgan out here one day. Jumper figured it was the most advantageous place to be if Morgan was planning something clever. Either Morgan himself would show up to skip town on his boat, in which case Jumper would deal with him in person. Or Morgan would go to the cops about his kidnapped wife thinking they would trace that back to Jumper, in which case Jumper would leave her corpse and the mistress's on Morgan's boat. Any jury in the country would convict a man whose wife and mistress turned up dead on his boat. Or, and this seemed the most unlikely scenario, Morgan would actually call Jumper and tell him he had thirty thousand dollars for him. Jumper wasn't entirely sure how he would play that one, but he was confident it wouldn't come up.

Right now, though, he had the phone number for a man named Hector and someone who was possibly valuable to him. Jumper felt the vibration of Óscar's approaching footsteps on the dock.

"We go now," Óscar said. "Deliveries come soon."

Jumper checked the time on his phone. Óscar and Ángel needed to get back to the bar. The morning's daily deliveries would be arriving. It was important they all keep the regular shifts going and have people see them at work.

"You be okay with Puto and that fucking pendejo?" Óscar asked. Like everyone else, he hated Bevel.

Jumper nodded. "What would you name a boat?" he asked. "If you had one?"

Óscar studied the name on the back of Morgan's cruiser and shook his head. "Mi barco se llamaría 'OcéanOlé,'" he said.

"OcéanOlé?"

"Sí."

"That's pretty good."

"Tú?"

"Boat Milk?"

Óscar hissed. "Mierda. Do better." He walked back down the dock.

Jumper typed the number for "Daddy" he'd gotten from Nina's phone into his burner and started sending pictures.

Chapter 10

"Morgan! Come in and grab a drink," Hector Simpatico bellowed, handing Morgan a champagne flute and pouring a measly couple inches of Dom Pérignon. Morgan knocked it back and held the flute out for another hit. *The upper classes and the stingy offerings they camouflage behind the idea of respectability, be damned,* Morgan thought. *If we're drinking in the morning, then top me up.* He felt like he was in the last round of a boxing match, moving forward with the clock on brute indifference fueled by the fire of exhaustion.

Hector raised an eyebrow at Morgan's proffered glass, but he poured the refill. "Tougher than you thought getting the old goat to part with his land?" Hector asked. "You look like hell, kid."

"He's downstairs signing over the title now," Morgan said.

"Roger called up and let me know. Have a seat." Hector waved Morgan to the same chair where Edison had splinted his broken thumb a couple weeks back. "That bag there is for you. Congratulations. You did it."

Morgan set down his glass and pulled the small nylon duffle bag onto his lap with his good hand. His good hand was on his bad side though, and the weight of the cash shot a ribbon of pain through his wound. He unzipped the bag and examined the banded stacks of bills. One hundred and fifty thousand dollars. It was a lot, Morgan knew, but it wasn't much. One year's salary for the upper middle class. Four year's salary for the working class.

Absolute peanuts for Hector and this bank. The stitches in his side would have taken half of it if he wasn't on Carrie's insurance.

Right now, though, it was enough to get out of town. He gingerly slid his broken fingers through the loops of the gym bag and hung the bag from the crook of his elbow. His good side with the bad hand.

"You can count it," Hector was saying. "It's not insulting. It's good business honestly." His phone chimed from his desk and Hector crossed the office to look at it. As he picked it up, his desk phone started ringing as well.

Morgan finished his champagne and gingerly rose to his feet. He was sure Hector had all sorts of slightly malicious business advice to offer him, but he was done here. Done with this bank, the development, his wife, his mistress—the whole fucking town. He looked over at Hector, who was standing at his desk staring, unmoving, at his cell phone, while his desk phone rang and rang.

Morgan shuffled out of the office past Hector's executive assistant, who was getting up from her desk as he passed, apparently concerned over the unanswered phone. "Is everything alright in there?" she asked.

Morgan shrugged and kept shuffling. Behind him, in the office, he heard Hector finally answer the desk phone. "Not now!" Hector shouted. Then, "Roger, not now. I don't care." There was the sound of the receiver being slammed down. Morgan pushed the button for the elevator. The phone on the executive assistant's desk started ringing. He wondered if it was Roger. Not his problem.

Morgan heard Hector's cell phone ring and Hector answer it, shouting, "Who the fuck is this? Do you have any idea what I'll do to you?"

The executive assistant came hustling back out of the office, looking rather calm considering the vibes coming out of the room.

Not her first rodeo, Morgan figured. She was a pro. He watched her answer the phone. "Hello? Roger, it's not a good time." The elevator doors dinged open, and Morgan stepped inside.

Hector shouted into his cell phone. "What do you mean 'I seem to think the stakes here aren't real'? Do I sound like a man who thinks we're fucking around? Do I sound like someone who thinks the stakes aren't real?"

That caught Morgan's ear. Where had he heard that? Jumper. That was it. Jumper said almost that exact thing to him just the day before. Weird. But not his problem. He pushed the button for the lobby. The elevator doors closed.

Morgan rode to the first floor, stepped out of the elevator, and limped into the bank's lobby. His hip ached where the van hit him. He glanced over at the office where he had left Butch and Roger Blankley. To his surprise, he saw a police officer in there with them through the office's glass walls. Butch appeared to be yelling at him. Roger Blankley had his hand out in the universally useless gesture of people trying to de-escalate while staying uninvolved. He was holding a phone to his ear with his other hand.

Morgan knew Butch was a son-of-a-bitch, but he had expected him to behave more passively with his daughter's life on the line. *What a rotten family*, he thought, turning his back on the scene in the office and limping past the spectators in the lobby, all turned to watch the proceedings in the office, which were growing in volume. Morgan put his shoulder from the side with the bad hand and aching hip against the bank door and pushed with the leg attached to the functioning hip. He needed to lie down.

At the top of the bank's steps he paused to fish his sunglasses out of his sport coat pocket. They were Ray Ban Clubmasters. He studied them for a moment, wondering if he could get a hundred bucks for them. Between the sunglasses and Nina's laptop he could probably generate enough for a tank of gas for the boat. Every dollar counted. Morgan was thinking this through when he heard a car door slam and the sound of feet charging up the steps. He looked down and saw a woman in a garish floral patterned shirt running at the steps, heading straight toward him. It took him a moment to realize he knew her, under the deep black bruising that spread around her eyes and across her face like a superhero's mask. It was Sailor.

Morgan had just enough time to comprehend that she was not coming toward him, she was coming at him. For him.

What a rotten family, he thought again. Then Sailor shoved something into his crotch. His brain misfired, and he went down.

•••

Sailor gently pulled back from kissing Lula through the bars of the police car.

"Feel better?" Lula asked.

"Better," Sailor confirmed. It was true. Things were no better at all, but she felt a little calmer, her mental state tipped slightly more toward whatever condition drove Tusk and her sister.

"Hey look, someone's coming out," Lula said, pointing through the windshield at the bank entrance.

Sailor turned. It was Morgan, the focal point of all the anger she had been generating since talking to JP and learning about Carrie going missing. No. Even before that as the man who cheated on her sister. *Calm*, she thought. *You can be calm and rational like Carrie and Tusk.*

"That's him," Sailor said. "That's Morgan."

"That's Morgan?" Lula asked.

"Yeah."

"So what are we sitting here for? Let's go get him."

God damn right, Sailor thought, liking Lula more by the minute, and kicked open her door. She ran up the steps of the bank, pulling out the stun gun as she went. She didn't wait for Morgan to speak. He was at the top of the steps, and she was lower than him. She crammed the stun gun between his legs and sparked it.

Morgan went rigid. His sunglasses fell from his hand, and he shuddered with the current. Sailor pulled the stun gun away, and he pitched forward and fell down the concrete steps of the bank. He laid on the ground in front of the police cruiser, which was when Sailor saw Lula was still in the back of Tusk's car.

"I forgot I can't get out on my own," Lula called through the cage and the front passenger door Sailor had left open. "Go get Officer Knight."

Sailor nodded and holstered the stun gun. She smoothed the front of her shirt. She felt immensely better looking down at Morgan crumpled on the pavement. She turned to go into the bank and caught her reflection in the glass doors. *Yeesh,* her face looked rough. Her dad was inside. There was enough stressing him out without being immediately confronted with his daughter's assaulted face. Morgan's sunglasses were by her feet where he dropped them. She scooped them up and put them on.

•••

Tusk made Sailor stay in the car because he wanted to limit the potential for confrontation and a scene with Morgan, but now he wished he had sent her in alone to deal with her father. Tusk had never met Mr. Cassidy before, but he had heard the comments and remarks over the years from JP, Dex, Carrie, and even Sailor about what a bear he could be. Still, he thought having his daughter kidnapped would have filed down his edge a little. As soon as Tusk came into the office and asked to speak to him and Morgan, Butch started shouting.

"Mr. Cassidy, I need to speak with you outside for a moment," Tusk tried again.

"Hell no. You need me to come somewhere, you arrest me. Arrest me in front of all these people. But you can't. You don't got nothing to arrest me for. You're the one breaking the law coming in here without a warrant—"

"Mr. Cassidy please, your daughter—"

"My daughter is none of your goddamn concern!" Butch screamed. "I know my rights!"

Well that settled it, Tusk knew. Once they start screaming that they know their rights you've passed the point of no return. They weren't going to listen to reason, and you could guarantee they definitely did not know their rights.

"Gentleman, please," the stooge at the desk was saying. His desk phone was against his ear. He had been trying to call someone since Tusk walked in the door.

"Dad!" Tusk and Butch both turned and saw Sailor at the door, wearing sunglasses, trailed by one of the bank's security guards. The guard looked harassed. "Do you know this woman? Is she with you?"

"*With* me is strong language," Tusk said.

"Is she police or not, man? She's runnin' through my bank shoutin' into people's offices sayin' she's with the police."

Butch threw his arms around Sailor. "Your mother and I were so worried," he said. "This is the daughter you were asking about? You found her? Did my wife call you?" he asked, the anger gone from him now.

Tusk preferred this Mr. Cassidy to the one who had been screaming at him, so he just said, "Yes, sir. I found her." He looked at the bank stooge who seemed to have finally gotten in touch with whoever he was calling. Tusk turned back to the security guard. "I'm really sorry Officer...."

"Sanford."

Tusk cringed inwardly calling a security guard "officer," but he knew it would go straight to the guy's dick and plug any holes in his ego, grinding off a little of his own edge. "Officer Sanford," Tusk repeated. "She's not police, but she's helping with an investigation. Can I come find you when we're done here? I could use your help as well."

Sanford got so puffed up Tusk was surprised he didn't burst out of his uniform. "I'll be up front when you need me."

Tusk turned to the bank stooge who was off the phone now. "My apologies Mr...."

"Blankley. Roger Blankley."

"Mr. Blankley. I need a word with Mr. Cassidy before you finalize your business here. And Mr. Childress too."

"Our business is final, actually," Roger Blankley said. "It seems there was a misunderstanding."

"We're not finished," Butch said. "We didn't transfer over the title. Where's Morgan? He didn't get the money yet, did he?"

"I'm sorry," Roger Blankley began and then stopped, looking up through the glass walls. "Ah, here comes our own Mr. Simpatico. He'll be able to clear this all up."

Everyone in the room followed Roger's gaze through the glass walls, as a man wearing a suit with a phone to his ear sprinted toward the office, then turned and continued across the bank's lobby to the front entrance and out the doors. They all turned back to Roger. "Mr. Simpatico is a very busy man," he said.

"Morgan is outside," Sailor said to Tusk.

"What's he doing outside?" Butch asked.

"He was leaving," Sailor said to her father. "And I, uh, stopped him."

"How did you stop him?" Tusk asked, leading the way out of Roger's office.

"Some carefully chosen words? He may have fallen down the stairs," Sailor said.

Tusk pushed through the doors of the bank. His cruiser was where he left it, the passenger door wide open, Lula pressed up against the cage yelling, "He ran off. I yelled for him to stop. It didn't work." *It never does*, Tusk thought.

The man from the bank, Hector Simpatico, was in the parking lot staring down the road that ran past the bank, phone to his ear.

"That's where I left him," Sailor said, pointing to a spot on the sidewalk. "He was lying right there."

Tusk crouched down and looked. A few drops of blood stained the gray concrete. Two times this guy had been lying on the ground, bleeding, and two times now Tusk had lost him. He was starting to think he might not be a very good cop.

•••

Jumper sat on the back of one of the vans, his feet scraping in the sandy soil that lined the banks of the Intracoastal Waterway, the back doors of the van wide open to his sides like a trick of the animal kingdom, a snake unhinging its jaw. At a small folding table a few feet away, Puto had finished boiling water on the small camping stove and poured it into the French press. The table held the stove and the coffee maker, coffee, and a few select bottles from the bar.

"A little Sambuca boss?" Puto asked.

"What's Mickey say?"

"Half past noon."

"A little Sambuca then."

Bevel paced the dock a little ways off from where they were parked. He was itching to get into the cabin with the captives. Jumper told him to stay on the dock, it was just light guard duty. Jumper saw Puto watching Bevel as well, shaking his head.

"Every crew needs a guy no one likes, Puto," he said to him. "Someone who's expendable. He's like a pair of underwear you don't mind ruining if you've got a stomach virus."

"Boss, can I ask a question?" Puto said, pressing the plunger on the French press.

"Go ahead."

"Why'd you only ask for a hundred grand at first? I mean, that's a lot of money, but a banker with ladies who do like, shady work for him or whatever them ladies do, he's probably got a lot more than that."

Jumper had let Puto listen to his call with Hector Simpatico. "Maybe he does, maybe he doesn't," Jumper said. "You ask the waitress for a burger, not a drill press. You know what I mean?"

Puto considered this. "No, definitely not," he said. He handed Jumper his coffee and Sambuca.

"What I mean is, you ask for something you think you can actually get. Is this guy worth a million dollars? Maybe. Let's say he is. Does he have a million dollars in cash lying around that he can get his hands on today by six o'clock? Probably not. So we ask for a hundred grand. Like asking a waitress for a hamburger, we're more likely to actually get the thing we asked for. Look at me."

Puto looked up from the table where he was tidying. "There are no big wins," Jumper told him. "There's no jackpot. People get rich the same way they go broke. In little pieces. We get ten grand from some guy on the hook for a bad run out to the county, someone else has to unexpectedly shell out three grand for a new fuel pump for their Nissan. We get twenty grand for holding onto a guy's wife, someone else has to pay half a million in medical bills one monthly statement at a time because his wife got breast cancer. It all happens in drips and drops."

Puto nodded. "You pushed him to two hundred G's, though. So this might could be a baby jackpot, sounds like."

Jumper looked down at his phone. He had actually expected Hector to push back at the sudden doubling of the ransom. The man's situation—the respectable position from which he conducted shady business as Puto had put it—indicated he should be a sharp negotiator. He should have counter-offered, even if it was just a formality. Or pushed back on the six o'clock deadline, claiming he needed more time to gather the money.

Jumper stared at the boat rocking gently against the dock. Bevel was leaning over, as though listening through the windows of the cabin. He saw Jumper watching. "Hey, I think they might be plotting something in there," he called over. "I'm just going to go in and check. Make sure they're not up to something."

"Shut the fuck up and stay on the dock," Jumper yelled back.

"Right, sure, okay," Bevel said.

Jumper replayed the conversation with Hector in his head. The man dismissed the ransom demand at first. Then he came around when Jumper threatened to torture Nina and dig into his operation. Jumper accepted this, merely assuming his threats were effective, but if pictures of a woman bound and blindfolded hadn't meant anything to Hector, why would broken fingers? Hector had agreed too fast, too easily. He wanted Jumper to think this was going to be simple. Same thing Morgan wanted him to think. Two days for a bank loan based on some bullshit title transfer. Jumper wondered idly if the bank Morgan was lying about was the bank where Hector worked. Probably. The two men likely knew each other. Nina was a connection point.

It clicked.

Jumper thumbed into the messages on his phone and looked at the pictures he had sent of Nina. There were three, using multiple angles to make sure there was enough photo-evidence for Hector to understand it was definitely Nina, for him to recognize her. In the background of each one was the high-polish wood paneling. The beige separation curtain with the snaps at the entrance of that tiny bedroom or whatever it was. The curve of the two steps that led into the cabin from outside with their inlaid teak grips on the top. Boat shit. The kind of shit specific to a specific boat. And while Hector might know a lot of people with boats, he probably had some specific ideas about what boat Nina was on.

That's why he changed his mind. That's why once he changed his mind he seemed almost impatient to get Jumper off the phone.

"He knows where we are," Jumper said.

"What's that, boss?" Puto asked.

"Pack up. Now. We're leaving," Jumper got up and ran for the dock. Behind him, he heard bottles and the French press clinking as Puto unquestioningly did what he was told. Ahead of him, Bevel was leaning into the boat's deck like he might be able to see down the entrance to the cabin. He scurried back to the dock when he saw Jumper coming.

"I was just—"

"Shut the fuck up, Bevel," Jumper said.

He boarded the boat and dropped down into the cabin. He took a folding knife from his front pocket and cut the ropes tying Carrie to the small table. He grabbed her roughly by the back of her shirt and hauled her to her feet, dragging her up the steps. "Your lucky day, lady," he said, hoisting her into his arms and dropping her back on the dock in front of Bevel, who looked scared and twitchy. What else was new? "Put her in the van," he said to the tweaker. Jumper leveled the folding knife at Bevel's eye. "Straight to the van," he said. Then he dropped back down into the cabin. He dug ear plugs from an inside pocket on his jacket and fitted one into each ear.

Nina tried to pull away when he grabbed her arm. He sliced through the ties on her wrists as well and hauled her to her feet.

"What's going on?" she asked. "Did you talk to Hector?"

Jumper shoved her into the small bathroom in the cabin and pressed her, face first, against the wall. Her voice came through the earplugs, small and distant, like someone speaking to him from the other end of an airplane.

"Oh no. No no no no no no no!" Nina screamed.

Jumper took his pistol from his jacket pocket. "Sorry, lady," he said, and shot her through the back of her head.

•••

Bevel figured he had been about as patient as any man in the history of the Earth, and Jumper was not showing much grace or appreciation for that effort. Like how Bevel saw Jug with the wife out behind the bar the night before and stayed on task, even though it was his perfect chance. But Jumper had given him a promotion and he wanted to show he could handle it. The women had been on the boat for a whole day now. Bevel just wanted to get in there and use them while he could. Two bitches they were most likely going to kill anyway, what was the harm?

Jumper wasn't cooperating, though. He wouldn't let Bevel into the boat with the women. They were just sitting in there. They weren't doing anything but waiting. He got Jumper what he wanted, why couldn't Jumper give him what he wanted? It was selfish, is what it was. And now Jumper had gone and shot one of them. Why couldn't Bevel have ten minutes with her before he went and did that?

So Bevel changed plans. He had done his part of things and received nothing in return. That was going to change. He was going to get satisfaction.

•••

Carrie heard Nina yelling "No no no" followed by the gunshot as she stumbled along the dock. The mundane sounds of their location, the water, the birds, seemed almost a roar in the wake of the gun's report. She was nearly sick. It was a simple *bang*, and Nina was gone forever. It happened between footfalls as she was tugged along by the same sour smelling man who had tossed her into the van the previous night. Nina died and Carrie's hope died with her. She let herself believe Nina's cajoling and finagling would work. That someone named Hector would take care of things. That they would be set free. Now she knew, absolutely, that she was going to die.

Nina had a powerful financial backer and she was dead. All Carrie had were her working-class parents and a collection of dangerously stupid siblings. Well, Dex seemed smart, but he was a broke student. What was he going to do? Sailor was high all the time, and JP was a mess in a bunch of his own unique ways. Neither of them had any money, and she wasn't sure either could give any coherent help to the police.

The sour smelling man was talking, she realized. "You can swim. Of course you can swim," he was muttering. "People look like you, they can always swim. Better hope you can, anyway." He jabbed Carrie in the side. It hurt. She instinctively flinched away from him and the jabbing, stumbling and unsteady on her feet because of the blindfold. The man wrapped an arm around her waist and pressed against her. She was nearly sick again at the thought of what must be coming, but then she felt his hand snake around to her waist and grasp her tied wrists. Her hands were bound together. Another cord ran from her hands and was cinched around her waist, barring her from moving her tied hands any higher than the belt buckle of her jeans. The man's fingers worked the knots as they walked. She felt the cords loosen momentarily before he gripped them tight again.

The relief in her hands and wrists was immediate and exquisite when he loosened the knot. More importantly, she felt a spark of hope flare and kindle.

"Bevel!" another man's voice shouted behind them, back by the boat. It was the voice of the man in charge, the one who had just shot Nina. "Get your hands off her, Bevel."

"She's falling," the man called Bevel said. Then, quieter, for Carrie's ears only she realized later, he said, "Should be loose enough you can flounder some till he gets you." Then he pushed her.

Carrie was weightless in the dark of her blindfold, then she smacked the cold water. The shock was all-consuming, a fierce cold that enveloped and stunned her. Her clothes soaked and her boots filled, conspiring with the water to keep her, to pull her down. Panic, as pure as she had ever felt it. She didn't get any forewarning to take a breath and was out of air as soon as she hit the water. She knew as certainly as she had ever known anything she was going to drown. Her bound hands were looser, but still binding. She jerked at the bonds with adrenaline strength but she couldn't get free. Her lungs burned with the need for air, burned past the point of endurance, then settled. She felt dreamy and calm. She pulled one wrist against the other and felt it give, felt the space she needed to wriggle a hand free. Before she could though, she was wrenched back into the air and onto the dock.

Carrie landed on her side like a caught fish, flopping, coughing, and gasping. Her blindfold held in place, she still couldn't see. Like her wet clothes it was plastered firmly to her now, an icy weight across her eyes. She heard the sound of tires on dirt and gravel, a voice yelling, "You okay, Boss?" Feet running along the dock. Hands lifted her.

Carrie felt the slack in her bonds. She pressed her hands and wrists against her waist to hold the cords in place, keeping the appearance they were tight. The man in charge said nothing, but hoisted her off her feet, carrying her in two arms. Carrie, pressed against him now, could tell he was big, hulking. He ran with her along the dock. Somewhere ahead of them an engine started.

She didn't understand what was happening or why. The urgency of the man in charge was the only thing that made sense. He had just murdered someone, after all.

•••

Bevel hauled ass up to the van as fast as he could with his stiff leg, jumped in, and spun tires toward the narrow dirt lane that led back to the highway. Fishing the wife out of the water would keep Jumper and that little rat fuck, Puto, occupied long enough to keep them from coming after him. With her ropes loose, she should be fine for however long it took them to haul her out. He didn't personally care if the bitch drowned or not, but he knew if she died it would cross a line with Jumper that might mean the end of him. This way, he was pretty sure he could walk it all back. Say she fell, say he was scared Jumper would be angry with him so he took off to give him time to calm down.

Meanwhile, he had carved out some time to finally get a little revenge.

•••

Carrie heard vehicle doors open. She was placed back in the van, she assumed. There was the slamming of the two back doors. The front doors opened and the van shifted as two men climbed in. Their voices were audible but muffled through the divider that separated her from the front.

"How hard is it to keep a grown woman from falling into the waterway? Plus he gives everybody the creeps, Boss," said a man Carrie had not previously heard speak. His voice was mild and soft through the partition. It came from the driver's side. The engine came to life and the van started to roll.

"He won't be an issue much longer," a second voice said. Carrie was pretty sure it was the big man in charge. "Problematic people have a habit of returning. When he shows up again, I'll deal with him."

"Can I ask something, Boss?"

"Is it about the girl?"

"Yeah. The one still on the boat."

"What do you want to know?"

"How come we couldn't get some money for her? Why'd we... *leave her there*?"

"The money man agreed too fast. He didn't ask questions. He seemed to know something."

"Did he know where we were?"

"Maybe. I think so. But he knew *something*. Something that gave him confidence. That's not ideal for the kind of negotiation we're involved in here. They should be in the dark, confused, desperate for information. That way, they follow the path you set.

The process you give them. You don't want to deal with someone who knows something. And he seemed to know something. So, we divested ourselves of that particular asset and that particular deal. It was a secondary play anyway."

Carrie tested the freedom of her hands while the man talked. Between Bevel's efforts and her frantic struggling in the water, the cord around her wrists was loosened enough that she was able to slip a hand free. She raised her blindfold, sopping with water. She was in the back of a van again, the two windows on each side covered with a dark tint that let in only dim light from outside. It was enough. She wasn't sure if it was the same van, but the interior door handles were missing again. The back of the van was empty except for her. The boss in the passenger seat was still speaking. She guessed he was on the phone now since the driver did not respond as he talked.

"Yes...I thought you said three business days...Sounds like you have a strong relationship with the bank."

Carrie shook her foot until she dislodged Jug's knife. It had been pressing painfully against her ankle for the past twenty-four hours. She tipped her leg up and the knife slid from her boot into her free hand. She opened it and checked the blade. There was dry blood on it, but it was sharp and solid. Carrie closed the knife and tucked it into the top of her jeans.

"Tomorrow works," the man in charge was saying, up in the passenger seat. "No, not the bar. I'll call and tell you where... Morgan, wait. Do you want to know how your wife is doing?"

Carrie stopped arranging the thin paracord around her wrists and listened. Did he just say Morgan?

"She's fine," the man said. Then, "Tomorrow. Pay attention to your phone. I'll call in the morning." He must have hung up because then he said, "Now that's a man who doesn't know something. Might not know anything, actually."

"He got the money?"

"Says he did. And early to boot."

"Where do you think he got it?"

"Hard to say. The thing I'm sure of is, it was one hundred percent not the bank."

"He ain't even asked about his wife, huh?"

"Between having her kidnapped and the sidepiece, I think we can safely assume it's not a strong marriage."

"She could do better."

"Most of them could."

They drove on in silence for what felt like a long time to Carrie. She worked at her restraints, wrapping the paracord back the way she was pretty sure it had been tied, arranging it so it looked tight but she could slip her hands free when the time was right. She practiced getting her hands out, learning how long it would take.

She also thought about Morgan. That scum. Her anger over the affair, her embarrassment about it, seemed stupid now. An affair was nothing. This kidnapping, this abduction, was a matter of life or death. One down, one to go, Carrie thought. She heard the half-second gunshot again in her head. The one that zeroed out Nina's life.

The van drove along what felt like an unpaved road for a while. Carrie checked her bonds one last time. They looked as good as they were going to look. She worked the blindfold back down over her eyes by rubbing her head against the van's wall, then laid down on her back near the doors. Finally, the van slowed, then stopped. Carrie heard the two front doors open and close, then the back doors opened with a flourish. It was quiet for a long moment.

"Feeling a little less froggy this time, I guess," said the voice of the man in charge. The one the driver called "Boss."

They got Carrie out of the van. She could feel the dampness in the air and smell the water nearby, wherever they were. It smelled of natural decay, fallen logs going spongy and leaves turning to black muck. The air was cool, filled with the nighttime sounds of the woods, the ceaseless hum of existence.

The two men led her to a door, then inside. No one checked her hands. No one commented on her restraints. Inside, the forest sounds were replaced by sounds of digital anarchy. Carrie figured it was a video game. A new voice from somewhere in the space in front of her said, "Oh, hey. Uh." And then stopped. Either cut off by one of the other men or that was the extent of their vocabulary.

Carrie was led away to her left and sat down roughly on the floor in what felt like a back room. The sound of the video game came to her from a distance now. She was pressed against some piece of furniture and another rope was looped around her throat, not so tight as to cut off her air, but tight enough to keep the thought of her air being cut off top of mind. Like a thumb pressed just too hard against her windpipe. Enough to keep her still. It was secured to something behind her, a bed post maybe. She heard the sound of whoever tied her around the throat crossing the room, then a door closing.

Carrie was about to work her hands free but she hesitated. Something felt wrong. More wrong anyway, since the whole situation was awful. Her brain was looking for something. It was the same sensation as having a song cut off midway and her mind needing to finish a well-known lyric. Except her brain couldn't pinpoint the thing it was looking for. She stayed still. She thought about Morgan. It went beyond merely hating her to do something like this. He didn't think of her as a human. She couldn't believe she had felt bad about her time with Tusk. About filing for divorce. About disrupting their lives with her anger over his affair with Nina. Even in the state of prolonged aggravation she had been in with Morgan, she assumed their actions and feelings at least reflected an acknowledgement that the other's life was meaningful enough to impact their own. She thought Morgan's surprise appearance and outburst at Big Lock's at least pointed to him caring about her seeing someone else, and therefore caring about her in some sense, even if he had it all wrong. But no. She was nothing to him. Less than human. Less than real. She began to cry a little thinking of just how sad that was.

"Okay then," the boss's voice suddenly cut through the sound of her sniffling and she yelped in genuine surprise, jumping slightly, choking herself against the rope around her neck. "Take it easy," the boss said. "A man can't be too careful."

The door opened and closed again. This time, she heard the thing. The gently shushing sound of the boss walking back down the hall, receding from the room, toward the gibberish sounds of the video game. The missing thing clunked down in its slot, the way her brain wanted it.

Chapter 11

Morgan once heard his brother-in-law, JP, describe his hangover as feeling like "if dog shit had the flu." At the time, Morgan forced a thin chuckle and inwardly rolled his eyes at JP's pathetic habit of dramatizing the aftermath of his excesses to highlight how hard he partied. Now, staggering from the Range Rover along the dock to *Boatacious*, a name he was proud to have come up with on his own, JP's phrase kept running through his head. There was no more appropriate way to describe how he felt. His stab wound throbbed and he was pretty sure he had ripped some, if not all, of his stitches when he fell down the bank steps. His hip hurt. He wondered if it was fractured. His broken fingers also hurt from landing on them at the bottom of the steps. The pain downpouring throughout his body was draining any reserves of energy left in his battery. He was half-asleep on his feet.

Sailor messed him up good. He had regained his senses on the ground by a police car, with some Myrtle Beach wastoid yelling something at him from the prisoner section in the back. He hadn't been able to focus on whatever she was hollering. Honestly, he hadn't been able to focus on much at all really, and he chalked it up to what he believed were his innate killer instincts that he made it to his boat, the last place anyone would think to look for him. The Cassidys and Jumper didn't even know it existed. The scene in Roger's office back at the bank didn't look like it was going all that well, so there was a chance Hector was looking for him too, wanting his money back. Hector knew about his boat of course, it was docked at a piece of Hector's property. He had even come out on it with Morgan and Nina a few times back when things between them were sunnier. What were the odds he would remember? But out of an abundance of caution, Morgan stashed his bag of money in a place no one would ever think to look. Between his pursuers and the fact he might pass out at any moment from blood loss, he didn't want to risk losing the only money he had in the world. His killer instincts again, keeping him one step ahead.

Morgan left the Range Rover unlocked and the keys on the driver's seat. The repo man could come collect it whenever suited him. Morgan was done. He was going to move *Boatacious* somewhere farther south where he could get some sleep and recover, then slip back into town to pick up his cash. After that, he was continuing south, and he wasn't stopping until he got to the Keys.

He limped down the steps into the cabin. He wanted to lie down and go to sleep right then, but he needed to move. He needed to get out on the water and away from this slip he was borrowing from Hector. A quick trip to the head to empty his bladder and he would be on his way.

Morgan didn't scream when he opened the door to the head and Nina's stiffening body toppled into him like a felled tree, but only because he was so scared he couldn't pull the necessary breath. He fell and Nina landed on top of him. Blood jarred into motion by the fall spilled from the bullet hole in her head and onto his chest. He scrambled from under her, trying to breathe, trying to understand what was happening. He sort of managed the breathing part.

Nina lay on her back, blood pooling under her head. She was bedraggled and rougher looking than Morgan ever saw her in life. There was a bruise along her jaw like she had been punched hard by an enthusiast, and her perfect blond hair darkened with blood and brain matter splayed grotesquely beneath her head. She was looking up at him with the surprised expression that had been her last. The one that seemed to say *I can't believe this is happening.* It was a permanent version of the expression Morgan was wearing as he staggered up the cabin steps and threw himself off the boat and onto the dock.

Morgan thought he might pass out. His brain tried telling him the dead body of Nina Capaldi couldn't really be there on his boat. But even as that desperate rationalization spun itself through his tired mind, a somber and serious part of him—what might be called a conscience in a more scrupulous person—assured him it was not only real, but that he could suss out what happened. He had killed her. That wasn't the literal truth, but his culpability in the chain of events that caused this was too immense, too immediate, for him to ignore. The bruise on Nina's jaw was the most damning. The image of it kept returning to him. He had put violent men into motion pretending he could control things. He sent those men after his wife. They had her now. Or was she on the boat too? Beaten and shot and stuffed into some other compartment he simply hadn't opened yet.

Morgan took a moment, kneeling on the wooden dock to steady his breathing. That's when he realized someone was watching him. Two moderately large men waited patiently at the foot of the dock. Parked above the dock, not far from the Range Rover, was a black Cadillac Escalade. A man Morgan recognized leaned out the front passenger window, also watching him.

"Hey, Morgan," Edison called out. "Do you remember me? I set your thumb when you broke it in Hector's office?" Morgan nodded. "Great! I think you'd better come with us. There's some parts of our deal that need a little attention. Cross the t's, dot the lower-case j's, that sort of thing. Can you come on up to the car?"

Morgan looked back at the boat with its terrible reality, then at the two unsmiling fellows at the foot of the dock. Finally he looked over his shoulder, south along the waterway where the afternoon sun brightened the far side of the shore and lit the seagulls in white commas punctuating a blue sky that ran on and on to the horizon. The world called to him to swim for it, but between his hip, his hand, and the stab wound he knew he would drown before he got ten yards from the dock.

Morgan stood and shuffled toward the Escalade. "Really appreciate the compliance here, Morgan," Edison called to him. "Mr. Maroney, Mr. Daniels." The two men at the end of the dock looked up at Edison. "Let's help him and be supportive, okay? Mr. Childress is already a little worse for wear it looks like and, well, there's still a lot of daylight ahead of us."

•••

Sailor answered police questions in the parking lot of the bank, then she answered more police questions at the station. Police went to her parents' house and got statements from her mom and brothers. Police talked to Hector Simpatico and Roger Blankley and the bank security guard whose full name was Curtis Sanford.

Lula took an Uber back to her hotel. "I can't imagine how bad the worry you're going through must be," she had said to Sailor when they exchanged goodbyes in the bank's parking lot, before Sailor went to the police station. "If there's anything I can do, like from a legal perspective or personally, just call me, okay?"

"Any calls from me are going to come from random numbers until I get a new phone. You'll never know if it's me or a scammer trying to convince you to renew your car warranty," Sailor said.

Lula lifted the Ray Bans and ran her fingers gently over the bruises around Sailor's eyes. "Try to let yourself be sad about it a little bit," she said. "It'll help you think about things from a new perspective. Maybe you'll get an idea you hadn't thought of."

Lula had ridden away in her Uber and Sailor went to the police station where she and her father answered a million questions about Carrie and Morgan and Nina. The police gave up dealing with Butch pretty early on and gave him a lift home. They kept Sailor for the rest of the day until Chester got out of a hearing he had been stuck at and stormed in, demanding to speak with his client. The detectives cleared the room for them.

"They're building a case against you," Chess said. "You admitted you were at the scene, you admitted you were following one of the victims."

"I didn't *admit* those things, Chess. It's not stuffing my training bra. It's not behind an embarrassment paywall. It's just what happened," Sailor said.

"You waited till the next morning to report the incident to the police."

"Do they not see my black and blue face? My car with the smashed windows still in the parking lot? I didn't do things exactly right. I wish I had. But I had help fucking it up. I took a serious shot to the head. And not one of the sugary ones."

"There are no other suspects, Sail. Besides Morgan, and he's in the wind right now. And even if they find him, there's no reason, from their perspective, you two couldn't be working together. Secret lovers conspiring to get rid of the people in their way."

"Oh for fuck's sake."

"It's what they see over and over," Chess said. "It's what happens to people in the world. The cops, they're not paid to be imaginative. To think that this time might be an outlier. Don't talk to them without me again. Ever. They're letting you go to Butch and Pam's but you have to stay there. They want to be able to bring you in for questioning again when they surface Morgan. Call me immediately. Do not, no matter what they say, no matter what bullshit they tell you, speak to them until I'm with you. Go against your genetics and clam the hell up, understand?"

Sailor seethed. Chester opened the door and called into the hallway, "We're finished here." He turned back to Sailor. "Let's go."

One of the detectives stepped into the doorway, blocking it, and said to Sailor, "We're going to need you to stay at home where we can find you. Do you understand? Don't leave your parent's house."

"Excuse us," Chester said, stepping into the doorway as close to the detective as possible without touching him. The man didn't move.

"Am I a suspect?" Sailor asked.

"We're considering all possibilities," the lead detective told her. "Your attorney has secured your release to your parents' house. We're placing an officer outside to watch both you and for the man who slipped custody today."

"The man you let walk out of your police station this morning you mean. You know, restaurants do a better job watching the diners to make sure they don't bounce on the check than y'all do with a violent criminal," Sailor said. "Maybe you should consider hiring a couple waitresses in the interest of actually keeping the city safe."

"Don't leave the house," the detective said, finally stepping back, unsmiling. "We're watching."

"At least get a few busboys," Sailor called back as Chess pulled her from the room and down the hallway.

Tusk was waiting outside to give her a ride.

"Home?" Tusk asked as he started the cruiser.

"Big Lock's." Sailor said.

"Big Lock's?"

"Carrie's Sidekick is there. I need a car until mine is fixed."

Tusk drove her to Big Lock's. He stopped out front. Sailor reached for the handle but didn't open the door. She leaned back in the seat and closed her eyes. Tusk put it in park. They sat in the cruiser next to Carrie's Sidekick watching people trickle into the bar.

"I knew she was married," Tusk said eventually. "And I knew there was some problem with them. She didn't want to tell me about it. I only even asked because it seemed like the thing to do. It wasn't something I felt like I had to be involved in. I thought I could sit out that part of things."

"What are you trying to tell me?" Sailor asked, though she knew he was trying to tell himself something. She was just his excuse to say it out loud, to have someone confirm his suspicion that he could have stopped all this if only he asked the married woman he was sleeping with more questions.

"Just that I'm sorry."

"You didn't kidnap her," Sailor said. "You didn't miss the signs. Feeling bad about it's just going to get in the way of you doing something about it."

"The Investigation Unit will find her. They'll follow up on the information you all provided today and they'll find her," Tusk said.

"What about you?"

"I'm patrol. It's best if I stay out of their way. Let them do their jobs. Besides, I couldn't even find Jug without your help."

"You knew to ask for help. That's how you found him," Sailor said. She opened the door and got out. "Thanks for the ride."

Tusk pulled away as Sailor crouched by the back bumper and fished out the magnetic box where Carrie kept a spare key. She got into the driver's seat and the familiar smell of her sister's car hit her. It all landed on her heart then. She started crying. Carrie drove them to school every day in this car. The two of them plus Tayto and Julie, listening to music, laughing and singing. She looked in the center console and found the Neil Diamond CD, the one that had *Cherry, Cherry* on it. Such a corny musician but they loved that song. They would scream along to the line, *Girl, we do whatever we want to*. Sailor learned to drive in this car, Carrie showing her how to work the clutch and the gears. A skill that was essentially obsolete even as Sailor learned it. Carrie had cried in this car, like Sailor cried now, telling her about Nina and Morgan and asking what was she supposed to do now?

Sailor thought back to Lula's parting words. *Try to let yourself be sad about it a little bit. It'll help you think about things from a new perspective. Maybe you'll get an idea you hadn't thought of.* One more in a lifetime of admonishments to take things more seriously. To straighten up, don't joke so much. But Sailor took everything seriously, always. She just didn't think it was prudent to let everyone know that. Well, now she was crying and letting herself be sad, so bring on the great ideas because she wasn't done. She started the car, backed it out and pointed it at the highway.

•••

Sailor's parents were both asleep early, exhausted and sad. Her mother slept with both her cell phone and the portable house phone against her chest, waiting for a call from the police department or her daughter telling her things were going to be okay. Butch was on the couch, asleep in the blue light of the muted television, half a beer sweating on a coaster on the coffee table. Sailor showered and changed into clothes left behind in her and Carrie's old bedroom. She rifled the dresser in the boys' room for a sweatshirt and pulled it on over the Janelle Monae T-shirt she had worn holes in back in high school.

The house was quiet. She looked out the front window and saw the patrol car parked across the street watching theirs and Nana Jean's house. She walked back to the boys' bedroom and looked out the window into the backyard. There was light glowing from the old treehouse their father had built twenty years ago, in the yard's one substantial tree in the small yard. She went out the backdoor. She heard their voices from the base of the ladder, low and hushed. The voices of men now. They were too deep and heavy for the thin plywood walls of childhood. She could smell the marijuana before she came through the trapdoor. There was Jug, JP, and Dex sitting Tetris-style, carefully arranged to fit the elongated versions of the boys they used to be into the space where they used to sprawl and wrestle. One good body slam now and the whole treehouse might collapse.

"This looked pretty unsafe from the ground," Sailor said, stretching her legs to slide next to Dex, the two of them on one side of the trapdoor and JP and Jug on the other. "But I thought I'd better come up and confirm for myself." She wiggled a little and the treehouse groaned and creaked. "Yep, definitely unsafe."

"You want to get Mom and Dad up here too, just to get another opinion?" Dex said.

"I can wake Nana Jean and we can drag her up here too, get her take on it," Jug said.

"Tell her to bring her bowling balls," JP said. "We can test if the floor is level while we're at it."

"Carrie'll be our final judge," Dex said.

Carrie's name took the smile off Sailor's face. The boys fell silent for a moment too, until JP said, "Fucking Morgan."

"I can't believe she married that dork," Jug said.

"None of us can," JP said.

"I can," Dex said. He waved off the joint Jug was holding out to him. "Carrie's smart. She's serious. Morgan was nice and had a decent job and tucked his shirt in and cleaned his fingernails and finished college. Who was she supposed to marry? All our friends are the kind of people who get high before funerals. Or run drugs as a side hustle." He looked at JP and Jug.

Dex and Carrie were the most alike of the four of them, Sailor supposed. Dex was modeling his own choices on Carrie's, now that she thought about it. He would finish college with a professional degree, something in business.

"Damn, Dexy," JP said. "The guy fucking kidnapped her. Or had her kidnapped. Or had some part in it, anyway."

"I'm just saying it's not her fault she married a guy who seemed normal. Just 'cause y'all think success is for losers."

Sailor thought again of Lula's exhortation to let herself be sad. That's what Dex was doing, the most emotionally mature among them in the treehouse. He was sad and scared for his sister. "They'll find her," Sailor said to Dex. He nodded. She sounded like Tusk, pinning the outcome of her sister's life on someone else's actions.

"For what it's worth, I'm not proud of my association with Jumper," Jug said. "The guy kind of fucked my life up for the last three years."

Sailor, JP, and Dex all gave him a look.

"Of course, I had a lot to do with that as well," Jug said.

"It's too bad Morgan doesn't know Jumper or we could blame Carrie's disappearance on him too, as long as we're taking off our bad decisions and hanging them on his coat rack," Sailor said.

"Morgan knows Jumper," JP said.

Sailor sat up straight. The treehouse creaked a protest as though admonishing her to keep still. "What'd you say?"

"I said Morgan knows Jumper," JP said. "He came and asked me about getting coke once. This was after I was sober so—"

"Sorry, did you say after you were sober?" Dex said.

"After I was *allegedly* sober. Fuck's sake, Dex, what'd I do to you?"

"Lied about being sober, obviously," Sailor said. "Go on about Morgan and Jumper."

"Well, Morgan didn't know I had lied about being sober, so it was a dick move asking me for a coke connection. But whatever, the man was employing me and he said it was a one-off for a bachelor party. I told him I didn't know where to score anymore except for Jumper's and that he didn't want to go there, that the place was bad news."

"You sent him to Jumper's?" Jug said. "After everything that happened you sent him to Jumper's?"

"I told him it was bad news. I used those exact words. I only mentioned it in case he asked around and someone else put him onto the place."

"But," Sailor prompted.

"But, he went there anyway. He told me a couple days later. Said he met Jumper and everything. He was real excited. His walk on the wild side I guess."

Sailor's brain was firing. She started to get to her feet and the treehouse gave a shudder.

"Sail," Jug said. "I just got back home. You mind sitting down and not killing us by knocking this thing out of the tree?"

Sailor slowly retook her seat, saying, "If Morgan knows Jumper then that's it. There's got to be some connection there."

"Why's that?" Dex said.

“I don’t...I don’t totally know why, but I *know*. I just know. Look, Morgan shows up all fired up and gets in a fight with Jug last night at the bar. What’s he even doing there? Watching Carrie?”

“He was coming to my show?” JP said, hopefully.

“Get real. Morgan’s as interested in your show as he is in non-pleated pants. And he didn’t come with Carrie. She was inside getting faced because someone,” she glared at JP, “broadcast a private conversation about her potentially having a tryst. He’s only there to make sure she gets snatched. He sees her with Jug and...I don’t know. He goes off-book. But the snatch still happens. The woman he’s having an affair with is also kidnapped. I mean, Morgan’s not doing it himself, so someone is in on it with him. Then he shows up here the next morning pretending not to have been stabbed the night before. Telling everyone the last time he saw Carrie was when she was on the way to the bar and he was going to a client dinner. He owes the bank money. That guy today, Hector whatever, said so. He said Morgan told him he wanted to sign over some real estate to shore up his debt. Morgan’s in on the whole thing and Jumper is the guy helping him. Or making him do it. Or something.”

The boys stared at her. “Maybe...but...” JP said.

“But what?”

“He went to Jumper’s one time.”

“One time that you know of,” Sailor said. “You both got involved with him and ended up owing him money, having your fingers broken...”

JP looked down at his hand and flexed it a few times. “Now that you mention it, Morgan’s fingers are actually broken. All four of them. And his thumb.”

Sailor hadn't seen Morgan since Carrie told her about the affair. She hadn't been able to stomach the sight of him. She remembered now, his bandaged hand at the bank.

"That could be a coincidence," Jug said.

"All fucking day you walk around the world and no one you see has five broken fingers. You think it's a coincidence that the two people who do are both involved with the same drug dealing bar owner you fled town to avoid? When you got those tattoos did you think it was a coincidence everyone who worked at the parlor also had tattoos? When you see people at the beach do you think it's just happenstance you all wore bathing suits that day?"

"What I mean is, our situation was kind of specific and a guy got killed who—"

"Who never made it into the papers or the police blotter or the obituaries," Sailor said.

Jug ran a hand through his hair. "No. But I saw him get shot. Bevel shot him."

"Bevel who never got caught for it," JP said quietly. "Bevel who must have showed up at a hospital with his own bullet wound. And no one ever tied it back to a dead body in the middle of the road because no one ever found that body."

Jug shook his head. "Y'all weren't there."

Sailor pulled open the trap door and swung her legs down onto the aging ladder.

"Where're you going?" JP said.

"I'm going to stake out Jumper's and find our sister," she said, and dropped the last four feet from the ladder down to the yard. She had gone a few steps when she heard someone else hit the ground behind her. She turned and saw Dex jogging to catch up with her. "I'm going," she said. "You're not talking me out of it."

"Talk you out of it? Hell," Dex said. "I'm coming with you."

•••

Tusk sat in a chair next to Jamie's hospital bed—on the side without the ruptured eardrum—staring passively at *SportsCenter* playing without sound on the small TV on the wall. Twice, Morgan Childress was lying on the ground, wounded, and twice, Morgan slipped away from him. Morgan wasn't exactly a criminal mastermind skilled in the art of evasion, either. He was a badly hurt real estate developer with a physique that suggested he drove to his mailbox. And Tusk lost him. Twice.

Jamie was pouring Tusk's gift, a bottle of the new Dirty Myrtle whiskey that was getting pushed hard in every liquor store and bar in town, into two plastic cups.

"That was meant for when you get out of here, man," Tusk said to him. "You can't drink that with a head injury."

"My head ain't injured anymore, they fixed it," Jamie said, handing him one of the cups. "I've been trying to find a bottle of this stuff for weeks. It's sold out everywhere I've been."

"Is it that good?"

"Nah, word is it's damn near gasoline but, you know, it's called Dirty Myrtle. It's just the vibe." He bumped his cup against Tusk's. "Bottom's up, boy scout." They drank. Tusk's entire esophageal tract flooded with rough heat. Jamie clutched his throat and coughed. "Oh shit," he wheezed. "That brought my concussion back."

"It's not back," Tusk said, wiping the tears out of his eyes. "That shit caused a second one." He took a breath. "It's for real, legitimately incredible that whiskey can even be this harsh. I'd think I swallowed hot gravel if I hadn't seen for myself it was liquid." He put his cup back on Jamie's tray. "That's it for me."

"Yeah, I'll take a breather on that too," Jamie said. "Where'd you get it?"

"I had to talk to the owner of Big Lock's to get security footage from one of their cameras. They got boxes of it from the distributor. I begged one off him."

"Oh yeah, your kidnappings."

"You heard?"

"Two kidnappings, financial malfeasance, ransom. You got involved with nine months' worth of crimes in one day."

"There's also a potentially unsolved murder out in the county," Tusk said. He repeated Jug's story about Jumper and Bevel and Randy. "I did some research. There's nothing, and I mean nothing, on record about this. There's no body, no missing person, no call to the local precinct about gunshots in the night. Nothing. It's like it didn't happen."

"Maybe it didn't."

"It's an awfully specific story for this guy to have invented, then left town over."

"Shit, I worked at a call center once with this guy, real fuck up, always right about to get fired. So he gets written up one day, goes to HR, the whole bit. Comes back and tells our manager he's been assigned to a performance plan and has to do training down on the first floor each morning till eleven. So for like a month he comes up every day at eleven and starts work. Then one day I come in and everyone's whispering and shit, turns out the guy's been fired. But the reason everyone is all excited about it is, the guy never got put on a performance plan. Never had to go to training. He was just sleeping in every day and showing up at eleven, getting paid for an extra two hours he didn't work. Our manager had never checked. He only found out when he saw the HR lady on the elevator one day and asked when the guy was going to be off his performance plan. Turns out the company didn't even do performance plans, but everything about the way this dude presented it seemed legit.

Right down to the phrase 'performance plan.' So, you know, my point is, your county murder, maybe it didn't happen the way that Jug dope thinks it did."

Tusk thought about this. "How'd you hear about the kidnappings and all that, anyway?" he asked.

"Craig Daniels was up here before you."

"You friendly with him?"

Jamie shrugged, reaching for his plastic cup and the bottle of Dirty Myrtle. "He's alright, I guess. He was mainly performing the act, you know? Another cop gets injured, you go see him, right? He had that dipshit Maroney with him, though. I could have skipped that. That guy has two brain cells and they're fighting for third place."

"The hell's Daniels doing with Maroney?"

"They work together, I guess."

"At the restaurant?"

"What?"

"Isn't Maroney a waiter?"

"Oh. Yeah, he was. No, not at a restaurant." Jamie took another belt of Dirty Myrtle and winced. "Second one isn't better, but you're more prepared," he reported. He exhaled loudly and leaned back in his bed. "They're doing private security work for some swinging dick over at Grand Strand Bank. Harvey Simp-something or other."

"Hector Simpatico?"

"Yeah, that's it. You know bankers now? Daniels is doing it for the extra cash. Maroney is doing it because he got fired for being a shitty waiter. Probably bringing extra bread to the owner's daughter's table or something."

Tusk tried to fit this new information into the events of the day. "A cop and a former cop are doing security work for a private citizen? A finance guy? He's paying them?"

Jamie looked puzzled by his incredulousness. "Yeah? Not sure if you've noticed, but we get paid jack shit." He pointed to his damaged ear, with the white panel of gauze taped over it. "Definitely not enough for this. They still ain't found him, you know that? Crazy motherfucker's still out there. Your boy Jug better watch his back."

"There's a patrol car watching his grandma's house where he's staying," Tusk said. Jamie stared at him. "What?" Tusk asked.

"I was in a goddamn police station. What do you think a patrol car's going to do? That tweaker wants to get in that house, he's getting in that house."

Tusk pushed Maroney and Daniels and their part-time employer from his thoughts. Jamie made a good point. A lot of good points. Bevel was still out there, clearly violent, clearly resourceful and, now that he thought about it, unlikely to be dissuaded by a patrol car parked in front of a house. The captain had specifically asked Tusk to keep an eye on Jug, which he was doing because he wanted to be a detective. Because that came with a pay raise. Because he made jack shit.

Tusk stood. "I need to go. I'll swing by your place tomorrow when you get out. See how you're holding up." He dapped him up and headed for the door.

"Try and snag another bottle of this Dirty Myrtle," Jamie called after him. "My momma's giving me a ride home and she's not going to let me stop at the liquor store."

On his way out of the hospital, Tusk's phone chimed. It was an email from the owner of Big Lock's with the security footage attached. He stopped on the sidewalk in the cool evening and sat on one of the benches in front of the hospital. He hit play and the night-vision footage of the back of Big Lock's by the dumpsters filled his phone screen.

The camera was pointed at the cluster of vehicles in the space that constituted Big Lock's staff parking. Tusk immediately clocked Morgan sitting in his Range Rover. He appeared to be glaring at something or someone off camera. Tusk watched as Morgan exited his vehicle and crossed the dirt lot coming toward the camera. He was angry and yelling and Tusk supposed that Jug and Carrie were off camera at the bottom of the screen. Seconds ticked by on the clock in the corner of the screen and suddenly Jug and Morgan spilled back into view in front of the staff parking, fighting and falling to the ground. Morgan had Jug in a choke hold. Tusk watched like a man who could see the future. There was the knife, the flailing stab to Morgan's side, Morgan stands and falls, Jug massaging his throat, Carrie kneeling over Morgan, Morgan back on his feet and then the white van blasting into frame and hitting Morgan as it skidded to a stop. A man exited the van and grabbed Carrie. Tusk watched, getting angry as the man appeared to hit Carrie in the throat before banging her head into the side of the van. The man grabbed her and began dragging her to the back of the van and in that moment he turned in such a way that his face was clearly visible to the camera. Tusk paused the video and zoomed in. Bevel Sloot.

Tusk got up and ran to his car.

Chapter 12

"What'd they do with the boat?" Michael Simpatico asked.

Hector sat on one of the couches in the three bedroom oceanfront condo in a complex approximately half a mile from Nina's, speaking with his brother over the phone. He had the sliding glass door to the patio open, letting in the cold night air. He loved a chill. The waves pulsed white noise in the background. "It's still there," Hector said. "It's our insurance policy, to make sure our friend Morgan here stays in compliance tomorrow. Isn't that right, Morgan?"

Morgan was laid out on a table in the middle of the room, absolutely looped on the painkillers Edison had provided him. Edison assured Hector the only thing keeping Morgan half conscious was the adrenaline his body was producing as Edison restitched the stab wound Morgan had acquired. Once he was done, Edison said, they could look forward to Morgan passing into unconsciousness. For now, Morgan replied to Hector with a slurred, "Righty-o, Chief."

"If he keeps cool and does what he's told, we'll take it offshore and sink it. If not, it's going to conveniently wash up on the beach for the Marine Unit to find, corpse and all, and trace back to Morgan off the registration."

"Is there a reason he can't just sink along with the boat and the corpse?" Michael asked.

"Not totally off the table. But there's a different play I have in mind."

"Where's our money?" Michael wanted to know.

"Morgan stashed it in the back of his missing wife's car."

"Where's the car?"

"We're working on that. It was in the parking lot of Big Lock's Bar and Grill. Morgan figured with his wife MIA the vehicle wouldn't be going anywhere. But, lo and behold, Morgan is gifted with the planning and foresight of the Donner party."

"What happened with the father-in-law's land? It's a bust?"

"Apparently he sold all but an acre years ago to a private hunting club. Whatever workfare clerk they have at the records office failed to file the paperwork they were sent. So the land records never got updated."

"Welfare has to be cheaper in the long run," Michael said. "It costs too much time and money for these people to have even simple jobs."

"Run for Congress."

"It's not totally off the table, as you say. There's money to be made there. Doesn't really get me away from the workfare people though, does it? I'm not sure I'd enjoy the company of my colleagues. Government attracts a lot of best-regional-door-to-door-salesman types. Cream of the crop, but the crop is shitweed. I think the play is to have someone we control run for Congress."

"Meanwhile..." Hector said, pulling Michael back on track.

"Right, lawyers, guns and money and so forth. Intel says Jumper is actually a seventy-year-old Black man living in North Myrtle Beach who sold his bar to a man whose name, at least on the deed, is Miles Rainey Blanchard. Miles started calling himself Jumper after he bought the bar. He tinkers. Apparently really good with electronics. Credit card skimmers were his play for a while out in Newberry. He was putting them on gas station pumps. He showed up in Myrtle Beach about five years ago."

"Was he a serious man back in Newberry? Or is that a developing characteristic?" Hector couldn't be sure what prompted Jumper to shoot Nina after Hector agreed to his ransom. Murder was serious. The only thing that made sense was that Jumper realized Hector knew where they were. Which would be unfortunate. It would mean he was smart. But maybe there was a chance he wasn't naturally a killer and Nina's death was a fluke. Plain old panic on the part of Miles-turned-Jumper.

"He was serious," Michael said, confirming Hector's fear. "At least three fellas dead that were likely his doing. Could be one or two more."

"He has resources?"

"Seems to. Doesn't spend extravagantly. Stays mobile. He's not deeply leveraged into any of his enterprises so he simply leaves when things get heavy. My guy says there's a rumor he used to be a restaurant manager in Asheville, North Carolina but I can't confirm that. Solid Assistant Vice President of crime. Plenty capable but not C-suite. How'd he get the kid over a barrel?"

Hector got up and stepped onto the balcony, sliding the door closed behind him. Drugged or not, there was no reason to talk this kind of business in front of Morgan. Or Edison, for that matter. "Same way we did it, sounds like. He gave him an opportunity, then turned it sour. Apparently Jumper or Miles or whatever he calls himself deals out of his bar."

"Weight?"

"Morgan doesn't really know, but signs point to yes. He sent Morgan on a drug run to let him make a little cash, which he needed because we have him over our own barrel. Morgan drops off the package, brings back the money is how it was supposed to go. But Morgan got robbed on the way back with the cash and that put him into Jumper for ten thousand." Hector heard the familiar sounds of his brother working his espresso machine. "Michael, for Christ's sake, it's nearly ten o'clock."

"Yep, that's what it says right here on my coffee maker. Quarter to ten. A lot about that drug run doesn't add up. Why would Morgan be on the hook for the robbery? It could only be someone who knew the delivery was happening and that Morgan would be the guy with the cash at the end of it."

"I agree it's suspicious. Even by the standards of drug runs. Morgan of course doesn't have ten grand and, you know, he's a fucking genius obviously, so when I told him I had an interest in his father-in-law's land—"

"Which doesn't actually exist," Michael interjected. Ever since they were kids Michael couldn't resist an, *I told you so.*

"Well even if it did exist, his father-in-law would prefer to pass shredded glass kidney stones than give it to Morgan. Apparently he hates him."

"That's understandable."

"So, Morgan tried to consolidate his debt into a single payment stream by getting Jumper to kidnap his wife so his father-in-law would have to sign over the land, so Morgan could get out from under us and use the pittance I offered him for the deed to pay back Jumper. You follow all that?"

"How'd he get stabbed?"

"Some stupid shit with a local hick. Who cares?"

"Obviously you do if you're having Edison patch him up."

"I need him to live long enough to get his wife back now that the cops are involved and the bank is loosely associated with the whole thing. And I don't trust this Miles Jumper creep not to just shoot Morgan and his wife and disappear with his money back to Newberry, or some other nowheresville in western South Carolina. Clemson or Pickens. Or fucking Gaffney."

The espresso machine hissed on the other end of the line. "So what's the plan for tomorrow?"

"Morgan follows through with the money and his wife is turned loose, sent back to the bosom of her family. Unfortunately, Jumper double-crosses Morgan, shoots him in cold blood. Then Jumper disappears."

"He disappears?"

"As far as the police are concerned, he disappears," Hector said. "In reality, he takes a trip with me to the low country."

"Well, well, well," Michael said, the sound of a first sip coming through the line. "That's interesting to hear. You've been somewhat reluctant to take that kind of action lately, if you don't mind me saying so."

"I mind. It's not reticence, it's thoughtfulness. It's strategy. It's weighing a strong play that's quick against a smart play that requires patience."

"Yes, I'm familiar with your business philosophies of violent action. What tipped the scales toward the effort of getting him all the way out to the low country? As opposed to just him and Morgan shooting one another and it's all wrapped up on the ground for the cops to sort out."

"I liked Nina."

"It's personal."

"Of course it is. You know why?" Hector said, prompting his brother.

Michael demurred though. "No you do it. You do Dad better than I do. Plus I get sad whenever I try to imitate him. I like hearing you do him, though."

Hector cleared his throat and pitched his voice just so. "Because business is always personal. If your business isn't personal then you don't have a business. You're just an asshole with a job."

"Amen," Michael said. "May he rest in peace."

"May he rest in peace," Hector echoed.

"Call me in the morning. Let me know what I can do and so forth."

"Alright. Love you."

"Love you too."

Hector ended the call and watched the small white lines of froth tear their way into existence from the black void of the sea, like seams bursting open and spilling to a frayed mess along the shore. They had to get Jumper tomorrow. It was an appropriate name he had stolen for himself. He made some money, kept his overhead low, and jumped to a new place before the incidents of his own creation crashed down around him. Hector felt a momentary pang of envy at that freedom, but he quickly dismissed it. There was a certain appeal to that kind of flexibility, sure, but it was a low-impact, small stakes mentality and he was a builder, a creator. You had to put down roots to grow to any meaningful size. For someone like Jumper, though, Morgan's thirty grand plus whatever else he had squeezed from this town would be enough to compel him to leave behind the consequences of a double kidnapping and a murder. His kind of money would go pretty far in Gaffney. Not as far as it used to, but still.

•••

Tusk parked down the street from the Shaw and Cassidy residences. He radioed up to the patrol car. "This is Officer Knight, radioing car 54C. Over."

A voice crackled back a moment later. "This is Officer Benson Groves in car 54C. Go ahead, Knight. Over."

"I'm parked down the street from you." He flashed his headlights a couple times. "I'm going to do a walk-around on the Cassidy and Shaw places. Over."

"Okay," Groves radioed back. "You want a buddy or something? Over."

Tusk couldn't wait to make detective and never have to work alongside patrolmen again. "No, I don't need a buddy for the walk-around, Groves. What I need is for you to know I'm doing it, so you don't shoot me. Over."

"Why would I shoot you? Over."

"Because I'm an armed Black man walking around the properties you're monitoring in the middle of the night, Groves. Over."

"Don't be shitty, Knight. I'd shoot you no matter what color you were. I'm a good cop. Over."

"Well don't shoot me, is what I'm saying. Over."

"Not till you take back that shit you said about me shooting you because you're Black. Over."

"Groves, are you saying you won't agree not to shoot me until I accept that the shooting wouldn't be 'cause of the color of my skin? Over."

There was a pause while Groves presumably ran that back to himself to make sure it tracked. "Yeah, that's the tall and skinny of it," he said finally.

"Fine. I take back what I said. I'm sure it would be an equal opportunity shooting. A colorblind shooting, purely out of the goodness of your heart. Over."

"Thank you. I feel heard. Over."

Tusk clipped the radio to his belt and walked through the backyards of the neighbors, not entirely convinced Benson Groves wouldn't shoot him. Tusk wanted to approach the houses surreptitiously, the way someone with ill intent and a little ingenuity would. A cop sitting out front was a deterrent, but criminals did stupid shit all the time.

Tusk had to climb a low chain-link fence to get into the Cassidy's backyard. There was a gray-boarded treehouse near the fence in the back corner. He felt a pang of envy seeing the treehouse and imagining the Cassidys as children. He wondered what it would be like to have siblings. Built-in friends. Allies. He felt a broad and nebulous wish to have been a kid with them, here in this treehouse. To be connected to a childhood that still retained a physical location—weathered for sure—but complete and tangible, nestled in the branches, held by arms that kept growing.

Tusk was balanced on the top of the fence, holding the bottom of the treehouse, negotiating the quietest way to jump down when he heard something between a scream and a moan coming from the Shaw house. He froze, listening, trying to find the sound again amidst the hum of HVAC compressors, the low-level white noise of cars on the roads, and the leaves collectively generating their small tearing sounds against the breeze. He heard it again. A high-pitched moan, muffled, nearly a whimper. Could be some dog worrying about the man on the top of the fence, not committed to barking just yet. But it rankled a part of Tusk in a way he didn't like. He dropped from the fence top and sprinted across the Cassidy's backyard, getting the necessary speed to vault the fence on the far side by the Shaw house with one hand.

Tusk took all three porch steps at once and pulled out his flashlight, checking out the back door. It was open, pulled to the frame but unlatched. He heard the moan again, followed by a man's voice. He got on the radio.

"Groves. Has anyone come or gone since you've been on watch? Over." He spoke in a whisper then turned the volume down for Groves' reply.

"Three people left from the Cassidy residence. Over," Groves said.

"Was one of them Jug? Over."

"Knight." Groves sighed audibly into the radio. "Was one of them a jug? The fuck are you talking about? Why are you whispering? Over."

Okay, that one was my fault, Tusk thought to himself. "Who did you see leave? Over." he said.

"Three caucasian males, since you're so into like, racial stuff. And zero caucasian females, who I have been instructed to specifically look out for. All in their twenties to early thirties I'd say. They left in two cars from the Cassidy residence. A Toyota Previa minivan and an old Suzuki Sidekick. They have not returned. Over."

Tusk sorted it out in his head. Three males had to be JP, Dex, and Jug. "There's someone in the Shaw house," Tusk whispered into the radio. "The back door is open. I'm going in, come back me up. Over." Tusk heard Groves start moving immediately, the door to the cruiser opening.

"Copy that. Coming in the back. Over," Groves said.

Tusk drew his weapon and entered the house. The back door opened into the kitchen. He saw what looked like a pistol on the counter and trained his flashlight on it. A lockpick gun. He heard the male voice distinctly now that he was inside. It was coming from his left, which looked like the way to the bedrooms. He crossed the kitchen and stepped quietly down the hallway.

"He'll be back," the voice was saying, almost chanting. "He'll be back, he'll be back, he'll be back. And when he's back he'll find you here. Yep, yep, yep. He'll find you here and see the blood and he'll run over and I'll be here. I'll be here waiting. Waiting, waiting, waiting. I got time. Plenty of time."

Tusk looked into the bedroom. A small night light weakly lit the room. In the thin glow, Tusk saw a man with one arm wrapped tightly around an older woman, Jug's grandmother presumably. The man's hand was pressed firmly across her mouth limiting her to moans and whimpers. The man's other hand flipped a large hunting knife steadily between his fingers. He held the woman roughly, absently, the way a child grips a stuffed animal as they focus on some other task. The man bounced on his feet, jerking the woman this way and that, her feet not quite on the floor. The sounds she was making were a combination of pain and a struggle to breathe in the harsh hold of the man who Tusk could tell was higher than a giraffe in a hot air balloon.

Tusk heard the smallest sound behind him and turned to see Groves, weapon drawn, coming down the hall. Tusk gestured that he was entering the room. Groves nodded.

Tusk stepped through the doorway and shouted, "Drop the weapon! Drop the weapon! Hands up!"

The man looked up and Tusk saw his whole face for the first time. Bevel Sloot.

Bevel let go of the woman. Nana Jean is what Sailor had called her, Tusk remembered, as she fell in a heap on the floor and didn't move. Tusk shouted again, "Drop the weapon!"

Bevel put up one hand in a gesture of compliance. He crouched as though to place the knife gently on the floor. Instead, to Tusk's great surprise, he sprang up from his crouch and launched himself through the bedroom window. He went headfirst, arms to his sides, smashing through the glass and wooden grills with the top of his skull. For a moment, Tusk saw Bevel sailing through the night like a comet, shards of glass twinkling around him in the moonlight. Then he landed in the yard, scrambled to his feet, and took off running. Tusk took a quick moment to reflect on how much he hated meth heads, then climbed out the shattered window and went after him.

•••

JP and Jug had soon followed Dex out of the treehouse and also agreed to come. They took two cars. Sailor went over the fence, through the yard of the backdoor neighbor so the patrol car wouldn't see her, and JP came around the block and got her in Carrie's Sidekick, lurching along in jerks and starts, no good with a stick shift. He yielded the driver's seat to Sailor. Dex followed in the saggin' wagon. They would watch Jumper's in shifts, they decided, using the van to stretch out and get some sleep as they rotated being lookouts. They parked single file across the quiet intersection where Jumper's Bar and Grill occupied a corner lot. The small parking lot out front held five vehicles.

Dex and Jug took the van first, flattening the back seats and stretching out to doze for a couple hours while Sailor and JP staked out the bar from the Sidekick.

"I really am sorry about the call on the live stream," JP said. "It was just for a joke." He rolled down the window and lit a cigarette, exhaling his small fog into the night.

Sailor snorted. "It was certainly hilarious. Tell it again. Tell it again," she chanted. She remembered when they were kids, Dex coming inside in tears from the treehouse or the yard, hurt and angry and JP behind him a minute later always with that same excuse. *We were just wrestling.* Or, *We were just playing soldiers.* Always with a *just.* Sailor had come to think of his initials as standing for Justifying Permanently. Though his real name was Jules Patton Cassidy, which he had hated from the time he was old enough to speak according to their mother.

"It would have been funny if you'd come to the show and I'd had some bits prepared from the whole thing."

"Am I supposed to appreciate that you gambled with my privacy?"

JP fiddled with his cigarette. Sailor stared at him but he didn't respond. When she turned her attention back to Jumper's he said, "Not appreciate it, no. But if it had worked, and it was something funny I made out of our conversation and everyone was laughing and you were a part of the show, you'd have felt special. Probably. I thought it might cheer you up a little."

"Things like that are only funny if both people are playing along."

"Is that how you think you do it? With all your sarcastic little jibes in every conversation. You think the people you're talking to are playing along?"

Sailor knew he was being defensive, Justifying Permanently as always. There was some truth to what he said, though. She was self-aware enough to know she forced space into her interactions with people, to feel like she was controlling at least one side of the conversation. She wanted some base layer of protection and felt she was the best person to provide it. The protection, of course, was also from herself. A guard against discovering people disliked her—found her too weird, too gay, too Sailor.

"Why'd you want to tell me about Carrie's affair anyway?" JP said.

"I wanted to ask if you thought she was having one. And if you did, maybe we should do something. And maybe you'd know what that something was."

"Sailor, my life is a mess. Why would I know what to do?"

"Because getting cheated on is a mess. Having a revenge affair is a mess. No one wants dental surgery from the guy who it's his first day on the job. You want someone with experience."

Sailor studied the people going in and out of the bar as they spoke. Stooped men and women, little gray question mark people, went in and stayed in. So did most of the rangy and irritable looking younger men who stalked across the parking lot like the bar was one more thing in the world that owed them something and wouldn't pay up—the kind of day-labor guys Air Down There and Isaac always had to let go after a couple days for fighting with everyone and arguing over every job. The kind of guys they had to ban from the job sites and watch out for afterwards for a week or so until they moved on to the next conflict. Sailor saw one lurching around the parking lot with a hammer shoved through his belt, dangling at his waist. He opened the door and looked in then shut it and didn't go inside. Probably a good call, maybe he was managing to hang onto his job for the time-being. There was a younger crowd too. Guys who looked like they should be going to the clubs. These patrons went in and came out ten minutes later, got in their cars and drove off. These were the people coming just to score.

JP laughed. "You thought that as a fuck-up, I'd be able to advise on Carrie potentially fucking up?"

"I don't mean it like that. You just...you got sober. Or so we thought, anyway. Got out from under working for Dad. Started doing your own thing, actually making a go of it. You seemed like you knew how to bail water from a sinking ship. And you're my big brother. I mean, I didn't even know you had paid back a drug dealer and had your fingers broken and all that. I was just going off your self-styled career as a performer."

"Well, thanks I guess. I know you're still mad. But I really am sorry. I'm sorry."

"I don't know how you do it. The shows, I mean. Aside from stealing material from conversations with me, of course."

"A performance is, at its most basic, just being there. If you bring literally anything in addition to your presence, you're operating above the baseline."

"I don't know what that's supposed to mean."

"You're a performer doing a performance as soon as you're up on the stage, or in front of the camera. Bang. That's it. Soon as anyone's looking at you, you're performing. The people watching you expect an incident and are there to witness it. You, the incident, and the witnesses. That's it. Those three things are all you need. At their lowest, most savage level, the witnesses will accept a disaster as 'The Incident.' That's the bottom. That's someone in a home video getting whacked in the balls by a toddler, or a plane crash, or an above-ground pool breaking open, or you simply choking and forgetting your lines and melting down. Or you fall off the stage, maybe."

"I heard you fell off the stage last night."

"Yeah, well, there you go. You heard about it. The audience will accept it as the incident to which they bore witness. So there you are performing. There they are, watching. You start off holding nothing but disaster. You go from there."

Sailor watched a couple guys come from around the back of the bar, like maybe they came out an employee-only door. "Look at these two," she said. "I think they work there."

"The thing is, people kind of enjoy a good disaster," JP said as he leaned forward in his seat and peered out Sailor's driver-side window. "So what you want to do is, try to weigh your material against that. Like, is what I've written at least slightly more entertaining than the schadenfreude they'd experience if..." he trailed off, frozen, staring at the two men.

"Dudeface, you still in there?" Sailor said, punching his arm. The two men appeared to be bickering, though they couldn't hear them. One of them had a baseball cap pulled low and was maybe Hispanic. The other was a bare-headed white guy dressed in pajama pants and a hoodie, like he didn't leave the house much. They approached a Kia Soul parked along the curb. "What is it?" Sailor said to JP, punching him again. "Do you know them?"

JP blinked back to life and sat back, a stunned look still slapped across his face. "Yeah, I know the guy in the hoodie. He's dead. That's Randy the Random."

•••

Tusk was fast but he wasn't meth-energy-with-a-head-start fast. He radioed back to Groves as he charged across the lawns after Bevel, hurdling children's toys and juking birdbaths. "Pursuing suspect," he puffed as he ran. "Over."

"Backup and an ambulance are on the way. Victim appears uninjured. Rest of the house is clear. Over," Groves replied.

Tusk kept running. He caught glimpses of Bevel ahead of him as they crossed the yards. They moved down the block for a few houses, then Bevel turned and ran to the street behind the Cassidy's, up through a front yard, and disappeared behind a house. Tusk slowed to a stop in the street as Bevel vanished behind the house. There, parked in the road, was a familiar white van, ladders stacked on its roof, two orange, two silver. Bevel had run right past it. It was the same van he had chased behind Big Lock's.

Tusk leaned against the side of the van and tried to think. Procedure dictated that he continue to pursue Bevel on foot until he either caught him, or the inbound backup could find the chase and join in. Bevel had run straight for his van though. Probably partly just retracing the route he had taken to the Shaw house, but also keeping close in case he had shaken Tusk's pursuit. That's what he was doing. Run Tusk around some yards, over some fences, through some trees until he either lost him or gained enough space that he could circle back to his ride and drive out of here.

Tusk pulled the door handles of the van. Locked. He stood in the street trying to decide, painfully aware he was losing time. Bevel would have noticed he wasn't behind him anymore by now. He'd hide for a minute or two at least. Be sure he was safe. Then he'd start picking his way back to the van. At least that was what Tusk hoped he'd do. Follow procedure or his hunch?

Tusk debated, finally figuring he wasn't even officially on duty so he didn't owe anything to procedure right now, he was off the clock. *Fuck it*, he thought, *let's ball*. All around him were open front lawns. There was nothing close enough to hide him besides the van itself. He looked at the space under the van. He wasn't fitting under there. He put one foot on the back tire, grabbed the roof rack, and hoisted himself up onto the top of the van. He wedged himself into the space between the two stacks of ladders. In the dark, nestled in the roof gear like this, he was out of sight no matter which way Bevel approached. He reached down to the radio clipped to the front pocket of his sweatshirt and clicked it off so chatter wouldn't give away his hiding spot. He waited.

Anxiety hit Tusk about sixty seconds after he turned off the radio. This was stupid. What the hell was he thinking? His suspect was out there sprinting across Myrtle Beach's south end, getting farther and farther away and he was on top of a van in a working class neighborhood. It could belong to literally anyone on this street. Of course there were orange and silver ladders on it. Those were the two colors ladders came in. It's not like purple was an option. He was blowing it. He was absolutely blowing it. Just get down, start running in the direction you saw Bevel go. You can lie and say you lost him. Meth heads are fast and they never get tired. No one expects you to catch a meth head, he told himself.

Tusk didn't get up. He stayed on the van. He told the voice in his head to take it up with his gut instinct if it wanted to complain. He waited. And then, he heard it. The slap of shoes running down the street. Bevel was coming.

Tusk heard him skid to a stop at the van and the sound of keys. He didn't want to get up too soon and have Bevel run away on him. That would bring him right back to where he started. He would pop up and drop over the side by the driver's door once Bevel got inside the vehicle.

Bevel unlocked and opened the door. Tusk felt the van shift with Bevel's weight as the druggie hoisted himself inside. Time to perform. Tusk tried to sit up and only managed to get to his elbow. He tried again. He was stuck. His belt. He was wearing his duty rig over his jeans and something on it was caught under the ladder in front of him. Or maybe under the ladder behind him. He couldn't actually tell except to say he was stuck. Below him, Bevel started the engine and dropped it into drive. The van pulled away from the curb with some speed and didn't slow down. Tusk was along for the ride now.

The little voice in his head told him to take it up with his gut instinct if he wanted to complain.

•••

Dex's Saggin' Wagon peeled away from the curb and shot down the street past where Sailor sat in the Suzuki Sidekick, listening as JP stammered and shook his head trying to comprehend the man across the street in pajama bottoms and the hoodie. The man in question, Randy the Random JP called him, looked up from his argument with his companion as the van tore away and made a quick right hand turn out of sight, then turned back to his argument and resumed pressing his point as he slid into the driver's seat of the Kia Soul and started the engine. The man Randy the Random was arguing with removed his hat long enough to gesture some point to Randy with it while he smoothed back his dark hair, then he got in the passenger side.

"Where are they going?" JP wondered aloud at the same time his phone began to vibrate and Dex's name appeared on the screen. Sailor put the Sidekick into drive and started after the Kia Soul pulling out ahead of them. "Where are *you* going?" JP asked her.

"We're following them," Sailor said.

"We're what? No, don't do that. Follow them where? And do what? We need to call the cops," JP said.

"And tell them what? We saw two suspects in our sister's kidnapping but we don't know where they are now? We'll call the cops when we find out where they're going," Sailor said.

"What are you talking about? Randy's not a suspect, he was dead until just a minute ago. I mean—you know what I mean."

"The guy he's with makes him a suspect," Sailor said.

"Who's the guy he's with?"

Sailor had caught a good look at the guy's face when he took off his hat. She recognized him. It hit her like a punch. A second one. "He's the guy that did this," she said pointing to her black and purple face. "Now answer your phone and see what's going on with those two."

•••

Tusk was terrified but he was also freezing and to his surprise, freezing took precedent in his brain. The late November air poured over him ceaselessly at seventy miles per hour as the van tore through the night. He wanted to get on his radio or cell phone and call for help but that presented a buffet of problems to work through. Even if he managed to get his radio or phone out with one hand while holding on with the other, would anyone be able to hear him over the wind? Maybe at a stop light, but Bevel managed not to catch a single red light between the Cassidy's neighborhood and the highway. There was also the concern of Bevel hearing him as he called for help. Tusk might be able to get himself dislodged from the ladder—he was pretty sure it was his Taser that had snagged—and get the drop on Bevel if the twitchy fellow stopped the van and got out to investigate, but it was no guarantee. Besides, Bevel might not even stop. He might just stick his whole torso out the window while the van cruised along and see a man riding on the roof between his ladders. A single bullet fired straight up through the roof of the van would do him in.

Once the van got some speed on 501 though, Tusk's thoughts focused solely on how cold he was. The night had been only a little chilly, sweatshirt weather, before he was stuck on the roof of a van doing seventy. It was arctic as far as he was concerned, and his jeans and sweatshirt were no match for arctic. The only thing he could do for himself was hang on and wait. It wasn't going to be a short trip he could tell. Bevel had taken 501 to 31 to International Drive, headed northwest. Wherever they were going it was rural, likely isolated, and Tusk was pretty sure whoever was out there wasn't going to be inclined to invite him in to warm up.

Chapter 13

Jumper hunched at the small breakfast counter in Randy's double wide out in Dam Swamp, smoking and contemplating the glass of Sambuca in front of him. Puto busied himself by straightening up the living room and cleaning the kitchen. The television was off now, it was quiet. Óscar was outside watching the front, circling the trailer from time to time. They were in the middle of nowhere, in a place few people even knew existed, but a man could never be too careful. Especially since Randy was mostly an idiot.

It was Randy who gave him the idea of robbing his couriers though, so Jumper had to give him credit for at least one good idea. Randy came to him saying he was a buyer by proxy. Randy himself didn't know the word "proxy" but that was the general idea. Two other guys came in and bought weekend party coke for their friends. Randy was one of the friends. He knew Jumper had these guys doing runs for him sometimes and one of these guys, JP, was floating the idea of pretending to have been robbed of the cash on the run and well, hey, Randy just thought that information might be worth something to Jumper. Like, maybe it was worth an eight-ball or two?

"I thought you said these guys were your friends," Jumper had said to him.

"Friends, acquaintances. They're just some guys I know," Randy said. "So what do you think? I mean, that info must be worth something, right?"

It wasn't. JP was simply a loudmouth who couldn't help verbalizing every thought that came into his head. He wasn't organizing a robbery. It gave Jumper an idea though, of how to generate a debt without having to first make a loan. These local guys who bought from him, who wanted to wade waist-deep into the criminal life they saw in movies and heard about in songs, didn't have the power or backbone to shirk a debt once they were in over their heads. If they got robbed of Jumper's money, Jumper would hold them responsible for paying it back. And Randy gave Jumper a way to guarantee they got robbed without actually losing his cash.

"There is something you could do that would be worth a couple of eight-balls," Jumper told Randy.

"Yeah? What?" Randy asked, wary. He had obviously hoped he could just sell out his buddies without getting his hands dirty. Too late, of course. He was already waist-deep, Jumper pulled him under.

In retrospect, it was a mistake to involve Bevel. He was only there to add verisimilitude, but he couldn't stop himself from improvising. Randy would pull his car across the empty road, stopping Jug and Bevel—JP wasn't available that particular night—then perform a quick, unimpressive robbery. Stick a gun in Jug's face, grab the bag, drive away fast. That was it. But Bevel was worried to the point of being preoccupied that Jug would think he was a pussy if he didn't at least pretend to defend the money, so he pulled his own gun during the stickup. He claimed later he only meant to fire at Randy and miss on purpose, an improvisation Randy didn't appreciate being on the receiving end of. The second problem arose when Jug grabbed Bevel's gun, apparently wanting to prevent an escalation of violence. Bevel tried to wrestle it back with his finger on the trigger and it went off like four times, one of those times into Bevel's own leg. Randy hit the deck when the shots began and lay still until he heard a scream as Jug shoved the wounded Bevel out of his truck and tore out of there into the night.

They stopped including Bevel after that.

All in all, Jumper had made over two hundred thousand dollars with Randy. With an additional thirty grand coming from Morgan tomorrow, plus the money from the houses, the cocaine, the handful of credit card skimmers they put up on gas pumps around town, and the bar itself, Myrtle Beach had been a good score. It was time to consider moving along, now that he was going to have a pile of bodies. But with the bodies being Nina, Morgan, and Carrie, maybe it wouldn't matter. A love triangle that ended badly, like they always did.

Jug never resurfaced after that first robbery set up, but Jumper got his ten grand out of JP. It made sense he should be the one to pay for it. After all, it had been his idea.

•••

Hector was dozing. There was no way to actually sleep in a situation like this, his brain hummed along too quickly on plans and anticipation. Edison answered his phone out in the condo's living room.

"Yes," he heard Edison say. "That's quite the development, any idea what they're up to?" A pause while Edison listened to the caller. "There's a significant likelihood they'll call the police." Another pause. "What would the response time be? It's your area of expertise seeing how you work for them." A pause. "I'll huddle with him and call back. Just monitor the situation for now." Pause. "No, just you two." Pause. "No." Pause. "No. Same plan for the next ten minutes, just watch and we'll call back." Pause. "Thank you."

Edison was always so polite, Hector thought. He was a good employee, he moved the needle, got things done. He knew what the smartest people all knew, cordiality went a long way. He would knock on the door in a few seconds, after checking on his patient, Morgan. Hector got up off the bed where he was lying on top of the covers in his pants and shirt. He pictured Edison checking Morgan's pulse, counting beats, looking at his watch. Hector slipped his suit jacket back on and tightened his tie. There was Edison's knock.

"Open it," Hector said.

Edison opened the door and stood silhouetted against the lamp light from the room behind him. "Daniels and Maroney have been staking out the bar like you asked. They caught sight of a Suzuki Sidekick doing the same thing."

"You're kidding."

"Two of the other kids. The girl and the older boy." Edison gestured to the unconscious Morgan. "His in-laws."

"What on earth are they doing?"

"Might be they're doing the same as us, looking for Jumper. It's possible they figured out a connection between Jumper, their missing sister, and Morgan."

"The pothead and the podcaster?"

"He does more of a stand-up comedy thing with some modern livestream and video elements," Edison said. Hector gave him a look. "I have a wide range of tastes," Edison said. "Two men left the bar and the Sidekick followed them, so Maroney and Daniels followed the Sidekick. The whole caravan made its way out past Conway into an area Google Maps only describes as Dam Swamp. The two men the kids were following pulled up at a double-wide out there off an unnamed dirt road. There's a white van parked out front. Like the kind you might kidnap someone with. Daniels did a little recon. Says there's an armed fellow outside doing the laziest job of guarding a perimeter you've ever seen."

"Where are the kids?"

"They drove past the trailer when the other car pulled off. Maroney is out looking for them now. If the siblings think their sister is in that trailer—and she might be, along with Jumper—they're probably going to call the police," Edison said.

"That would throw a wrench into our finely laid plans, wouldn't it?" Hector said.

"Most definitely."

"How many men total?"

"Daniels thinks four to six possible. That includes the lazy perimeter guard. There is a possible additional player. Daniels thinks the two men might have also been followed by another man they spotted at the bar. An unknown. They'll keep us posted, naturally."

"Four to six guys with minimal discipline, lazy habits, and a false sense of security," Hector said. "What do you think? Can we swing that with me and you and the two off-dutys?"

Edison nodded brightly. "I'll get the gear bag out of the floor safe." He turned and stopped, saying over his shoulder, "What about him?"

"Bring him along," Hector said. "You never know. Maybe we'll need a human shield."

•••

Sailor picked her way through the woods with the night vision app JP had downloaded onto her phone. JP plodded along beside her with his own app. He was scared and unhappy with the plan, but he didn't want to let her go alone. Now that they were out here in the dark with two half-charged phones and her packing nothing but a couple of stun guns, she appreciated his reluctant accompaniment.

Dex had called and filled them in on his and Jug's sudden departure. Nana Jean was shaken to her core but she was okay. JP told him what they were up to and Dex made both of them turn on the location tracking on their phones.

They had followed Randy the Random and the other man, turning off their headlights once they got onto the unnamed dirt road. Sailor navigated by the twin red stars of the other car's taillights while JP frantically downloaded the night vision app for her saying, "Shit, shit, shit. This is so stupid. We're doing something so stupid." Finally, he got the app working. Sailor held the phone up and, now that she had a wider field of vision, put on a little more speed as they bumped along after the no-longer-dead Randy and the man who smashed in her face.

They watched Randy and the other man pull into the front yard of a double-wide trailer, set back off the dirt road, surrounded by forest. Sailor stopped on the road, fairly certain they were hidden by the dark and the foliage and the incessant chirp and chatter of swamp life. They watched on their green and black screens as the two men exited the Kia Soul. They were greeted outside by a third man.

"He's holding a gun," JP whispered. Randy and the other guy went inside the trailer, leaving the armed man outside. As the door opened, they glimpsed a giant sitting at a counter, then the door closed. "That was Jumper," JP said.

Sailor drove them farther down the road and pulled over at the edge of the forest.

"Okay, let's call the police," JP said.

"We need to know she's in there. We need to get closer. Peek in the windows. See if we can see her so when we call the police we know she's there," Sailor said.

"Remember when you said earlier that I've been through some shit and gotten myself straightened out and that's why you wanted my advice? Because I've had some experiences that have given me wisdom?"

"I don't recall using the word *wisdom*."

"Because I'm your big brother? Well as your big brother, I'm saying that going anywhere near that trailer with the armed fucking guard in front of it is a mistake."

Sailor had listened and nodded. "You stay here then," she said, and got out of the car. JP had followed though because, she figured, at the end of the day he was a decent enough big brother.

They picked their way through the woods and approached the double-wide from behind. The guy with the gun must have still been in front, Sailor didn't see him anywhere. "The windows are too high. You're going to have give me a boost," she whispered to JP.

"This is insane," JP whispered back.

"This is family," Sailor said.

"Same difference," JP said, but again he followed her, out of the safe cover of the tree line.

JP made basket-hands, interlacing his fingers, and Sailor used them to step onto his shoulders and look through the first window. "It's the living room and kitchen," she whispered down to JP.

"Fucking fascinating, do you see our goddamn sister or not?" he hissed back.

She stepped backwards into his hands and then to the ground. "No Carrie," she whispered. "The giant is sitting at the breakfast bar."

"Jumper."

"You're lucky he only got your fingers. He's like a bodybuilder."

"And a body breaker," JP said. "Which in no way felt lucky."

"There's three other guys," Sailor said as they slid along the trailer toward the windows at the far end. "The two we followed and a skinny little bean pole." They checked the other windows on the back side of the trailer. They looked into two empty bedrooms. "There's one more room on the front," Sailor whispered. JP shook his head and pointed back to the cover of the tree line around the trailer. He went into the darkness and Sailor followed him. He got his phone and night vision app back out. Quietly, they moved around the trailer so they could see the front from the woods. JP pointed to the green figure on his phone screen, leaning against a car hood.

"The guy with the gun is still in the front of the place," JP said. "We'll have to like, lure him away I guess."

"I don't want to be a lure. You know what happens to lures? Things try to eat them."

"I'm not leaving here without—" Sailor stopped as headlights washed out the screen. A white van pulled off the dirt road and into the parking area in front of the trailer. The headlights cut out. They both looked as the screen adjusted and focused again. A guy climbed out of the van, crossed to the trailer door and stopped with a yelp as the guard slid up, unseen, beside him and grabbed his hair, settling his gun under the man's chin.

"Bevel," JP whispered to Sailor.

"Shit," the man yelled. "Óscar. Shit man. You scared the hell out of me. You want to take it easy with the gun, man? There's no need— ow, OW, shit, okay, okay, I'm walking. I was going in the house anyway. That's where I was headed before you—" the trailer door opened, swallowing the two men and the one-sided conversation.

Sailor looked at JP in the dark. "Fast as we can," Sailor said, and the two of them ran out of the woods to the front of the trailer.

•••

Tusk dropped down off the roof of the van as quietly as he could. He opened the driver-side door with shaking hands and climbed inside. He slumped down so his head was hidden by the dashboard and steering wheel. There was residual warmth in the small front seat. He sat shivering with his arms across his chest, hand tucked into his armpits. He had heard Bevel encounter whomever had been out front and raised his head in time to see that person escorting Bevel inside at gunpoint, urging him along via a fistful of his greasy hair.

Tusk fished his cell phone out of his pocket and called the station. He gave his code to Kiya, who was answering the officer line that night, and laid out the situation.

"The suspect fled in a white van, license plate KLWJ-21. I pursued and lost contact with officer Groves in the pursuit. I need to drop you a pin. I don't know where I am. Somewhere north of Conway I think," Tusk said.

"Is the GPS in your vehicle not working?" Kiya asked. "Or the radio for that matter?"

"I'm not in my vehicle," Tusk said.

"How were you able to pursue the van from downtown Myrtle Beach to somewhere north of Conway without a vehicle, Officer Knight?" Kiya said with mild impatience.

"I was able to climb onto the suspect's vehicle as he fled. I rode out here on the roof." Tusk decided the part about his belt getting stuck wasn't an important detail.

There was a long pause on the other end of the phone. "I know that's bullshit," Kiya said.

"Negative," Tusk said, irritably. "I'll sign an affidavit. Did you get the pin I just sent you? I need backup sent to this location. Suspect is here with possible accomplices who are armed. I have a visual on that."

"You rode all the way out there on the roof of a suspect's van?" Kiya said.

Tusk noted from the tone of her voice that she believed him. She was impressed. He was freezing, tired, and had nothing but dead ends and failures the last forty-eight hours and found, suddenly, that he needed Kiya's thin semi-skeptical admiration desperately, the way he needed water for a hangover, or aloe for a burn.

"On the roof of the van with the suspect driving?" Kiya continued.

"Goddamn right I did," Tusk said, rising to the occasion. "Now I'm freezing my ass off, alone at a trailer in the woods, and I'd love some support."

Kiya laughed and hooted in excitement. "Well shit, cowboy! How many desperados you want me to send?"

•••

Sailor stood on her brother's shoulders, angling her head to look through the small gap in the bottom of the blinds. A bed was pushed under the window. There was a floor lamp and not much else in the room. She could see the closed door and a small closet set into the wall. Otherwise, the room was empty. She felt sick. How could Carrie not be here? She had been certain. The fake dead guy, the man who had knocked her out when Nina was kidnapped, the fact they were coming out of Jumper's—these things had added up to finding Carrie. The little radar inside her that let her know things had pinged. Now she was in the woods in the middle of the night, peeping in windows and her sister was still out there somewhere. Or worse, she was—

Then, Sailor saw it. A small movement at the top corner of the bed. A patch of brown hair peeking out from behind the pillow. Carrie's hair color.

"I see her. I think I see her," Sailor hissed down to JP

"Seriously?" JP said.

"We're in the swamp avoiding men with guns looking for our kidnapped sister, you lump of mud, of course seriously."

"So get down so we can go call the police."

That's what Sailor told him, wasn't it, she thought. Locate Carrie, call the police. But now that she could see her, now that she was so close, she just couldn't hop down and run back through the woods, leaving her in this shitty swamp trailer.

"Hang on, let's make sure it's her," Sailor said, pawing at the window screen, trying to remove it.

"Are you insane? Stop that, someone'll hear," JP said. "Of course it's her. Who else would it be?"

"I don't know. Nina maybe? They could have kidnapped anyone," Sailor said, trying to buy some time on JP's shoulders. The screen came loose with a little finagling the way all screens are desperate to do from the moment they're installed. Sailor flung it away and pushed at the window. Incredibly, it was unlocked. It slid upwards.

"The police like hearing about anyone who's been kidnapped. Just get down before I pull you down."

Sailor opened the window. She raised the blinds as quietly as she could and whispered, "Carrie!" as loud as she dared. The small brown patch of hair turned at the sound. "Carrie!" Sailor whispered again. "It's Sailor."

"Sailor?" the small brown patch replied.

"It's her!" Sailor said to JP, pulling her head out of the window. She stuck it back inside.

"Yeah, it's me," Sailor said. "Are you okay?"

"No. I mean yes, but obviously no. What are you doing here?"

"Rescuing you."

"Sailor, go call the police. They shot Nina, they'll shoot you."

"JP is with me."

"They'll definitely shoot him. Then they'll shoot you twice for bringing him along and making them listen to him."

"What's she saying?" JP said from under Sailor's feet.

"She's glad you're here too," Sailor whispered back.

"Sailor, listen," Carrie said. "Go call the cops. These people are—" There was a crash and a thump from the other end of the double-wide. Someone screamed. There was more crashing and the trailer shook.

Outside, the front door of the trailer was jerked open and a trapezoidal light, as though from a refrigerator in a dark kitchen, spilled out into the night about twenty feet from where Sailor stood on top of JP.

•••

Jumper heard the van door slam and knew it was Bevel even before he heard his jagged, whining voice trying to negotiate with Óscar. Bevel simultaneously could not adhere to the requirements of belonging to a group of people and also couldn't function without the group, couldn't stay away. You would ask him to do something, he would fail or refuse to do it because he wanted to do something else, then he would vanish in anger or under threat. A contrariness ran through him. He always needed to take his own action whether there was any real reason to or not. Like when he pulled the gun during Randy's first staged robbery. His only job had been to sit quietly and get robbed, then act worried about having been robbed on the way home. It was very little work. But because he was asked to do it, he simply had to do something else instead. He only got himself shot, so there was no real loss on Jumper's side, but it was indicative of Bevel as a criminal partner. Jumper would have gotten rid of him earlier except he was expendable and Jumper had tasks for expendable people. Today though, peeling off in the middle of a kidnapping when the only thing he had to do was follow Jumper and Puto from one place to another—that was the final sign that sooner or later, Bevel's way of zagging when anyone smarter than a donut would zig was going to have consequences that would impact the rest of them.

Randy and Ángel were back. Jumper had sent them both to the bar. He wanted Ángel to work his shift for the purposes of an alibi should they need them, and Randy he just wanted out of the trailer because his anxiety over the kidnappee was getting on his nerves. He made him drive Ángel. Ángel was on the couch now, looking at his phone. Randy was next to him, back on his PlayStation doing something in space when Bevel arrived. They all heard him wheedling outside with Óscar.

The door opened. Bevel came indignantly into the room, Óscar holding a gun under his chin and gripping him by his hair. Puto cleared away the ashtray Jumper had been using and replaced it with a clean one. He topped up his Sambuca.

Randy paused his game, dropping the trailer into quiet. Everyone watched Bevel and Jumper. Bevel immediately started jabbering excuses.

"Jumper, she fell in and I was just scared you'd think it was my fault. She ain't had no water or nothing to eat. She was just dizzy probably. So I just thought I'd get out of there and give you some time to calm down is all," Bevel said.

"Some time to calm down," Jumper repeated, lighting a cigarette. "And where have you been since?"

"You didn't say you needed me out here right away, Jumper, or I'd have come sooner. I thought, you know, it'd be alright if I just come out here at some point tonight, which I done. Here I am. Van's outside. No problems."

Óscar still had Bevel by the hair. The gun remained under his chin. Jumper said, "Where'd you go? While you waited for me to calm down some."

"I had to check on my momma. She's sick. You know? And she needed to see me. So I had to go check on her and take care of her some."

Jumper put on a tone of grave concern. "Your mother's sick? Bevel, I had no idea. And you were caring for her?"

"Yeah, yeah," Bevel said. "I had to bring her some soup and some medicine and blankets and change her sheets and get her some water and crackers for the soup."

Jumper put down his cigarette in the ashtray and stood, coming around the counter. He waved Óscar away from Bevel, who stood up straight finally. He looked uncertainly at Jumper, who said, "I apologize for the way you were greeted just now." Bevel's face relaxed. Jumper swung his meaty left fist and connected right under Bevel's eye, knocking him sideways into the front wall of the trailer. "It should have been something more like that," Jumper said.

He stayed right on Bevel, another left, two quick rights and Bevel hit the floor. Jumper knelt on his chest. You can't waver fighting a meth head, he knew. They're too wired, they have stores of inhuman energy. If you leave space in the assault, they'll either get the better of you or get away entirely. Even now, after those shots to the head, Bevel was still thrashing a bit. Jumper knelt on Bevel until his weight began affecting the scrawny man's ability to breathe. Bevel moved his arms away from his face to try and shove Jumper off of him. Jumper brought his fist down again, a carefully targeted shot, and shattered Bevel's nose. Most of the fight went out of Bevel then. Jumper hoisted the bloody man to his feet, gripping him in a near-strangulation headlock. He yanked open the door to the double-wide and began dragging Bevel outside behind him when he remembered himself. He shuffled back a few feet and faced Óscar.

"Could I borrow your gun?" he said to Óscar. "I don't want to have to fumble through my jacket." Óscar handed over his pistol. "Thanks," Jumper said. Ángel was back on his phone, unperturbed. Randy was ashen, staring at the floor. "Randy," Jumper said. Randy didn't look up. "Randall!" Jumper shouted. Randy looked up, his eyes going from Jumper to the top of Bevel's head tucked under Jumper's arm like a football, the man's body limply trying to hold its footing behind him. "If you'll help Puto find some cleaning supplies—bleach, carpet scrub, what-have you—I'll clean this up when I'm finished," Jumper said. He pointed with the gun at the smears of blood that crossed from the plastic kitchen tile to the thin carpet of the living area. More was dripping from Bevel's nose onto the carpet as Jumper spoke.

"I don't...I don't have...anything like that," Randy said.

Jumper gave him a look. "That's disgusting, Randy. That's how you get bugs. And," he gestured again with the gun, "blood stains, of course."

With that, Jumper turned and dragged Bevel out into the night.

•••

Tusk hung up with Kiya. He slipped his phone back into his pocket and raised his head to peek over the dashboard at the trailer into which Bevel had been taken. He was thinking how he would need to find a place to lay low until backup arrived, when movement on his left caught his eye. Two people, one standing on the other's shoulders, were pressed against the front of the trailer. The one on top seemed to be leaning into an open window. The one on the bottom was facing him and was definitely JP Cassidy. Which meant the one on top was more than likely Sailor Cassidy. Also more than likely, were their odds of getting themselves killed.

You have to be absolutely shitting me, Tusk thought as he quietly opened the van door and slipped back out into the chilly swamp air. How had the two of them found this place and gotten out here? Presumably not on the top of a moving vehicle, he figured.

Tusk was creeping around the back of a car parked near where the siblings were doing their circus act, being quiet, practicing situational awareness, unsure if there was another guard outside, when he heard a ruckus start up in the trailer. The door suddenly flew open, yanked inward. Framed in the doorway's rectangle of light was a behemoth. A man far too large to be considered with calm rationale after appearing with such force.

Tusk had never laid eyes on the man before but he was certain, beyond all doubt, that he was finally looking at Jumper.

•••

The trailer shook, there was a crash and a scream and the front door was pulled open. JP grabbed Sailor by the cuffs of her jeans, balling the fabric in his fists, and with a strength he did not own, rented from the panic-laced adrenaline spurting out of some buried gland, he lifted her from his shoulders up into the air through the window. Sailor didn't resist, her own panicked clawing at the bed covers helping the effort as JP lifted. Her torso made it through the narrow space. Once she was part way in, JP was able to turn and help shove her the rest of the way, pushing her feet until she was safely out of sight.

JP turned once his sister was safe—well, not *safe*, but safer than he was anyway—and saw someone breach the plane of the doorway gun first. He knew he would be seen and shot in the next moments. Before that could happen, though, he was yanked bodily off his feet and slammed to the ground behind a car. The wind was knocked out of him and he hit his head. From the ground, he saw up the length of the arm attached to the hand pressed over his mouth. At the top of the arm was Tusk.

Tusk held a finger to his lips and JP nodded. They pressed themselves against the side of the car and heard footfalls coming down the three wooden steps at the front door. The footfalls found the ground and came their way, an additional set of feet making scrabbling sounds. Jumper passed under the open window Sailor had gone through and past the car. He was moving quickly, and didn't see Tusk or JP in the dark as he went by. After two more strides, they were at his back, watching Bevel's dopey legs stagger along, trying to keep up as Jumper dragged him by the head.

JP peeked through the car's windows back toward the trailer. The front door was still open. He turned to Tusk, "Where did you come from?"

"I'm trying to catch criminals and find your sister," Tusk hissed. "Where did you come from?"

"I'm trying to avoid criminals and find my sister," JP said. "She's in there, by the way." He gestured at the window. "Both of them, actually."

"I saw. You doubled the number of Cassidy women trapped in that house."

"Well what was I supposed to do?"

"Stay home and let the police handle it."

"Well that's...valid," JP said. "I can't argue with someone who's going to throw logic in my face."

"I bet you'll try."

JP had actually been trying to think of a good argument for why they should be out there in the woods—something better than *my little sister bullied me into it*—but now that Tusk had goaded him he wanted to be contrarian. "I would but— Shit, you got me in a box here. Look, the point is you're here now. You're the police. It'll be fine. It's all working out."

The screaming erupted then, first from behind the trailer, then from inside it.

Chapter 14

Jumper dragged Bevel around back of Randy's trailer, humming quietly to himself. He did not generally take pleasure in killing people. He had no particular feelings about it to be honest, it was just housekeeping. Maintaining order. General cleanliness. The ashtrays simply had to be emptied from time to time, to do otherwise was messy and gross and bad for business. This time, though, there was a little spring in his step. He hated Bevel.

He felt good about the beating he had laid on the man. Solid contact was made on each strike. Jumper could feel the impact in Bevel's limp countenance as he pulled him along by the head, his firm grip around his neck slightly limiting air supply and blood flow, ensuring a meek and docile victim. It was too dark to see properly around the back of the trailer. Jumper clicked on the light mounted to Óscar's pistol and tossed Bevel out into the circle of light it threw at the base of two trees, where the small lot ended and the woods began again in earnest.

Bevel flopped to the ground. He tried to achieve hands and knees but couldn't manage, and fell over onto his side. He put up a hand, poor defense regardless of what Jumper might rain down, but utterly meaningless against a bullet.

"So long, Bevel," Jumper said. "It was absolutely not nice knowing you."

Before he could pull the trigger, a bush to his right seemed to come alive with movement and a scream. Jumper got the light up just in time for it to flash off the hammer that swung down and took apart his jaw.

•••

Carrie watched her sister come pouring through the window with a mixture of relief and horror. On the one hand, she had never been so happy to see someone as she was to see Sailor right then. For two days, Carrie had felt utterly isolated and hopeless and now here was her family, doing the impossible, somehow finding her. On the other hand, now they were both in this room surrounded by armed men.

Sailor rolled off the bed and hit the floor with a thump. Carrie flinched, hoping the sound would get attributed to whatever was going on outside, where she heard someone descending the front steps and passing beneath the window. After the close call with the giant boss silently waiting in the room with her, Carrie had been too scared and unsure to attempt anything. Her hands were still only bound in appearance, she could free them pretty easily, but what was she supposed to do with that freedom? There was a guard outside. She heard him singing softly as he walked around the house. And there was utter silence from inside until only a little while ago, when the video game sounds came back. She thought they might give her some sound cover to make a move, but while she was working up the nerve a van pulled up outside.

Then Sailor appeared at the window. Then she came through it. Carrie saw her sister's lovely face, black and purple and swollen, staring at her.

"What happened to you?" Carrie said in a whisper. "Are you okay?"

Sailor stifled a laugh and threw her arms around Carrie's neck. "Am I okay?" she repeated. "You're asking if I'm okay while you're tied to a bed in this shit-shack?" She let go and looked at Carrie. "Yeah, I'm okay now."

There was a scream outside. They both looked to the open window, frozen, but nothing came in. Carrie took her eyes off the window, meeting Sailor's gaze again and saw, behind her sister in the doorway, that they were no longer alone in the room. There was a man in the doorway, Ángel, though she didn't know his name. He was watching them, a thoughtful expression on his face.

"Ahora hay dos," he said, with a tone of mild wonder. Then he crossed the room in two quick strides and grabbed Sailor around the throat, jerking her up against the wall.

Carrie watched him holding her sister against the paneling, his back to her. He studied Sailor for a moment, the same befuddled curiosity in the tilt of his head as he took in her bruises.

"La mujer del gato infernal," the man said.

Carrie's Spanish was decent but she couldn't concentrate on translating as she slipped her hands from their rope and pulled Jug's Buck 110 from the waistband of her jeans. Sailor made gurgling sounds against the wall. Her feet were off the floor, all of her weight hanging from her throat where the man had her pinned. Carrie opened the blade of the knife and sliced through the rope around her neck. Ángel pulled a handgun from the waistband of his pants and held it up to Sailor's red, struggling face, saying something in Spanish that, again, Carrie didn't have the mental bandwidth to translate. He pressed the barrel of the gun to Sailor's forehead. Carrie pulled her neck free from the rope and stood. Holding Jug's knife with two hands, she raised it above her head and brought it down with everything she had left in the tank, burying the blade in Ángel's back up to the hilt.

He shrieked, dropping Sailor as the muscles in his back contracted and pulled his elbows backward, his arms out to his sides like he was frozen in the middle of the chicken dance. He turned and focused on Carrie. She could see the rage in him overtaking the pain as he managed to reach out for her. Behind him, coughing and choking still, Sailor got to her feet, pulled out one of the stun guns she was packing, and fired it against Ángel's neck. He seized and shook on his feet for a moment before pitching forward face-first into the wall.

There was the sound of running down the hall as another man came sprinting toward the bedroom. Sailor threw herself against the door, slamming it shut. She managed to flip the privacy lock just as the man hit the door. Carrie heard the repeated banging of him throwing his shoulder against the hollow door, still working the knob with one hand. She put both hands against the door and leaned into it, adding her weight to Sailor's in holding it closed. Sailor holstered the spent stun gun, pulled out her second one, and placed it against the knob, which was jerking back and forth as the person on the other side tried to force it to turn. Sailor sparked it. There was a soft thump from the other side of the door, the banging stopped.

"The window," Carrie said.

"You first," Sailor said.

Carrie poked her head out the window and felt her forehead bang against something hard and living. She watched JP clutch his nose where she had just headbutted him. He toppled backwards into the dark yelling, "Shit." Then she heard him hit the ground and shout, "Fuck."

"Oh JP! I'm sorry," she said. Carrie looked down to see what JP had been standing on to be at window-level. Tusk looked back up at her.

"I'm really sorry about how things ended the other day," he said.

Then he turned and fired three shots into the open front door of the trailer.

•••

Hector switched the phone to the car's speaker system and said, "Go ahead. Tell us what you see." Edison was driving. Morgan was slumped over in the back seat, still unconscious.

"Jumper dragged someone outside a few minutes ago and hauled them around to the edge of the woods," Daniels said. "Maroney had to run down the road to keep them in view. He didn't have the greatest angle on 'em, but says it looked like Jumper was setting up to take the guy out execution style, then Jumper got jumped."

"Sorry, did you say Jumper got jumped?" Hector said. "Someone jumped him? In the woods?"

"Craziest shit I ever saw," they heard Maroney say in the background, Daniels's mic picking up the commentary.

"Best guess: It's the unknown third party we saw. Still no idea who that guy is," Daniels said.

"Hit him in the face with a fucking hammer, it looked like," they heard Maroney's distant voice say. "Just...*pwahh*! Right in the mouth. I mean, goddamn."

"What happened to the dead man dragging?" Hector said.

"Scrambled. Darted off into the woods somewhere's my guess, with a fresh load in his drawers and a renewed faith in Christ."

"Any idea who it was?"

There was a slight pause before Daniels said, "Can't confirm, but I think it might have been Bevel. My cousin."

Hector muted the phone and said to Edison, "Remind me how badly the cousin compromises Daniels's ability to follow instructions."

"I believe he mostly hates his cousin," Edison said. "Like everyone else."

"Still, it's family," Hector mused. "I suppose I could just ask him." He unmuted the line. "What's your situation now, Daniels, given your cousin's involvement here? You need the night off?"

"No sir," Daniels said. "There's still some hope a gator gets him in the swamp."

Hector looked at Edison who shrugged. "Alright, where are you two now?" Hector asked.

"Across the road, within sight through the binoculars. The brother or sister, one of 'em, went through the window of the trailer when Jumper came out. And there's a cop here. He's called for backup. I'm actually being texted to come back on duty and roll out here."

"How'd the cop get there?"

"Dispatch's message says he rode out here on the roof of a suspect's van," Daniels said.

"Hell yeah! That's some cowboy shit right there," Maroney's thin voice chimed in.

"It's fucking stupid, is what it is," Daniels said back to him.

"Just 'cause you don't like Knight. You saw him, same as I did, come off the roof after that van pulled up. Dude's a fucking berserker, man. That's what policing's about. Hanging onto the roof of cars, jumping out of planes and into boats and shit."

"None of that is what policing is about. Boats?"

"While I appreciate your rights as Americans and cops to be dumbshits," Hector said. "Can you tune back into the situation at hand? The one I'm paying you to deal with."

"Right, sorry. And Maroney's a *former* cop, just to be clear."

"Dick," Maroney said.

"Sir, can I make a suggestion?" Daniels said.

"Think carefully before you do," Hector said, trying not to lose his cool.

"I'm pretty sure Jumper's still lying back there behind the trailer with half his face smashed in. The cop is in a fire fight with some goon inside the trailer. The siblings are— I don't know, one of them's rolling around on the ground with a broken nose or something. While this is going on, Maroney and I can slip back there and grab Jumper. Meet you up the road, hand him off along with Maroney, I come back to support my fellow police officer. Bing, bang, boom."

Hector muted the line again and said to Edison, "You see drawbacks?"

"No. That's the play."

"The money's still in that Suzuki."

"We don't know where, exactly, the car is," Edison said. "Police are inbound. You can definitely have Jumper or maybe have the money. I don't see a scenario where you get both and I see long odds on the money."

"Okay, do it," Hector said, unmuting the line. "Is your colleague and those kids going to make it out of that fire fight, just out of curiosity?"

"The hammer guy is creeping around the side of the trailer, coming in a window behind the goon in the doorway," Daniels said. "Looks like it's going to sort itself out."

•••

Tusk was trying to apologize to Carrie when he saw movement out of the corner of his eye and went into motion out of Pavlovian reflex, like he was taught. He clocked the gun in the man's hands and drew his own, firing into the doorway then stepping back behind the fender of the parked car, where JP was on his hands and knees, clearing his bloody nose on the ground.

Tusk looked over the hood of the car. From where he was crouched, he could see into the front door at a slight angle. The front door itself was opened inward and appeared to be moving slightly. *Like someone is hiding behind it, reloading,* Tusk thought. He took a steady breath, then another, and got into position—two-handed grip braced on the car hood, aim locked on the sliver of space in the doorway where the shooter was most likely to appear. Another breath. He waited.

•••

Sailor grabbed Carrie and yanked her inside when she heard the shots. They rolled off the bed and hit the floor next to the man Sailor had last seen from the ground, looming over her before unloading a jackhammer shot down onto her face. The man was conscious but lethargic. Sailor assumed it was the combination stabbing, electrocution, and blow to the head when he fell into the wall. Sailor felt something hard underneath her and looked down. It was her Hellcat, fallen from Ángel's hand when Carrie stabbed him. She picked it up and checked the clip, slid it back into place. Checked the chamber. Good. Safety off.

The man on the floor moaned and moved. Sailor gripped the knife handle jutting from his back and pressed the barrel of her Hellcat against his eyeball. "Pendejo," she said. "Acuéstate o te dispararé en la polla y te dejaré vivo." The man nodded.

Sailor stood.

"What are you doing?" Carrie asked. "What did you say about his dick?"

"I told him to stay still, or I'd shoot his dick off and leave him alive. Grab that knife handle and joystick the shit out of it if he tries anything," Sailor said.

"Where are you going?"

"We are getting the hell out of here," Sailor said. "We're not dying in this shitbox. The carpet is disgusting, there's a hole in the wall from this asshole's face, and, and, and, it smells like boy."

Carrie gave her a look. "Okay, have you been to your own apartment recently?"

"I bought a scented candle!" Sailor snapped. Carrie raised an eyebrow. "I planned to, anyway. It's on my list. I'm going to get one." She flipped the privacy lock and opened the bedroom door, leading with the Hellcat.

The hallway was empty. A stripped-down symphonic score played on a loop from the living room. Sailor edged quietly down the hall. Outside a closed door, she heard hushed voices.

"...doesn't matter now. Just stay down and be quiet."

"The cops are going to come."

"Would you rather be dead? Shut the fuck up and stay down. The walls of this thing are vinyl and foam. Bullet'll come through like it's paper and..."

Sailor guessed it was a bathroom and that at least one of the occupants was the guy who had tried to shoulder his way into the bedroom. She took another step toward the living room. She could see the TV now, a video game paused on the screen, the looping score playing over a menu of game choices. She stopped. At the far end of the trailer, a man with a conical head like a bullet, gripping a hammer, was coming through the living room window with the concentration and intensity of a panther. The man's eyes were locked on something just out of Sailor's view. Something just beyond the TV. She leaned forward slowly, not wanting to draw the bullet-headed man's attention.

There was a second man, standing behind the open front door. He had his eye pressed to the crack at the hinge, the small space between the door and the door frame. This man was also deep in concentration, leveling a handgun to shoot through the door at something he was sighting through the crack. Sailor realized the *something* was a *someone*, and that it must be Tusk. The man behind the door did not hear the bullet-headed man, who was now through the window. Who was raising the hammer with both hands. Who was bringing the hammer down into his head.

Sailor wished she had closed her eyes for the impact. She heard the muffled thud as the hammer connected and experienced a startlingly visceral sympathy timed to the blow. The man fell into the living room and as his gun hand, followed by his head, passed the edge of the door and into view from the outside, two gunshots rang out, at least one of which connected with the man's head, finishing off anything that was left of him after the hammer strike.

The man with the hammer jumped at the sound of the gunshots and pressed himself against the wall. Sailor stepped backwards down the hallway. She passed the bathroom again.

"...it's my gun, I'll be the one to hold it, thank you very much. You just try not to piss yourself again."

"It's water from when I jumped into the bathtub."

"I'm in the same tub. It's bone dry. Except for your piss which..."

Sailor stepped back into the bedroom and gently closed the door. She watched the hall as she closed it. The hammer man's shadow was moving slowly toward the hallway.

"Well?" Carrie asked.

"We can go now. The window. Tell Tusk he got him. And um," she looked over her shoulder at the door. "We should hurry."

Carrie called out the window to Tusk before popping her head out and risking it getting blown off. While she did that, Sailor studied the man on the floor. The one who had hit her. The one who had kidnapped Nina. Nina, who was now dead. The hammer blow to the head of the man in the living room flashed grimly through her mind with the attendant stomach lurch. She leaned over the man on the floor with the gun barrel back in his eye and said, "Shhhhh," then yanked the knife out of his back. The man squeaked a little. Sailor placed the knife on the floor within the man's reach.

"Hay un hombre por ahí con un martillo al que no le agradas ni tú ni tus amigos. Él viene hacia aquí," she said quietly. She tapped the knife for him to see.

"Por qué?"

"Me dejaste vivo. Te dejo con vida," she said, then stood, slipped the Hellcat into her waistband, and stuck her feet through the window after her sister.

Sailor threw her arms around Carrie again once they were out. Tusk still had his gun out, covering the window and the door. "Where's your car?" he said.

"It's down the road," Sailor said.

"Start running. I'll follow."

Sailor took Carrie's hand and they ran, JP alongside them. They darted around the cars and vans in front of the trailer until they came to the dirt road where they turned right and sprinted. As they ran, Sailor heard gun fire back at the trailer. She turned and saw Tusk was behind them. He waved for them all to keep going.

They got to the Sidekick and piled in, Sailor driving and Carrie up front. Tusk and JP climbed in the back. Dawn was slow-rinsing the night away, birdsong and soft light rose in the dew. Sailor started the car and peeled out onto the dirt road, pressing the pedal down. They rocketed along, the tires kicking up dust, the sun rising. Sailor realized she was still holding Carrie's hand. She looked down at their joined palms then up at her sister. Carrie smiled and laughed. Sailor laughed. She laughed and screamed, and Carrie screamed too.

Sailor said, "Wait, wait, wait. I was saving this," she hit the CD player. Neil Diamond's voice burst through the speakers already mid-song, singing, "...*got no right, no, no you don't / Ah, to be so exciting*."

Sailor and Carrie screamed again and sang along.

She got the way to move me, Cherry

(She got the way to groove me)

Cherry, baby!

In the rearview mirror, Sailor saw Tusk shoot JP a look. JP just shook his head and rubbed his face, smiling. Tusk looked out the back windshield one more time, then leaned back in the seat and took a huge breath, closing his eyes.

Up front, Sailor and Carrie raised their fists and banged on the ceiling as they sang, "*Girl, we do whatever we want to!*"

•••

Jug rode in the way-back of the Saggin' Wagon with his Nana Jean. He and Dex had gotten back to the house as the additional police arrived. He was absolutely wracked with guilt. He had left her again, disappointed her again, after being back in her life fewer than twenty-four hours. The Cassidys woke up with the lights and cops and all the activity, and of course Mrs. Cassidy had assumed it was something to do with Carrie and had her hopes raised and dashed in a matter of moments finding out that, no, Carrie was still missing, but the man the police now suspected as her abductor had been right next door in her neighbor's house and all the kids were gone. No one standing guard but Officers Grove and Knight who only barely got there in time.

Pam and Butch had obviously demanded to know where Sailor and JP had gotten to and, again obviously, lost their minds when Dex told them about his call with JP. Which, after the police left, is how they all came to be in the Saggin' Wagon with Pam up front, watching the digital dots of two of her children on Dex's phone, imploring him to drive faster every couple of seconds. She and Butch brooked no argument. They were going to retrieve their kids and no one was splitting up. They were all going.

"Mrs. C," Jug had said. "The police said they're already heading out there and for us to stay—"

"Get in the damn van, Judson, or so help me I will handcuff you to a tree and leave you out back for that maniac as bait," Mrs. Cassidy said.

"No man left behind," Butch had said, hoisting him through the van's sliding side door by the back of his shirt. "And you either," he added.

Now, they were all driving out to the swamp as the light gently broke the horizon, the sun putting its feelers out before fully committing to dawn.

They all recognized him as they passed by, even through the blood that coated his face and shirt—the bedraggled thin man lurching along the side of the road. Bevel. He was the only thing there was to see in the thin light on the empty road. There was nothing but him and the minivan. Jug heard his Nana's breath catch as they passed. "That's him," she said, squeezing Jug's arm. "That's the man who came in the house. That was him."

"I saw him, Nana. That was Bevel," Jug said.

"That's the man that took Carrie," Butch said from one of the captain's seats in front of Jug. Butch was in the one on the driver's side behind Dex.

"Turn around up here," Mrs. Cassidy said to Dex. She pointed to a level spot on the side of the road.

"Why do you want to turn around?" Dex asked. "Call the police. We've got the cards of like ten detectives at this point."

"Keep him in sight, okay?" Mrs. Cassidy said.

"Do what your mother asked please," Butch added.

Jug saw Dex clock his dad in the rearview. *Please* wasn't a word they heard from Butch very often. "Alright," Dex said. He reached to take his phone back from his mother. "You want me to call the detectives?" he said.

"Just drive," Butch said, as Dex swung the minivan around and started slowly back the way they had come. Bevel was maybe one hundred yards ahead of them. "I'm calling right now."

Butch pulled out his phone and started dialing as Dex crept along behind Bevel. Jug moved up between the two front seats, between Dex and Mrs. Cassidy, to watch Bevel. Bevel turned around and looked back at the van. They had been spotted.

"We found him," Butch was saying into the phone. Someone must have answered. "The man that took our daughter." There was a pause. "This is Butch." A pause. "Herbert goddamn Cassidy, you gave me your card not even three hours ago. Who the hell else would it be calling about his missing daughter? My taxes pay for this lousy—"

"He's got a gun," Pam yelled, drowning out her husband.

Up ahead of them, Bevel had started running back toward the van now, a gun out in front of him. Jug moved back beside his Nana, shoving her over behind Mr. Cassidy as a shield. Dex stopped the van and said, "What should I—" Before the clear report of a gunshot cut him off. The shot missed, presumably because Bevel was running and firing at the same time.

"Drive! Hit him!" Pam yelled.

"Ma, I can't— Hey!" Dex's father grabbed him from behind, pinning his arms down.

"Pam, grab the wheel. Do it!"

Mrs. Cassidy was already moving. She grabbed the steering wheel, threw her leg over the center console, and punched the gas.

"Mom, no. Stop!" Dex yelled.

"Faster, Pam!" Mr. Cassidy shouted. The van picked up speed. There was another gunshot, another miss.

"Son of bitch. Kidnap my daughter. Fire a gun at my family!" Pam screamed, rodeoing the center console, one foot on the gas pedal, gripping the steering wheel in two hands.

"Faster!"

"Let me go!"

"What's happening?" Nana Jean asked.

"Aw hell," Jug said. He threw an arm across her chest, using his other to brace against the side of the van. "Hang on, Nana."

The Saggin' Wagon continued to pick up speed, bearing down on the man charging it, firing madly.

•••

Bevel walked along the road in the pallid light, his face throbbing, his neck sore and crimped. A minivan drove past him, the only vehicle he had seen since he had run from the trailer. When it passed, Bevel fished his baggy from his pocket and snorted back a bump off his fingernail to quiet the pain, drowning it in the rush.

He was going to set Jumper's bar on fire, there was no question about that. He last saw Jumper getting his face beaten in, but he knew better than to assume he was dead. It didn't matter anyway, alive or dead he was burning down the bar. Hopefully with Óscar, Ángel, and Puto inside it. Then, he was going back to Jug's house and he was going to kill that old woman. His grandmother or whoever. He had retrieved the gun Jumper dropped when the first hammer strike got him. Hopefully he would find Jug there too and he could kill them both, but he was definitely killing that old woman.

Bevel was deep in his own thoughts when a sound cut through them and caught his attention. He turned around and saw the van that had just passed by. It was following him. In the early light there was no glare to cut his view through the van's windshield. Incredibly, impossibly, he saw Jug, dead in the center of the two front seats, staring at him. He pulled the gun Jumper had meant to kill him with from his pocket. His blood rushed, his synapses burned, he started running. He fired at the van. Nothing seemed to happen, but he must have been running faster than ever before because the van was getting close really quickly. He fired again. Missed again. He was almost right up on the van now, sprinting full speed.

For one instant, Bevel registered that the van was coming toward him, that's why it was getting closer, not his incredible running power. He also noted he could no longer see Jug. The face of an angry and determined looking woman he did not recognize blazed through the windshield, vengeful and raw with hate.

Her look hit him first. Then the minivan.

•••

Daniels and Maroney had zip-tied Jumper's hands and feet several times over. The man's face was a mess but he was conscious and bucking when they opened the trunk of Daniels's Mercury. Edison administered a sedative and did a quick assessment of Jumper's injuries.

"Jaw is shattered beyond repair, ocular bones and cheek bones are all fractured it looks like. Nose, weirdly, not broken," Edison said.

"He'll live though?" Hector asked.

"Certainly."

"And feel pain?"

"Oh absolutely."

"Great," Hector said. He reached into the backseat and grabbed the still unconscious Morgan. He yanked him out of the car, letting him flop to the side of the dirt road. "Load him up," he said, pointing to the trunk where the sedative was draining the fight out of Jumper.

Hector stood in the road with his phone to his ear, watching the men struggle under Jumper's bulk. The day was breaking around them now, like cream dripping steadily into black coffee diluting the darkness slowly but unstoppably.

A voice answered on the other end of Hector's call. "Yeah, Boss?"

"Point it toward shore and cut it loose," Hector said.

"Perfect timing, boss," the voice on the phone said. "Tide'll carry it straight in."

Hector ended the call and looked in at Jumper, lying on plastic in the back of the SUV. Jumper met his gaze, did not look away.

"We're taking a ride to the low country, Miles," Hector said. "And we've got two full days before Thanksgiving. Two days, me and you. That's what I'm thankful for."

Hector crouched down, even with the back of the SUV and Jumper's eyes, dilated and white in the pink and red mash of his face. "And when I finally let you die on Thanksgiving morning, before my family's meal." He reached out and tapped Jumper's chest. “That’s the moment—the last moment ever—that you’ll be thankful for.”

Hector stood up and closed the back of the Escalade.

•••

Tusk had Sailor drop him off near the main road and sent the three siblings on their way. He waited for his backup to finish up with whoever was left at the trailer.

Groves was the first car to pull down the dirt road, lights on but no siren. Tusk waved him down and he stopped alongside him. Tusk climbed in the passenger seat.

“You know, that old woman cried on my shoulder for half an hour after you jumped out the window,” Groves said, starting down the road again. “You never came back and I was just stuck there with her bawling like that. Look,” he pointed at the shoulder of his uniform. “It’s still damp. I’m not emotionally equipped for old women bawling on me in their bedrooms. With their weird old furniture and all that.”

“I was pursuing the perp, Groves,” Tusk said.

“Yeah, you pursued him and never came back. I heard you rode out here on the roof of his vehicle. Is that true?”

“That’s true.”

“Damn, man, really? For real? Hanging onto the roof?”

“Really for real.”

“Hell yeah! So what I’m saying is, I drove all the way out here and if we go kicking the door of this place down and there’s a bunch of old people in there, this time you stay behind and let them weep their snotty noses all over your uniform and I’ll go out the window and ride on the roof. Okay?”

"Yeah, sure. Deal," Tusk said. They were approaching the trailer but something on the side of the road caught Tusk's eye. "Hey look," he said. "Stop here."

Groves stopped the car. They got out and stood over the man lying on the side of the road. "Strange place for someone to throw away a perfectly good white boy," Groves said. "You know this guy?"

"I do indeed," Tusk said. "Would you believe this man is a possible criminal mastermind, responsible for orchestrating multiple kidnappings?"

"Not wearing a golf shirt and suit pants like that, no. He's dressed like a college football coach."

"Looks can be deceiving. You want the collar? He's a person of interest."

"Really?"

"My treat. Since I left you to deal with the crying grandma."

"Well hell, Knight, that's awfully decent of you. You'll still let me pursue next time, right? In case there's a chance to hang onto a moving car?"

"Next roof ride is yours, Groves. Promise."

•••

Morgan felt something jab him in the side. *Not again* he thought as he swam to consciousness. A heavy haze threatened to pull him back under between each jab. He instinctually covered his stab wound. But the jabbing was on the other side. Finally, he opened his eyes to early morning light and saw a Black man he vaguely recognized standing over him. He couldn't place him, but he thought he recognized him from this exact same vantage point, which, now that he was coming to, seemed to be lying on his back in the weeds and grass on the side of the road.

Another man, a white guy in a police uniform, knelt down into Morgan's field of vision.

"Let's not go bitching and moaning about it, but you're under arrest Mr. Childress," the police officer said.

Morgan looked around. No Hector, no Edison, no Jumper, no Mr. Cassidy, no Sailor. He dropped his head back to the ground and felt the bandage over his side. He could see into the open back of the police car. The soft black vinyl of the seat.

"Thank you," he said to the cop. "Jesus Christ, thank you so much."

Chapter 15

Tusk accepted the tumbler of whiskey Captain Lewis passed him over the desk. The captain hoisted his own glass in the air and Tusk copied him.

"Here's to getting in the pipeline for a well-earned promotion to detective," Captain Lewis said. "Mostly self-driven too." He took a drink. Tusk followed suit. They both started coughing and wheezing.

"Is this Dirty Myrtle?" Tusk asked.

"Yeah," Captain Lewis said, sitting up and regaining his composure. "It's local. You know it?"

"The way you pulled it out of the bottom drawer and all, I just assumed—" Tusk coughed again.

"That it was something special? God no. This stuff'll kill you." He took another sip from his glass. "It's like they distill it into used cigarette butts. That's the flavor profile. You get used to it, though. Sort of start to enjoy how bad it is."

"It's like toilet stripper," Tusk said, trying a second sip and handling it a little better. "And what do you mean *mostly* self-driven?"

"Well, you said it was Jamie who got you off your ass to go check on the Shaws and the Cassidys. You lose points for him intervening."

"Hey, I rode on the roof of a van doing seventy for nearly an hour to make that bust."

"You got stuck up there," Captain Lewis said. Tusk had told his captain the truth about his journey on the van's roof. The captain counseled him not to let boring honesty get in the way of a career-defining event. "But you survived. You made the bust. So." The captain leaned forward with his glass and clinked it against Tusk's. They both took a drink. Tusk was prepared for the taste this time, but he didn't think the Dirty Myrtle was getting any better.

"Why'd you have me following Jug anyway?" Tusk said. "Am I allowed to know now?"

Captain Lewis leaned back in his chair and sighed. "I've known Jean Shaw for thirty years. We go to the same church. Get breakfast together sometimes after. She volunteers at all the police events. She worked hard raising that boy after his momma disappeared. And then he got into some trouble and vanished and it just broke her heart all to pieces. That happens to someone you know, someone you think is kindhearted, and there's nothing you can do. Your badge, your gun, years on the job, it doesn't matter. You start to realize that most of the time there's nothing you can do for anybody. A dumbass boy gets into the kind of trouble that turns him into a dumbass man. And you're sitting there, a police officer, telling your friend you can't help. Can't undo the trouble, can't find the dumbass. When he showed up again, I wanted to be able to do something. I thought if you kept an eye on him maybe we could find the source of the trouble and get it taken care of. And here we are."

"I heard the Marine Division found Morgan Childress' boat yesterday afternoon. With a body on it," Tusk said.

"They did. Do you think Morgan killed Nina Capaldi?" the captain asked him.

"I don't think Morgan has it in him to kill anything but his marriage and career."

Groves had booked Morgan the day before, along with the others they rounded up from the trailer in Dam Swamp. When two more cruisers arrived bearing four more officers, they had gone into the double-wide. They found Ángel Valero Vasquez, still alive on a bedroom floor, suffering from a dozen bodily contusions and a stab wound. He was clutching a Buck 110 folding knife in his hand that looked awfully familiar to Tusk. Then again, it was a popular knife. Next to Ángel, also still alive, they found Peter Barasco suffering from several small stab wounds and lacerations. He was clutching a bloody hammer that Tusk was pretty sure they would find out had been used on the head of Óscar Grimeldoza Mateo who they found dead by the front door. The bullet that killed him was Tusk's, but there was severe blunt force trauma to the back of his skull. A fourth suspect fled the trailer as they approached. Kiya, who had forced a rookie to take over dispatch so she could respond to the scene, chased him down and brought him back. That one was Randall Paul Brady. The trailer was in his name, which made him primarily responsible for the several pounds of cocaine they found on the premises.

They didn't find Jumper, nor another unknown person who Tusk had counted in his mental tally when he got a look through the opened front door while he sat shivering in the van. They did find Bevel. He turned up underneath Dex's minivan. The Saggin' Wagon, as Tusk had heard it referred to. Bevel had been thoroughly killed by the van, but all five passengers described being shot at. It was pretty clearly self-defense as far as the Myrtle Beach Police Department was concerned. It helped that Bevel's family member on the force, Officer Craig Daniels, wanted no further investigation. In fact, it seemed like his spirits had been lifted by the whole tragedy.

"It bothers me that Jumper hasn't turned up," Tusk said to Captain Lewis.

"He will," Captain Lewis said. "Alive or dead, one way or the other, he'll show up again, whether you want him to or not. For now, take the win. One kidnapping victim returned home safe, in time for the holiday tomorrow. Five suspects apprehended, and a drug ring dismantled. No officers hurt except fucking Jamie who shouldn't have been wearing his damn AirPods on duty, and he'll be fine. They fished the thing out of his ear canal. One suspect dead from a clean shot of return fire—perfect procedure—plus getting hit in the head with a hammer—not by us. Another suspect run over by a van, but the police bear no responsibility for that. One dead civilian but again, not our fault, and we caught the guys, complete with a photo from the scene of the abduction. A good quality photo too. And you're going to be an absolute legend behind that roof ride. Plus you'll make detective in spring as long as you don't do anything stupid between now and then. Take the win and shut up about the rest."

"I guess that's true," Tusk said. He took another sip of his whiskey. Still bad, but less jarring. Take the win. He couldn't remember the last time he had one to take. On his way home today he would buy a bike. When he got home, he would ride the bike to the beach. It didn't matter if it was cold. He would sit on a towel and look at the water. In four months he would be a detective. He would sit in the sun and think about that. His win.

"It's a good result," the captain went on. "Most of them won't be like this. Like I said, most of the time you can't help anybody."

•••

Carrie parked in the small beach access lot and dialed Chess's office number. He answered personally.

"This is the law office of Chester Hobbes, Chester Hobbes speaking."

"I love a lawyer who answers his own phone. It drips professionalism."

"Jesus, Carrie. I heard about everything. Are you alright?"

"I'm okay, Chess. Physically, anyway. How'd you hear already?"

"Tayto told me. She…I uh, saw her somewhere. I'm so glad you're alright. Is there anything I can do?"

Carrie herself had called Tayto the day before, when the whole family plus Nana Jean and Jug were at the police station giving hours of statements. Tayto brought them changes of clothes and sandwiches. She ferried Nana Jean back to her house and sat with her until Jug was free to go. She had spent her whole day as physical and emotional concierge for Carrie's family. It was the kind of thing that drained a person, and very likely brought up all kinds of anxious fears by proximity to trauma, Carrie knew. The kind of thing that often made someone seek emotional recharge through physical comfort. And now Chester was telling her he heard it all from Tayto.

"Did you see Tay last night?" Carrie said, probing.

"Oh, yeah, I was at the bar—"

"She didn't work last night," Carrie said. She put Chester on speaker and opened her message app. She texted Tayto: *Were you LEGALLY slutty last night?*

"Oh, she was just also there hanging out I guess," Chess said, fumbling his words.

Tayto texted back: *Seriously? I literally just left his place. Did he tell you? I'm gonna strangle him with one of his dorky ass ties.* To Chester, Carrie said, "You guess? What do you mean you guess?" She replied to Tayto with: *How many dePOSITIONS did you do?*

"No, I just meant—" There was a pause. Carrie figured he was reading an angry message from Tayto that had just popped up on his phone. "Are you texting her while you talk with me?" he exclaimed. "Jesus, okay, fine. Taylor was over here last night, you happy now?"

"Are you?"

"Yes, actually. But now I'm going to have to cage this tiger you've unleashed so thanks for that. You're doing alright, I take it?"

"Remember how we were going to have to get a private detective to follow Morgan? Document his infidelity and all that?"

"I'd say maybe let's table that until you've had a chance to process this whole kidnapping thing but yeah, I remember."

"Well, I think we can skip that part and go straight to serving him the divorce papers."

"Why's that?"

"'Cause he's in jail."

"Oh?"

"For kidnapping."

"Oh!"

"Yeah. I didn't get a chance to tell Tayto all the details."

"I'll have to see what he's charged with and how he pleas and all that but, yeah, that should make this pretty cut and dry. You saved yourself from a pretty messy process."

"And all I had to do was get kidnapped and nearly killed."

"I told you," Chess said. "The law is hell. Wow. Shitheel kind of describes him too mildly, huh?"

"It's legitimately incredible how poor of a husband he was." She thought about it. Past tense was wrong. "Is, I mean," she said. "Unfortunately."

"Not for much longer."

"Promise?"

They hung up. Carrie got out of her car and made her way down the boardwalk to the beach. Tusk was sitting on a towel, facing the gentle ocean with its small cold waves. He turned as she came up behind him and scooted over so she could sit.

"Is that your bike I saw in the lot rack?" Carrie asked.

"At least one of them's mine," Tusk said. He had a beer in his hand. There were a few more in a small soft-sided cooler next to him. He offered her one and she took it.

"There's only one in the rack. You got a girl's bike?" He had mentioned the bike when they planned to meet. It caught her eye as she crossed the parking area.

"It's black."

"Not the color. It has the low cross bar."

Tusk shook his head. "I'm not smashing my balls on a metal bar just because someone says it's a man's bike. I'm too old for that shit. Bike genders are a social construct anyway." Tusk looked over at her. "You don't want to talk about my bike."

"It would be easier to just talk about your girl's bike."

"You're here so we can break up."

Carrie drank from her beer bottle. There was an energy in a major traumatic incident that unlocked something in you, she had mused the previous night. The wall of hesitancy and consideration that you erected to keep from making rash decisions you might regret got kicked to pieces. The trauma also built a new wall around you, she supposed, that made people less likely to hold your decisions against you. That was freeing. Wandering her new mental interior the night before, with the renovations still underway, smashed walls littering the floor and new walls still wet with paint, she dragged out all the decisions that had piled up in her mind's closets and dealt with them.

Move forward with the divorce—she had spoken with Chess now and that was in motion. She was moving out of the house she had shared with Morgan and finding a new place. Break up with

Tusk—that one, she decided, was best handled as soon as possible. She wanted clearance from everything in her old life. Tusk was a decent guy but, who was she kidding, her relationship with him was the unhealthiest thing in her life besides her relationship with her husband. It had only seemed clean beside the wreckage of her marriage. It was like looking at a stable fracture next to a compound fracture with the bone speared through the flesh. Maybe not as gruesome, but a broken bone is a broken bone.

"Of course you figured that out," she said, partly to herself, partly to Tusk. "You're a good cop."

"Maybe I've just been broken up with a lot."

"No, you haven't. You just gravitate toward relationships that can't possibly work out."

Tusk sighed. "Of course you figured that out," he said, echoing her tone. "You're the married woman I've been dating."

They sat drinking their beers, watching the small waves. Finally, Carrie said, "You want to come over for Thanksgiving dinner tomorrow?"

"Absolutely not."

"C'mon, Captain Lewis is coming. Nana Jean and my mom were so insistent it was a borderline assault on an officer."

"You mean I could have Thanksgiving with my ex-girlfriend *and* my boss?"

"Sailor's bringing someone she met. You can watch Butch try so hard to be accepting of the gays that he circles back around to homophobia. It's a family tradition."

"Lula's coming?"

Carrie was startled that he knew this mystery person Sailor was bringing to dinner. No one else in the family had any clue. "You know her?" she said.

"My ex, my boss, and an ACLU lawyer?"

"Don't forget my dad who has antiquated ideas about race and sexuality."

Tusk sighed again. "What time?"

•••

"Hello JP-nuts! Welcome to a special Thanksgiving episode of the live stream, coming to you directly from Pam's kitchen on Thanksgiving morning. If you look right here," JP bent down and opened the oven, focusing his phone's camera on the turkey inside. "You'll see the star of today's meal."

"Jules Patton Cassidy, shut my oven door this minute or God himself will not be able to find all the pieces of you I scatter across this rusty earth," his mother said from the sink, just out of the shot.

"Ma, with the full name and all, c'mon."

"Oh you'll edit it out later. Besides, everyone'll know what it is when they hear it at your funeral if you don't stay away from my oven. And get that cat off my counter!"

"It's live, Ma, I can't edit," JP said. He swung the camera view around to the counter. "With me as always is my furry sidekick, Walnut." He stopped the camera on himself, with Walnut over his shoulder on the counter beside a casserole dish filled with uncooked green bean casserole.

"JP I swear to—"

"Ma, he loves green beans. You know this. You put them out on the counter like this, Walnut's getting on the counter."

"Jules Patton—"

"Alright! We're going!" JP scooped up his cat and carried the phone through the kitchen into the back of the house where Dex was finishing getting dressed in their old bedroom. "The whole Cassidy clan plus special guests are coming today. Here you see baby brother Dex, delinting his T-shirt in case any single ladies swing by for family Thanksgiving I guess. It's always a real meat market over by the cranberry sauce, you can understand why he'd want to look his best."

Dex smiled into the camera. JP was grateful that at least one member of the family could be counted on to lean into the performance a bit. "Hi JP fans," Dex said. "Welcome to our childhood bedroom. If you look behind me, you'll see the sad twin bed where a young JP explored his body, huddled beneath the covers looking at the ladies pajama section of the L.L. Bean catalog. There was many a night and early morning where I'd awake to the desperate and strained sounds—"

"Okay, moving right along," JP said, shutting the door and heading for the den. Between his mother and Dex, he was going to get nothing but harassment online. "Here we have the pater familias himself, Mr. Cheer and Sunshine, my dad, watching pre-game coverage at ten thirty in the fucking morning, the saddest of all television programming. Washed out old men in hilarious suits, commenting on football games that haven't happened yet." JP framed his father on the couch behind him, sitting next to Jug, both of them glaring at him. He dropped into a sports announcer voice. "Well Jimmy, what the Cowboys need to do today is move the ball down the field and score. They want a win here." He switched back to his regular voice. "Oh, should they keep breathing too? No shit they need to score and win, Howie. It's almost like that's the entire point of the game. It's worrisome that you and Jimmy have to keep reiterating the simple concept of a game you both played to one another over and over because you're both so—"

"Jimmy Johnson is a national hero, you little shit," Butch roared. "And he's on a real show, with cameras, and not a phone while he's holding a cat like some goddamn soap opera."

"There he goes. Today's trigger was besmirching Jimmy Johnson's legacy," JP said to the camera.

"Damn man," Jug said. "Do you got to rile him all up when I'm sitting here with him? We were just having coffee and enjoying the morning."

"Listen to Jughead," Butch grumbled.

"You see this tattoo, man?" Jug said, holding up his arm. "It says 'Think before you act.' You should try that sometime."

"Let's zoom in on that ink," JP said. He dropped Walnut gently on the floor and focused the camera on Jug's tattoo. "That motto of yours appears to be written in a thought balloon above an image of Garfield."

"That's right. Kind of a play on *think*, 'cause Garfield talks in thoughts, you know?"

"And it appears Garfield is holding a gun and has just shot and killed a man, whose corpse is also permanently drawn on your skin."

"That's Hamlet. In the tattoo, the message is kind of directed at Hamlet who Garfield has just shot."

"Who Garfield has just shot because..." JP tried to think of anything Hamlet could have done to have called down Garfield's murderous wrath. "...because he killed Polonius? Or Odie? Was there someone named Odie in the play? Nermal?"

"What? No. Because Hamlet is an actor. 'Think before you *act*.' Do you get it?"

"Great ink, brother."

"Thanks, man."

The door opened. Carrie and Nana Jean came in, Carrie hauling two cases of beer and Nana Jean with a Tupperware bowl of ambrosia salad. Carrie fixed JP and Jug in a mean stare.

"I know the two of you are not out here screwing off instead of helping," Carrie said. "Jug, I'm particularly surprised at you, after you showed me that tattoo last night."

"Think before you act?" JP said. "With 'before' spelled with the alphanumeric 'b4'?"

"I haven't seen that one," Carrie said. "I saw 'Be of Service.' It's a bee smashing an overhand serve to Serena Williams."

"Venus," Jug said.

"Sorry. Venus. Can't believe I mixed them up, what with the incredible likeness by whomever did the freehand work for your tat," Carrie said, rolling her eyes.

"You want to see?" Jug asked JP

"Let's not use all your A-material in your first week back home," JP said.

"Come be of service then," Carrie said.

"How come you don't harass Dex this way?" JP asked.

"'Cause I'm already in here helping," Dex called from the kitchen.

"I'm coming," Jug said, standing and following his grandmother.

"JP!" His mother's voice cut through the kitchen clatter. "This cat is going in the oven!"

"Oh, suddenly it's okay to open the oven door? Because when I did it—"

"JP!"

"Alright, fans. This is JP signing off. Appreciate your loved ones, think before you act, take care of yourselves, be of service to others, and have a happy Thanksgiving."

•••

Morgan Childress lay in a hospital bed handcuffed to one side and shackled by both ankles. He mostly thought of Nina, which surprised him. He was slowly coming to understand that his relationship with her was a fabrication. Something about being in a fight, then stabbed, then electrocuted, then drugged, then dumped on the side of a dirt road had jarred loose the realization. Bits and pieces half heard while under Edison's sedatives floated through his mind like ghosts behind an astral plane, unclear but insistent and pointed. He had been taken. He was a sucker.

This depressed him. It made him sorrowful, an emotion too fully realized and concrete for the screaming flippancy of his affair with Nina. Their time together had the same amount of depth as the pleats on his khakis. It was all surface—him posturing while struggling to stand on it and her skating across it with disdain for the ease with which she could do it while he could not.

Nina was cruel and unpleasant most of the time, and his own driving motivation was purely lust. It was pitiable that two people so disengaged with one another as humans should end up with one of them shot through the head, her body stood up like an ironing board in a hallway closet in the small bathroom of a heavily mortgaged boat. That the body he discovered so horrifically could have easily been Carrie's was a possibility that only depressed him further. He could reason that Nina's death was happenstance, but he knew that Carrie's would have rightfully been laid at his feet alone, and not just because that's where she happened to land when he opened a bathroom door.

He had been suckered, he reminded himself. Grifted. Hoodwinked. It was not entirely his fault. He had not understood what was happening around him, so it had been fairly easy to take advantage of him.

But now he saw clearly. Now he saw the pieces on the chess board—understood for the first time that a game was being played at all. He was ready to join in, as a player rather than a pawn. As his opening move, he was going to bet that Hector would be willing to move heaven and earth to cover up any connection between himself and poor dead Nina Capaldi. Because along with what a sucker he'd been, another realization was jarred loose during his time in Hector and Edison's care. He realized why the phone number that appeared so many times in Nina's call log seemed familiar. The call log in her laptop the police had recovered from his abandoned Range Rover. The one they couldn't access without the password. The password he knew.

So when the detectives came to question him, surrounding the small hospital bed prison he occupied before his inevitable move to a real prison, he was ready with a plan for the first time in a long time.

"I'm willing to talk," he told them. "I'd be happy to give you all the details you need. But I'm going to need a lawyer. Call Hector Simpatico. Tell him Nina's daddy told me to reach out. He'll send one."

•••

Sailor reached to hang up the phone back on its base on the hotel nightstand. She missed and heard it hit the floor. Sunlight streamed through the sliding glass doors that led to the balcony of this room she had rented Tuesday evening when the police finally said they were done with her. Sailor had gone back to her apartment for approximately twenty minutes. As soon as she walked in, she knew she would be moving out after Thanksgiving. The post-Harper squalor pad had to go. She had located a duffle bag and threw in clothes, toiletries, stun gun chargers and extra clips, a box of ammo, her favorite coffee cup, her stash box, all the lighters she could find, the Catriona Ward novel she was reading, sunglasses, a bathing suit, and a small transistor radio she managed to scrounge two batteries for from a bathroom drawer. She left her apartment, walking along Ocean Boulevard until she saw the Hilton with the Thanksgiving holiday special rates advertised on its sign. She had called her parents and siblings from the hotel room's phone. *This is the number where you can reach me. Room 1980.*

Sailor had put the Hellcat and stun guns in the safe and unpacked the rest of her things. She carried the radio, the hotel phone's portable handset, and her stash box out to the balcony. She found a classical station—she wanted calm music she wouldn't recognize and follow along with—and rolled a joint. While she smoked it, she stared at the phone number Lula had scrawled on a gum wrapper. Finally, she called.

"Hello?" Lula's voice had sounded wary, skeptical of the unknown number.

"Ma'am, have you given any thought to extending your car's warranty?"

"Sailor," Lula had said, with no hesitation.

Now, Sailor swung her legs onto the floor and scooped up the handset. She slipped on her bathing suit top and her shearling lined denim jacket. She slung the beach wrap she had picked up in a beachwear store across the street around her waist, and stepped out onto the balcony. The sun hung over the Atlantic, scattering light across the sea like falling gold coins. Sailor slipped on Morgan's stolen sunglasses against the beautiful glare, and dialed her sister's number. She found part of a joint poked through the tab of a White Claw and lit it while the phone rang.

The call connected. The first thing Sailor heard was her mother's voice shouting, "This cat is going in the oven!" Then Carrie's voice came through closer and more clearly saying, "Hey."

"Did she leave green beans on the counter?" Sailor asked.

Carried sighed. "I don't know why JP can't get organized enough to put a little bowl of them out somewhere else for Walnut. I mean, I guess I do know, he's a lazy idiot, but still. Every year with this shit." She must have stepped away from the kitchen into their former bedroom. The background chaos quieted. "What time are you coming?"

"Around noon. Did you talk to Chess?"

"Should be a slam dunk."

"No private detective needed?"

"Not anymore. The kidnapping and the dead woman on his boat should suffice in lieu of photographic evidence. Chess'll have him served after the holiday."

"Are you serious about living with Mom and Dad again?" Carrie had told her she was going to be staying at home until the house got sorted out and she could sell it or it got repossessed or whatever.

"I don't want to stay at that house. I never liked it anyway. I'm moving forward. One way. That house is in the wrong direction."

"I get it. I'm calling you from a Hilton. Dad is going to drive you crazy, though."

"I'm sure he will. I was thinking though, since you mentioned the Hilton. Why don't you stay there?"

"At your house?"

"Yeah, until you find a place. It's free. It'll be tied up in legal garbage for a month or so. There's a pool."

"It *is* nearly Christmas I guess, perfect time to be using an outdoor pool."

"It's heated, smartass."

"Damn, y'all were fancier than individual wrapped little cheeses." Her big sister, always looking out for her, Sailor thought. "Seriously though," she said, "that's a nice offer. I'll think about it."

"You can think on-demand. You don't need to wait until later. And anyway, you're staying there. No arguments. I left you something on the kitchen counter. Something I found in the back of my car, stuffed into the well where the jack goes."

"That's weird and ominous. What is it?"

"I can't tell you, it's a surprise. I have my theories on where it came from. I'll tell you one thing, though. It's fucking ours. It belongs to us now. You'll see. Check out of that Hilton when you leave to come to dinner. I'll give you the key to the house. Can't wait to meet your mystery date. Byeeee," Carrie said, and hung up before Sailor could get in another word.

"Guess I'm checking out," she said to herself.

The conversation with Carrie brought back a recurring thought that had been swimming through Sailor's head since the whole family had been reunited, and the singular focus of finding Carrie was gone. The private detective Carrie had been planning to hire was going to charge a couple grand just for photos, she had said. That sounded pretty good. Sailor didn't particularly want to keep running service calls for her dad.

Private detective—it certainly sounded cool, and after the last couple days she was thinking she might have a knack for it. After all, she knew things. Things people didn't say out loud.

Sailor sensed someone watching her and turned to the glass doors. There was Lula, sitting up on the far side of the bed, looking at her. Lula smiled. She climbed out of the big king bed and went to let the room service guy in. She blew Sailor a kiss as she passed by.

Well alright, Sailor thought. *Still got it.*

THE END

About the Author

Kennedy Weible was born and raised in Myrtle Beach, SC. His short stories have appeared in *Iron Horse Literary Review* and *Hanging Loose Magazine* among others. He is the author of the novels *Number One Loser* and *Prophet of Loss*, the short story collection, *How You're Not Funny*, and the children's book *Bed Critters*. His humor essays have appeared in *Men's Health* and *McSweeney's Internet Tendency*. He lives in Raleigh, NC with his wife and son.

Apprentice House is the country's only campus-based, student-staffed book publishing company. Directed by professors and industry professionals, it is a nonprofit activity of the Communication & Media Department at Loyola University Maryland.

Using state-of-the-art technology and an experiential learning model of education, Apprentice House publishes books in untraditional ways. This dual responsibility as publishers and educators creates an unprecedented collaborative environment among faculty and students, while teaching tomorrow's editors, designers, and marketers.

Eclectic and provocative, Apprentice House titles intend to entertain as well as spark dialogue on a variety of topics. Financial contributions to sustain the press's work are welcomed. Contributions are tax deductible to the fullest extent allowed by the IRS.

To learn more about Apprentice House books or to obtain submission guidelines, please visit www.apprenticehouse.com.

Apprentice House Press
Communication & Media Department
Loyola University Maryland
4501 N. Charles Street
Baltimore, MD 21210
410-617-5265
info@apprenticehouse.com
www.apprenticehouse.com

www.ingramcontent.com/pod-product-compliance
Lightning Source LLC
LaVergne TN
LVHW012338100826
845148LV00018B/2838

* 9 7 8 1 6 2 7 2 0 6 8 1 5 *